a novel

Ray Had an Idea About Love

Eddie Lewis

Simon & Schuster
New York London Toronto
Sydney Tokyo Singapore

SIMON & SCHUSTER
Rockefeller Center
1230 Avenue of the Americas
New York, New York 10020

SIMON & SCHUSTER and colophon are registered trademarks of Simon & Schuster Inc.

Designed by Carla Weise/Levavi & Levavi
Manufactured in the United States of America

10 9 8 7 6 5 4 3 2 1

Library of Congress Cataloging-in-Publication Data

Lewis, Eddie.
Ray had an idea about love / by Eddie Lewis.
p. cm.
I. Title.
PS3562.E9397R39 1995
813'.54—dc20   94-23909
CIP

ISBN: 0-671-88762-9

Acknowledgments

I would like to acknowledge the following people for their contributions to *Ray Had an Idea About Love*:

Those friends and family who were with me in the divorce trenches, for their understanding and support.

Natalie and Don, who as professionals and as friends had faith in me before I did.

Those who gave *Ray Had an Idea About Love* an audience when it most needed one: John Thorndike, Natalie Goldberg, Terry and Sonja Passalacqua, Graham Ward, Jacob Deegan, Kathleen Lee, and Mary Feidt.

Bruce Throne for being the voice of Zach.

Cara Stein and Matt Bialer of the William Morris Agency, for loving the book and for everything they did on its behalf.

My editors, Michael Korda and Chuck Adams, for loving the book and for everything they did on its behalf.

Cheryl Weinstein and the rest of the people at Simon & Schuster, most of whom I have never met or spoken to, for shepherding this book into its final form.

for Joey and Matt
and
for Mary

Part One
Fall 1982

Leaving

Ray sat on the coffee table facing the couch. Arrayed in front of him were his wife, Betsy, and their two boys: Jesse, five, and Zach, two. The moment was arranged, discussed by Ray and Betsy late at night.

"Boys, we have something to tell you."

Zach sat like a puppy in his diaper, a pacifier with a large white disk in his mouth. Jesse avoided Ray's eyes, uncomfortable with such formal discussions. Betsy put a bare, freckled arm around each one of them. They waited for Ray to begin.

Ray was nervous, not wanting this moment, wishing that it could all happen without it.

"Next weekend," he told them, "I am moving out and into another house."

He expected the need to explain, to elaborate what that meant, to talk about weekends and every other Thursday afternoon and night, but Jesse brought him up short. He looked at Ray quickly, his eyes unblinking.

"No," Jesse said, his back going stiff; then he began to whine. "I don't want you to move to another house."

They looked at each other for a brief, hard second; then Jesse cried out, "Why?"

He put his head against his mother's shoulder and cried and cried, gently saying over and over, "I don't want you to move to another house. I don't want you to move to another house."

His tears came easily, freely. Betsy pulled him into her shoulder, kissed his forehead. She and Ray exchanged glances. Ray sensed that she was trying to help, that she was working to smooth over this unexpected moment in this staged scene. It was her way of keeping them a unit. Ray closed his eyes and sighed. As Jesse wept, Ray began to see that what was happening had nothing to do with alternate weekends and every other Thursday night. Like the fragile wing of a bird-shaped kite, something had broken and would never fly again. Repair was not in Ray's nature.

He knew that he was leaving and would not be back. He did not know why. He only knew that somewhere between his stomach and his heart, a hard knot had formed and it would not soften. It twisted tighter and more painfully every night. Then his lower back started hurting, and he could not sleep. He woke in the middle of the night in such pain that he could do no better than roll off the side of the bed and crawl to the TV in the living room and turn on the all-night sports channel. Wrapped in a blanket he kept on the couch, contorted into whatever position gave him relief for that moment, his jaw slack with fatigue, Ray watched Ping-Pong from Japan, a rodeo from North Dakota, dirt-bike racing from the deserts of California. Whatever the event, one commercial reliably returned over and over, a commercial for a magic knife that diced, sliced, and pared the same onion, tomato, and lemon time after time. This knife could be bought only by dialing an 800 number; it was not available in stores. A million times Ray had wanted to buy that knife; yet, caught in the madness of his early-morning pain, he could never reach for the phone.

There was Julia. She had walked with him up the dirt road that led to the ski basin, listened to him talk on and on about Betsy; she had slept with him on the old mattress in her friend's cabin by the stream. Ray had told Betsy that he was not leaving her for Julia, but he did not know if that was true. Julia was a possibility, although he was not ready to admit it. What did it matter anyway? He was gone.

Ray knew Betsy did not understand it, did not believe it. She had insisted they visit a counselor. Ray had sat on the old green couch in the basement of a house, a room that must have once been remodeled as a TV or rec room, with dark paneling and low tile ceilings, and said only that he did not love her anymore. The counselor and Betsy asked him to explain, to say more, asked him how he felt, and like a sullen child he picked at what was left of the green fabric on the couch and said nothing.

"Does it have to do with Sean's death?" the counselor asked.

"No," he told her.

Sean was Betsy and Ray's first son, who had died when he was nine days old.

"Did you know," the counselor continued, "that somewhere around seventy-five percent of all couples that experience the death of an infant get divorced?"

"No," Ray answered.

Betsy was letting him go graciously, with a minimum of tears. It was their way. They did not fight. They did not wrestle. At other moments, Ray had imagined that this way of theirs was graceful, like the dance of the matador with the bull; that he was the matador, and the bull, carrying the horns of wild emotion, passed within inches of ripping open his soft belly again and again, each time missing neatly, safely. At this moment, Ray did not feel so graceful. As a matador, he had no taste for the kill. And it was not going well. His first sword thrust had hit bone.

Betsy still believed in the dance. The night before, she had suggested that Ray think of this move as a trial separation, an experiment. She asked him not to shut the door permanently. She was not ready to believe that Ray was really leaving. Jesse knew better. He smelled death and understood that things in life can drop away and never be seen again. Ray wanted to pick up the red cape and tease away the tears, to flash and dance until the crowd was once more on its feet, shouting *ole* with each pass, cheering and happy in a bright sun. But it was too late for that. He was leaving. He did not yet understand the carnage. He was only dimly aware of it. He, too, wanted to still believe in their way, wanted to see this moment as a simple, smooth changing of partners in the dance.

Jesse played in the backyard with a gardening trowel. He was digging up worms in the flower bed along the block wall. When he found one that he wanted to keep, he brought it to Zach, who was sitting in the middle of the lawn. Zach was in charge of the white plastic container. He constantly inspected its contents, picking up worms and holding them as they wiggled around his fingers. Occasionally he threw one back at the wall.

"Zach," Jesse yelled at him, "don't throw them away."

Zach only stared back at Jesse. His pacifier, which he called a "binky," was pinned to his OshKosh overalls with a ribbon and a diaper pin. He grabbed it with a dirty hand and stuck it in his mouth.

It was a mild October evening in Santa Fe, New Mexico, summer perfectly blended with fall. Ray sat outside in one of their white metal picnic chairs next to the round redwood table and drank a Budweiser. Beer had layered an extraneous twenty pounds on Ray over the last ten years, softening without altogether hiding his six-foot athletic frame. Betsy was inside cooking. Ray had spent the day packing. In three days he would be gone, erased from this tranquil domestic scene.

When they went to bed that night they had to step around the boxes stacked in the narrow aisles between the bed and the walls. Betsy took off Ray's underwear and licked his naked body carefully, slowly. With her tongue she played with his cock and sucked on it until it was hard. In their nine years of marriage, she had never done that before, as if his imminent departure was firing her passions. She stroked him as she sucked and licked. Ray was back and forth between amazement and excitement. Then he let his head fall back and got lost in the excitement. He almost came twice. Betsy straddled him and with her hands on his chest, eased herself down onto him. Her long, straight red hair hung around her head like a veil, and the ends brushed Ray's chest. With long, deliberate motions like a pump jack in a flat west Texas field, she made herself come, tightening her muscles and sitting up straight as she did. Ray grabbed her hips and thrust up in to her and came while she was still shuddering from her orgasm.

They lay collapsed against each other, wet with sweat. In the sensual fog between awake and asleep, Ray realized that they had just made love as they had never made love before. He could not remember the last time they had even had sex. Two months before? He could not remember the last time Betsy had come. Had she ever come?

At that moment the truth of things seemed distant and elusive. Once, early in their marriage, before Jesse and Zach were born, Betsy had tearfully confessed that she had never had an orgasm. They had been drinking and Betsy had gotten morbid and depressed. The confession had sobered Ray. He hadn't realized. And he didn't understand how a person could make love and never have an orgasm. And he didn't understand how he could not have known such a thing about his own lover. He had become enthusiastic about giving Betsy her first orgasm, turned on even, as if she were a young virgin, but his efforts only made things worse for her and the subject was eventually forgotten. Sex became a sideways thing for them, and Ray, in his sideways thinking, figured that maybe somewhere along the way she had gotten her orgasm. He had not known when she was not having orgasms, why would he know any better when she was? Until that moment, when she came so strongly that it got him thinking again that maybe this was it, maybe this was the first time.

"Is it that good with Julia?" Betsy asked, more curious than bitter.

He did not answer. The subject was long past the point of discussion. He was leaving.

Now You
Have
Nothing

When he woke from his first night at his new apartment on Silver Street, Ray wanted to contact two people. The first, of course, was Julia. Even though they had been lovers for four months, they had never spent the night together and they had not made love at all for a month. This, Ray was confident, would change immediately. The thought buoyed him, made him feel good about his new place. Leaving Betsy, his children, and his home scared him. If Julia was not his new love, his new life, she was at least hope that new loves and new lives existed out beyond this frontier of everything Ray had ever known before.

Ray sat in his one chair, a yellow cloth director's chair, and stared at the red telephone that he had just installed. It was his only link to the world. He had just discarded all others. He felt stripped of definition: no longer a father, no longer a husband. It was as if his entire past life belonged to someone else: college at Brown, small Massachusetts boarding school, small Philadelphia church school.

His first girlfriend, Wendy, had been in his fifth-grade class.

They never spoke to each other. Ray wrote her love notes on pages torn from his spiral notebook and he passed them to her through Wendy's little brother, Sandy, who was in the fourth grade at the same school. Wendy wrote him notes and delivered them in the same way. She also sent gifts: a pink ribbon in a small white box, the plastic eye from one of her stuffed animals, strands of blond hair wrapped in Kleenex. During classes they looked at each other frequently and with meaning. Years later, Sandy told Ray that he, not Wendy, had written him all those notes, sent him all those gifts. Ray had not believed him, but since Ray and Wendy had never spoken, he could never be sure.

His whole past life now felt like that early incident with Wendy, beyond his true touch, made up, outside what he could feel and who he was. His relationships felt as if they had all been negotiated by a middleman, like Sandy, an intruder, all conducted at arm's length. Now, he thought, now he could find the real Ray.

He picked up the phone and dialed Julia at work. They both worked at Prime Time Electric. More precisely, Julia worked for Ray.

"Hello, stranger," she teased him, "coming to work anytime soon?"

"Tomorrow," he said. "I'm still fixing up my new place."

"How is it?"

"It's OK. A little short on equipment, but it's got all the essentials." Ray felt not just the cavernous space of his new apartment but the wide-open spaces of his new life as he spoke. "Why don't you come over this evening?" he asked Julia. "I'll make some dinner."

Julia hesitated before she agreed. She recognized that this was a different invitation, that the two of them were operating under new rules. Ray was no longer a married man. Not officially divorced, of course, but neither was she. She had been separated from her husband, Roget, for over five months, living in her own small apartment, a converted garage in the Casa Solana subdivision. She had never invited Ray to her apartment. They had made love at stolen moments and in borrowed places, mostly her friend's cabin, but also in the woods and in abandoned fields and once in Ray's Toyota next to the Albuquerque Highway when a hailstorm had forced them to stop. Never in Julia's apartment. She had slept with pickups from the Alto Club there, and once with Roget, but never Ray. Now Ray had his own apartment; now things had changed.

As soon as he hung up, Ray regretted his offer to make dinner. He did not have any real experience in making dinner. He had volunteered in a nervous moment, to give his invitation to Julia an air of domesticity, a touch of the everyday. It is no longer just about fucking, he wanted to say, and dinner seemed like a good way. Only now he had to make it.

Dimitri would help. Dimitri was the second person Ray wanted to call, and he would have some ideas about dinner. Food was one of Dimitri's passions. Ray decided not to call, to just go over to his office and walk in. It was not far from his new apartment. As he started his car, Ray imagined sharing lunches with Dimitri at his new place, lunches of homemade Greek treats, and talking on and on about women, life, love, and suffering.

Ray and Dimitri had spent many such hours over the summer. On weekends, they had talked as they wandered through the piñons in the country around Dimitri's house. Ray had confided in Dimitri, telling him of his affair with Julia and letting loose all his frustrations with his marriage. Dimitri had listened, interested, had asked questions, and had slowly begun to talk about his problems in his own marriage. They developed a bond, two unhappy men sharing with each other their tales of woe.

But Dimitri had missed the climax of all their discussions, for in the month that Ray had decided to leave Betsy, told her that he was leaving, and actually left, Dimitri had been on vacation in Florida. He knew nothing about these accelerated developments, and Ray was driving over to reveal them, to present them, as a surprise.

Dimitri was editor of *VIVA*, a slick tourist magazine that the state of New Mexico published once a month. When he graduated from college he had been an artist, and when he got married he took a job with *VIVA* as a commercial artist. Over the years he had moved up until he was named editor fifteen years ago.

When Ray walked into Dimitri's office just before noon, Dimitri was on the phone. He was well tanned. They waved at each other and Ray sat down to wait. Behind Dimitri on the bulletin board was a glossy picture of the governor.

Dimitri hung up the phone. "Hello, my friend."

They stood and gave each other a hug. Dimitri's tan accentuated the fan of wrinkles spreading out from his eyes. Dimitri was fifty and shorter than Ray. He stood slightly curved forward. His hair was thinning in a wide swath across the top of his head.

"How was your trip?" Ray asked.

"It was good, and the sun shone. A day or two of rain, but not much. My brother drove me crazy, so I stayed with my nephew. I spent most of my time on the beach. Oh, the bodies, the bathing suits, my friend . . ."

Dimitri talked about women and food in the same way, with a resonating Mediterranean passion. His eyes closed halfway and he gave a little at the knees. It could be fresh shrimp sautéed in garlic and butter or a well-tanned thigh emerging from a yellow bikini: the lust and love sprang uncontrollably from the same Greek core.

"Listen, Dimitri, I have a surprise for you. Are you busy?"

Dimitri looked at his watch. "No, it's time for lunch. We'll go get some lamb at Torrento's and you can tell me."

"No, I have to show you. We'll have lunch afterward, OK?"

"What is this mystery, my friend? Let's go."

Ray parked in the space in front of the kitchen door of his new apartment. He looked at Dimitri and smiled.

"What?" Dimitri asked.

Ray waved his hand at his apartment.

"What?" Dimitri asked again, after looking. "What is this? Enough of this mystery."

"This is my new apartment."

Dimitri looked again, studying the exterior.

"What?" he asked again, bewildered.

"This is my new place. I moved out."

"You moved out," Dimitri repeated in a hushed tone.

Ray nodded.

"*Verdad?*"

"Come look," Ray said as he got out of the car.

"You moved out. Left Betsy, the kids?"

"Come on, look."

Dimitri followed Ray around his new apartment, dumb-struck. Every now and then he asked, "*Es verdad?* You moved out?"

Ray walked Dimitri through the small kitchen into the living room that, at the moment, had no furniture, not even a rug on the bare wooden floor. The sunlight streamed through the south window.

"This will be the boys' room when they're here. I'm getting some beds."

There were two steps down to Ray's bedroom. The double mattress he had taken from his old house lay on the floor with a gray sleeping bag on top like an abandoned cocoon. Boxes with books and clothes were stacked in the corner behind his one chair.

"I'm getting some sheets this afternoon," Ray said, remembering that Julia was coming over that night. Another errand. He would unzip the sleeping bag all the way and use it as a quilt.

Ray opened the door to the bathroom to let Dimitri look in: yellow linoleum tiles, an old-fashioned tub with feet, no shower, white toilet, white sink.

"That's it," Ray said, pleased.

"That's it," Dimitri repeated.

Outside, Dimitri looked over the stuccoed wall of Ray's new apartment as if he were trying to see if there wasn't more, as if he had missed something. They stood on either side of Ray's Toyota, looking at each other over the roof.

"If this is what divorce means," Dimitri said, "don't let me ever even think about it. This is the most depressing thing I have ever seen."

• • •

Over lunch, Dimitri told a story about a woman he had met in Florida. Normally, Ray loved Dimitri's stories, but he was stung by Dimitri's appraisal of his new apartment and had trouble concentrating.

"I spent most of my time on the beach," Dimitri was saying. "Oh, the bodies, the bathing suits . . .

"This one woman I met. She was so beautiful. She was visiting Miami from Orlando. She had a daughter there. We met at the beach two or three times and when I talked to her I got so hard I had to lie on my stomach so she wouldn't see."

Julia, after she had gotten to know Dimitri, once said, "He loves women." Ray thought this odd, and she explained. "Not any one woman. Not me, or his wife, or any one woman. He loves all women, the idea of women. Sun on a bare breast. Soft skin. On the right day, in just the right light, he can love any woman, adore her."

"Because he's Greek and wants to get laid," Ray said.

"That's part of it," she said, "but not all of it. It has to do with love too."

"Love?" Ray was interested in her ideas about love.

"He's a warm, soft bed that wants you to sleep forever. He wants to hold and comfort women."

"I thought of you," Dimitri said, "you and Julia. She was beautiful, like Julia. Long, tan legs. Not as young. But a perfect body. Bigger breasts than Julia. Oh, my friend . . .

"We had dinner one night. I figure this is it. At dinner, I make the mistake of telling her that I used to be an artist. Oh my God . . .

"It turns out she makes these cards, you know, like greeting cards or something. She carves wood blocks and then prints her design on the front, and on the inside she writes in that fancy writing, what do you call that writing?"

"Calligraphy?"

"Yeah, that's it. In calligraphy she writes these stupid little sayings. You know, like 'Love is caring enough to say hello,' or whatever. So at the table she starts pulling these cards out of her purse. Twenty or thirty different kinds. And this is an expensive place and our food has just come and here she is like some salesman with her cards all over the place. I ordered snapper and they what they called 'blackened' it. It was delicious."

The thought of the blackened red snapper caused him to pause, as if he could still smell it. The moment hung, his gesture frozen; then he went on.

"But she wants me to look through her damn cards. She was very excited about them."

"What did you tell her?"

"Well, I admired her energy for doing them. She was so happy to show them, you should have seen. But . . . they were so terrible, I can't tell you. These pastel-colored prints. I didn't even want to open them to look inside, but she opened each one for me to show me the little saying."

"So, for fear of receiving one of her cards every week, you lost interest?"

"No, no. Let me tell you. Finally she put the cards away. She was drinking a lot, the whole time, and I think because she spent so much time with her cards she drank too much before she ever ate anything. You know me, with my prostate, I only had one glass of wine and I shouldn't have had that, but she is drinking Jack Daniel's straight. She calls it 'J.D.' So by the end of dinner she is pretty drunk; I'm amazed she can walk, three or four drinks she's had, but she handles it well. She talks normally and walks OK. A real pro."

He laughed admiringly and touched Ray's arm.

"I ask her if she wants to rent a hotel room. She says 'sure.' Right away, no hesitation."

Dimitri's story was beginning to interest Ray. For all his talk about women, Dimitri had never taken any of it this far before. Ray noticed the shift. The waiter delivered their food.

"I've been away for a month," Dimitri told the waiter. "Every day, I think about George's lamb. You tell George that Dimitri is back, OK?"

The waiter smiled and nodded. Dimitri laughed. Dimitri continued his story after tasting the lamb.

"I should have known something is wrong when we are fucking, because she is throwing her head from side to side and making these moaning noises. At the time, you know, I just thought that's her way of being excited, but now I realize there is something wrong with it, like she is having a fit or something. It wasn't really in rhythm. You know, not right.

"Anyway, we fall asleep. I guess she passed out. In the middle of the night I become aware of something warm, like a hot water bottle. And then, I am half awake, you know how it is, you start realizing things a little at a time and at the same time you're not sure of anything. Not even sure of where you are. Well, I realize that this warmth is also wet and I wake up quickly. The crazy woman, she peed in the bed, all over."

Dimitri spread his hands out to demonstrate the puddle and laughed. He grabbed Ray's arm and laughed harder, stomping his foot and wiping the tears from his eyes.

"What did you do?" Ray asked.

"I took a shower. And I was just going to leave her. She is still lying there, in her pee, sound asleep, snoring. I felt sorry for her, though, and I try to wake her up. I shake her shoulder, but she is out. I begin to worry that something is wrong. She is definitely alive, but she is so asleep. I can not wake her up. I get undressed again and I carry her, drag her, really; she weighs as much as I do. I bring her in the shower and hold her up in there as the water runs over both of us. She is still totally out. This is hard work, holding her up and fooling with the knobs all at once. And she is all wet and slippery.

"I begin to get aroused. My dick gets all hard again." Dimitri holds his arm at his elbow and makes a fist to demonstrate how hard his dick had gotten.

"This is crazy, I think. I turn the water colder. She begins to wake up and she notices my hard dick and starts to play with it. She is still sort of drowsy, like she is on some drug, but she is getting me excited. We try to figure out how I can get in her but it doesn't work, then she turns around and puts her hands against the wall under the shower head to hold herself up and I stick it in her and we are slipping all over with water coming down on us but finally I come like that. I thought maybe I would fall and break my head." Dimitri laughed again.

"Still, I have to carry her out of the shower, she is all sort of loose, like she has no control of her body. I take the sheets off the bed and lay her down and wrap her in the bedspread.

" 'Are you OK?' I ask her.

"She nods that she is OK, drifting off to sleep right away. I get dressed again. It is four in the morning. I sit on the chair. She is asleep again, but I can tell that her breathing is more normal somehow. The room smells like pee. I leave her like that."

"You never saw her again?" Ray asked.

"That was last weekend, just before I left."

Dimitri began to laugh, full of the memory, and grabbed Ray's arm once more. "Can you imagine, waking up like that in all that pee?"

Dimitri laughed and shook his head, amused, embarrassed, disgusted, and delighted all at the same time.

Ray laughed too, but he was thinking about Dimitri's reaction to his new apartment again. Clearly, Dimitri thought Ray had gone too far.

"How do you feel?" Ray asked Dimitri. "Do you feel guilty? About Eleanor? Does it make you feel like something's wrong with Eleanor because you slept with this woman in Florida?"

Eleanor was Dimitri's wife. Dimitri thought for a moment, adjusting to Ray's change of tone.

"No," he said. "You are too serious. People sleep around all the time. Of course things are wrong with Eleanor, you know all about that, but this woman, she is nothing."

"Do you sleep around all the time?"

"No," Dimitri answered after a pause. "Never before."

"Then, isn't something happening? You've been married over twenty years and never slept around. And I, not so long, but I've never had an affair before. Now, Julia, and all this in Florida. Isn't something happening?"

"What is happening?" Dimitri asked, angry with Ray's persistence.

Ray shrugged his shoulders. "I don't know. I moved out. That is happening. That seems like a lot."

"My God," Dimitri said, "and now you have nothing. Just that apartment with nothing in it. I could not do that. Don't ask me to do that."

Ray forgot to get Dimitri's advice on cooking dinner, so he went to a bookstore and bought a copy of *The Fannie Farmer Cookbook*. He got it in hardback for durability, thirty-five dollars; he felt he needed to hold something that might last. He sat in the parking lot of the Safeway and wrote down the ingredients for beef Stroganoff. He would buy some rolls as well, the kind that pop out of a cardboard cylinder.

As he sliced the mushrooms he thought about the knife on the late-night TV commercials and laughed. Like a forgotten dream, that time seemed to hardly exist. Then he became aware of a cold darkness in the apartment. With his new, store-bought knife still in his hand Ray walked into the room off the kitchen that was to be Jesse and Zach's. The warmth and brightness of the day had passed and the thirty-degree night was beginning to penetrate. The windows were black holes in the wall. He turned on the light, a bare overhead bulb, but it was so harsh he immediately turned it off again. It was like being lost in the woods where every tree and rock is clear but none of it looks familiar, in fact, it all looks menacing. The room was four walls and a ceiling, but it had none of the qualities of home. He could not bring Jesse and Zach here, he thought, feeling the distance he had created between them and himself.

Ray retreated to the kitchen. He whisked the sour cream and poured it into the cast-iron frying pan he had bought at Empire Builders. He returned the beef and onions to the mix. His feet were tired and his back was sore. It was eight o'clock; Julia was an hour late. The beef Stroganoff was the consistency of soup with yellow drops of butter fat floating on the surface. Ray decided to hold off on boiling the noodles ("disregard the cooking times recommended on the box—they are almost always too long," Fannie Farmer said) and gave up on cooking the Hungry Jack dinner rolls since he didn't have a cookie sheet. He sat on his bed and propped two pillows between himself and the wall. He began reading a Civil War novel about the battle at Appomattox that his brother had left behind when he visited four years earlier. As Ray read he listened for a noise at the door, a knock, a shuffle of feet, a car pulling into the parking lot. He listened for the phone. Ray paid little attention to the description of Robert E. Lee's white horse making its hoof-weary way up the muddy road toward the worn canvas tent that held the other generals. A noise at the window made him look up and squint into the darkness. Anybody could be standing there looking in on him and he'd never know it.

When Ray next checked it was nine-fifteen. He looked in on his beef Stroganoff, which had cooled and now looked like one of Jesse's papier-mâché collages. He was not hungry, so he turned off the kitchen light, took his pants and shoes off, and slipped into his sleeping bag. Julia might still come. He picked up his book to read but could not focus. Ray turned off the light and lay back, looking up at the dark ceiling above as if he were at the bottom of a barrel. He was wide awake. Ray thought about Dimitri and the woman in the hotel. It was different with Julia, he thought. There is no comparison.

Ray kept listening for Julia until he fell asleep.

Suddenly
This Is
My Life

The next morning Ray was cheerful once more. One bad day was not enough to shackle the greater forces of liberation and joy. When he went to his car to go to work the early sun was beginning to melt the frost from the previous night. He took off his leather jacket and threw it across the passenger seat. His car, the same bleached-out white Toyota Corolla, felt like a 280Z. He zipped down Cerrillos Road to work, darting between cars, pulling his shoulder harness out and releasing it as if it was a suspender strap. "I OWE, I OWE, SO OFF TO WORK I GO," said the blue-and-white bumper sticker on the car in front of him at the stop light at St. Michael's Drive. Ray felt relieved of such sentiments, free of all definition. He turned on the radio and pushed the button for the country music station.

"Hello, Julia," he said cheerfully when he arrived, as if he had not waited for and wanted her less than twelve hours earlier, as if she were just a bookkeeper and he just her boss.

"Hello, Noni," Ray said to his secretary in the same way. Noni had a poster behind her on the wall which read, "Life is a bitch, and so am I."

Scott, his foreman, was at the drafting table in Ray's office nervously flipping pages of plans, looking for something that seemed to be lost.

Scott was a big Swede from Minnesota with hands as wide as plates. He always wore an undersized blue polka-dotted welder's cap that perched on his head as if it were about to fall off, which it never did. Scott had been a diesel mechanic in Minnesota and even though he was now a skilled electrician he still operated like a mechanic. He was comfortable with large wrenches, stuck bolts, and hard ground. He was impervious to cold weather, wet feet, and long hours. He was not comfortable in an office reading sets of plans and drinking coffee.

"How's it going, Scott?" Ray asked, still fiercely upbeat.

It was with obvious relief that Scott greeted Ray that morning. The previous week's responsibilities slid off him like heavy weights. He quickly unloaded the last few, necessary pieces of information.

"Bud brought these by yesterday," he said as he lifted the edge of the plans in front of him. "He wants a price by four this afternoon."

"Good job?"

"They're remodeling the kitchen at Arby's. It's a lot of work. There's a whole new three-phase service that I don't really understand, for the deep fryers. I went by there yesterday and worked on this thing all afternoon, but I haven't really figured it out yet. It's hard to know how this job will look, you know, when you start tearing stuff out and have to retrofit conduit and whatnot back in. I asked Bud about T & M, but he said he needed a firm price."

"I'll call him," Ray said. "How's the baby?"

Scott's face lit up. Mentioning Scott's four-month-old baby was guaranteed to cheer him up. Before he had gotten married, Scott had spent weekends racing sprint cars on dirt tracks in Albuquerque. That's where he had met Glenda, and after she had gotten pregnant they had quickly gotten married. They were an unlikely-looking couple; she was just over five feet and dainty, as if a strong wind might blow her away. They were both so blond that their son was almost albino. Scott had given up sprint cars and quickly converted to doting parenthood, with all the usual photos and stories about their son, Jonathan.

"Great," Scott answered, dutifully extracting the latest pictures from his front shirt pocket.

Even with pictures, Scott was not tempted to stay in the office any longer than necessary, and he left, ducking his head and cap under the door frame.

"He's not happy when you're gone," Julia observed. "He gets on the phone and he doesn't know how to get off, like he's stuck, always waiting for his brain to catch up with the conversation."

Ray sat down at his desk. Julia's yellow miniskirt and wide patent-leather black belt were at his eye level. She was wearing black stockings.

"We need some money," Julia said. She was chewing gum.

It was her job as bookkeeper to tell him things like that. He wished she wouldn't. They always needed money. Ray had become expert at the subtle levels of urgency. Whatever level, though, the whole issue was a constant shadow, a tireless, small voice telling Ray that no matter how sunny and successful his business appeared to be, underneath it was not healthy. Then, he always speculated, in an effort to not face that particular thought at that particular moment, maybe that's just the way it is in the world of money: a constant tug of war with Ray and all other small-business people, the knot in the middle of the rope.

"No check from Rankin?"

Julia shook her head.

"So how's your new place?" she asked nonchalantly.

"Fine."

"I'm sorry I didn't make it last night. Roget called me at the last minute."

Ray nodded, feeling his stomach tighten at the thought of the night before, and still feeling depressed about the money.

"He sounded desperate so I thought I better go over there. I didn't have your number or I would have called."

She spoke quietly, almost in a whisper. It was their habit to hide their affair and Ray noted its persistence even now, after he had moved out and there was nothing left to hide.

"You don't have to whisper," Ray whispered to her.

She laughed but shifted her weight from one foot to the other. She continued in a soft voice.

"Are you mad at me?"

Ray considered getting mad at her. He reached out and grabbed her behind the knee, running his hand up the back of her thigh. She pulled her leg away.

"Stop," she said. "Dirty old man."

"Let's have lunch."

"OK," she answered with some hesitation.

"What's wrong?"

"I just don't want some heavy meal, like hamburgers or something" she answered, making reference to Ray's favorite food.

"Let's go to the salad place."

"OK." She brightened at the thought of greens. "I'm leaving around ten. Can we meet there?"

After Julia left his office, Ray began his long list of calls with one to Bud Jackson. From Ray's point of view, Bud was one of the three truly professional general contractors in Santa Fe. The other eighty-six ranged from crusty old carpenters like Trane Rivet, who ran his business out of his garage and an old pickup simply because, as a matter of his constitution, he could not work for someone else, to hot-blooded real estate developers like Larry Robinson, who shuffled so much money so quickly in and out of banks and from one pocket to another that he was like a water bug breathlessly scooting ahead of a giant tidal wave. The wave had caught up with him at one point and the resulting crash had swamped subcontractors, suppliers, even one bank, but Larry had walked away with dry clothes and was still contracting.

"How can he get away with that?" Scott had commented when Ray told him the story. "That's not right. Things just shouldn't happen that way."

Ray had laughed at his bewilderment, but the truth was that Ray didn't understand it any better than Scott.

It would have been prudent never to work for either Larry Robinson or Trane Rivet (Trane almost always refused to pay some portion of his bill), but it was not always practical. Prime Time Electric always needed work and whenever anyone called, they answered the call like firemen. But it was a special situation when Bud called, and they gave it special attention. Bud paid his bills on time and his checks were printed by a computer with job account numbers on the bottom.

Two months earlier, the last time Ray had lunch with him, Bud told Ray his wife had thrown him out of the house and was suing him for divorce. She had a twenty-four-year-old lover, an artist, who moved in as Bud moved out, and she was so angry at Bud that she couldn't talk to him without yelling, accusing him of raping her soul. They had two daughters in high school; one of them had been Rodeo Queen at the state fair in Albuquerque the past summer. They were remodeling the kitchen and adding a laundry room when she "blew a fuse," as he put it, and wouldn't let him back in the house to work on the job. She had gotten a court order preventing it. He had to send the people who worked for him to finish the job and would sometimes ask one of them to fetch some clothes, a razor, a picture he had left behind.

Bud had sipped soup at lunch that day while Ray wolfed down an enchilada with red chile. Ray did not know him well and was disarmed by his frank and detailed descriptions of his problems. For a man in his late forties, he looked young. His face was smooth and boyish, his hair combed back neatly. He talked softly, elaborating on the events between himself and his wife in a litany of incredulous wonder.

"What happened?" Ray finally asked, confused. "I mean, why does she want a divorce? I don't understand."

"I don't know," Bud said simply. "Suddenly this is my life. She's got this guy, and I'm out. I'm the bad guy. Even Shana and Rachel treat me differently, as if there's something wrong with me."

He looked down the front of his neatly pressed and buttoned shirt as if he had just spilled his soup.

"Do you want a divorce?" Ray asked him.

"No," Bud answered quickly. Then, more thoughtfully, he added, "I don't know. I didn't think I did, but now I don't even know who Fran is. I was married to her for twenty-two years and suddenly she's some stranger, like someone I don't know, as if I just met her. Except she yells at me all the time. It's as if I had amnesia and lived some other life. This psychologist I'm seeing, she tells me to think of Fran as if she's crazed, someone different. I try, but I don't know. I mean, I don't even have a house. It's hard to pretend nothing's going on."

"What happens now?"

"I don't know. The lawyers have got their teeth into it and they're not about to let go. It could be years. I don't know what to do but go on working, I guess. The bills haven't quit."

Bud had experience with subcontractors who went out of business halfway through a job, suppliers who wouldn't hold their price on metal studs, architects who undersized roof joists, backhoe operators who ripped out gas mains, unexpected bedrock that had to be dynamited, owners who sued each other over who was meant to pay, windstorms that blew over entire pumice block walls, snap freezes that crumbled twelve truckloads of poured concrete, government regulations that sucked money out of his books with a large hose, and when he laughed you could hear it like boulders rubbing deep in his chest. But this, this business with his wife, was something he had never seen before, and when he laughed that day over lunch it was shallow and short, as if he didn't know where to make the noise. He knew the whole affair belonged in that category euphemistically referred to in contracts as "acts of God," yet it didn't quite fit. The loose-jointed, easygoing bemusement reserved for such disasters caught somewhere in his throat, and by the end of lunch Ray thought he might actually cry, but he just quit talking and shrugged his shoulders between sips of soup.

"Amazing," Ray told him shaking his head. "Maybe it's just a little fling or something?"

"Well, I think I've been flung," Bud had said.

"What's the deal with Arby's?" Ray asked Bud when he came on the phone.

"What's your price?"

"You really have to have it today?"

"I've got to call Chicago before five, our time."

"We've got questions."

"Cover yourself. There's no time for answers."

"OK. How's everything going?"

"You don't want to know."

"Want to get lunch next week?"

"Sure."

"Tuesday?"

"Sure."

The sun shone brightly, warming the inside of Ray's Toyota as the cool early-winter air blew in his hair. It was twelve-ten. He was late meeting Julia for lunch.

Ray took off his sunglasses inside the restaurant and scanned the tables for Julia. He did not see her in the main dining room and walked to the side dining room. People talked to each other earnestly over heaping platters of lettuce and spinach covered with thick, creamy dressings. Julia was not there either.

Ray got in line with a plate and tray. He began to think of Julia and Roget talking the night before as he waited in his new apartment. His stomach tightened again and the skin on his arms flushed. He felt petty and jealous and worked to overcome it as he grabbed some spinach leaves with the tongs.

Maybe she left, he thought as he sat down, got mad for having to wait and left without eating. Julia had a temper the color of her hennaed hair. The restaurant was bright. Suddenly the green of Ray's lettuce was greener, as if it had just been put under a color-enhanced light bulb. He could see the beams of light coming through the greenhouse-style windows that wrapped up along the ceiling. The air took on a static, enlivened quality. The hum of voices froze into a single tone. He paused and took it in, as if he were awake in a dream, the epicenter of a painted landscape.

A couple got up from a table, busing their trays scattered with dirty napkins and bits of corn bread. They stood at the cash register to pay without speaking. The woman was wearing a navy blue blouse with large red balloons on it and a white skirt down to the middle of her calves. Her collar was buttoned around her neck and she had fashioned a red scarf into something like a giant bow tie. She rubbed her lips together as if to spread and smooth her lipstick. Her eyes drifted around the room without looking at anything. Her husband, or boyfriend, had on faded, dirty blue jeans that were sliding down in the rear. He was wearing a tan striped snap-up cowboy shirt and there was a line along the back of his hair from wearing a cowboy hat. They live in a trailer near Cerrillos, Ray thought to himself, and he owns a backhoe.

Ray thought of Bud Jackson and wondered, if you scratched the surface of this couple at the cash register, what baroque tales might be discovered. He and Betsy had appeared just like them for so many years, an ordinary couple, out in the world having lunch, having babies, having all the things that ordinary couples have. The woman pulled a mirror out of her purse and examined her face with easy, familiar tilts of the head; she ran a finger along the side of her nose, rubbing at some smudge or blemish. Ray was drawn to her. He imagined her in front of the bedroom mirror in their trailer wearing only a slip, looking at herself in just the same way.

Julia walked through the front door and into Ray's line of sight. He watched her look around the first dining room, as he had, and then turn and come back toward him. Although she was tall, she slouched, her shoulders and head tilted forward. Ray let her look without signaling to her. She scanned by him twice before she saw him. Her large mouth broke into a smile.

"You creep. Why didn't you say something?"

She took off her jacket and left to get a salad. She was wearing a white, sleeveless man's undershirt. Her shoulders were large, brown, and rounded smooth as if they were sculpted and sanded with fine sandpaper.

Ray did not bring up the subject of the previous night; he had promised himself. But she began talking about Roget.

"Actually," she said, a favorite word of hers for beginnings, "it was ugly last night with Roget."

"What happened?"

"He called. I could tell something was wrong right away; his voice was so stiff, so distant. He asked me to come over. Demanded that I come over."

As she talked she ate with a vigorous appetite, popping cherry tomatoes in one bite.

"He put the classical station on the radio. He knows I don't like the classical station. Right away, when I kneel down at the coffee table, he puts it on. I mean, we've had fights, screaming and yelling where I've ended up leaving over the radio station; he wants to talk; so what does he do, he puts on the fucking classical radio station. I don't say anything. There's this tension and, frankly, I'm a little scared."

There was a righteous fury in her tone that Ray was used to, but it was muted today, chastened.

He smiled, absorbed, amused at the thought of Julia biting her tongue on the choice of music. Julia loved music, modern music: Talking Heads, the Police, Men at Work, Sex Pistols. She walked as if she were always listening to it, as if the rhythms and chords were attached to her knees and shoulders. Sometimes, she would do a skip, in the middle of a sentence or thought, a quick dance step, without even knowing it. Rock and roll ran through her as if her spine were an antenna and her heart were a tuner. Ray was not always sure that she was listening to him when he talked. Her hair fell halfway across her face, hiding the music in her eyes.

She was clumsy when she walked, tripping on curbs, but it was because she was torn between the beat inside of her, hard and clear, and the annoying irregularity of the concrete, glass, and metal of the world around her. On the dance floor at the Alto Club, she was at peace, one, like water over rocks, and she closed her eyes and lifted her head so that her hair fell back away from her face and the blue, red, orange lights swept across her wide forehead and her body moved with the music that was all around and through her, and she was alive.

She continued her story.

"Roget asks me if I have been seeing you. I don't know how he could possibly know. He says he's heard you've moved out, split up."

She looked up at Ray, slowing the pace of her eating, then went on.

"I told him I wasn't seeing you."

This caught at Ray as a betrayal.

"What fucking business is it of his anyway," she added hastily. "He started calling me names. He said it was just like with Damien."

"Who's Damien?"

"Damien was his best friend in Paris. A long time ago, when we lived there, we were very poor. Roget was working at a hospital for dying people, old, sick people. It was cold, winter. Drizzly, wet, always cold, and our apartment didn't have a heater. It was broken. Roget worked at night. Damien lived next to us. Damien would come over and talk when Roget was gone, and we started sleeping together. One night Roget came home and caught us in bed."

Ray made a face; it was painful to imagine such a moment.

"It was the most awful thing I've ever done. It was the worst I've ever felt. I wanted to kill myself. I couldn't believe I didn't think he was going to find out somehow. But when he did—*whew!* it was awful. Roget took me away. He quit his job. Actually, I don't think he ever took the time to quit, we just left the next day. First for England for two years, Wales actually. We rented a stone cottage way the fuck from nowhere—and I thought *Paris* was wet and cold. We burned cow turds to try to keep warm. We stayed mad at each other for over a year."

She paused, lost in her story.

"He was calling you names," Ray reminded her.

"He called me a whore. He said I enjoyed breaking up families, like Damien's, like yours. He called me a cunt. I finally snapped, I sat there taking all his insults and then I snapped and I yelled at him finally, I shrieked at him to turn off the fucking radio and he looked at me for a second. I think he was stunned that I said anything. Then he slammed his fist down on the coffee table. It's glass and when he hit it it broke and pieces flew everywhere. I didn't realize it, but one cut me here."

She pointed to a small, raw line running down from her left eye.

"His hand was all bloody. That's all I could see. He was waving his hand around and blood was getting splattered all over the house, on the white sofa. He went on yelling at me and I ran out of the house."

Her head was lowered, her hair covered her face. She had stopped eating. Ray took her hand.

"You should have come over."

"I thought of it," she said, not lifting her head. Ray lowered his head toward the table, trying to see her eyes.

"Julia," Ray said softly. No reaction. He said it again. "Julia." He tugged on her hand lightly. She looked up reluctantly.

"You're not breaking up my family," Ray told her.

Her lips were pinched together. She nodded.

"I know that," she blurted out, and dropped her head again, her shoulders moving with her silent crying.

Julia did not come to Ray's apartment anytime that week, but he did convince her on Thursday to go down to Albuquerque with him in the afternoon to help him buy some beds for Jesse and Zach at American Furniture. He wanted to be with her, but he also wanted to inject some of her sense of style into his life and thought that with her along he might pick out something other than the predictable when he chose beds.

He was right. With her help, he bought a large-tubed blue steel bed for Jesse, and a plain white crib for Zach. He thought Zach was too old for any of the hanging toys that attach to cribs. They would be delivered in Santa Fe the next day.

They were done early. Julia suggested they spend the rest of the day at a place she knew by the river. It was early November and, in Albuquerque, still warm.

"A friend brought me here once," she explained. They parked in a cul-de-sac and slipped through a hole in a chain-link fence.

Julia knew people, and she knew people who knew places. Ray was uncomfortable sometimes that she was so knowledgeable. It fired his imagination about all the places she had been, the people she had known, slept with. It was as if she were standing on the corner waiting for an interesting idea to drive by. She was easy in a way that made Ray uneasy.

"Who?" Ray asked her.

"A girlfriend."

Julia looked at her feet as she walked, as if she needed to see them to keep from tripping. The sun was bright and made Ray squint. He had left his sunglasses in the car but decided not to go back. Julia wore fluorescent orange sunglasses.

They walked down a path that snaked through three long rows of crisscrossed steel beams. They perplexed Ray; they formed a rusty, high wall that ran in between the flood-control ditch, which they had crossed on a wooden bridge, and the river, toward which they were headed. He thought for a moment that maybe it was a sculpture by the man who draped a curtain across Oregon. He felt displaced, as if he were suddenly in a war zone. Julia shuffled ahead and Ray trotted to catch up.

Down by the river the dirt was like sand and the ants were busy among the clumps of grass. Julia lay with her heels drawn toward her bottom and her knees in the air. The sun shone in her eyes and she squinted for a while and held her hand high above her for shade, to try to see while they talked. Soon she gave up seeing and rested her arm across her eyes. Her body was at just the right angle so that the sun fell full across her. It wasn't long before their conversation ended and she lay motionless, baking, a total offering to the warmth of the day.

It was always a surprise in November to be able to strip back to an undershirt and shorts. It wouldn't have been unusual if Julia had taken off her shirt altogether, but she thought better of it and just rolled it up to expose her belly.

The Rio Grande was desultory at best as it sat swamplike around the debris and mud islands on its run through Albuquerque. In the winter it was not much more than a dry creek bed, a wash set between two distant, verdant shores. The growth along the banks, the wild cane and salt cedar, gave definition to the whole river, the river that once was. In spots along the bank around them was evidence of a mighty river, one that knew how to flex its muscles. There was flotsam caught four and five feet up in the trees; gaping cuts in the side of the bank wild with hanging roots; the steel beams they had passed through earlier. It was hard to conceive of such thundering power on such a still day, a day in which the birds constantly chattering in a tree nearby were a rude disruption.

Ray was bored lying in the sun and rolled over on his side close to Julia. He rubbed her bare stomach with the flat of his hand, making a circle around her belly button. She whispered a small sigh of appreciation. Ray skimmed his hand across her skin just enough to stroke the invisible hairs, just enough to tease her senses. He decided that they would make love.

"Have you been reading about that woman in the paper?" Julia asked.

"No."

"You haven't?"

Ray felt her stomach tighten under his hand.

"No."

"Oh my God, it's incredible." She continued lying, her arm draped over her eyes. "This woman walks into a hospital with a newborn baby and says, 'Help me, I've just had a baby.' I mean new newborn, still covered in yuck. The doctors are suspicious right away. Something is wrong. They take care of the baby and then do an examination on the woman. No way she's just had a baby. I mean, you know, no tears, no blood, it's easy to tell something like that."

Ray slipped his hand from Julia's stomach up underneath her shirt and ran it over a breast. This was not the kind of story to put her in mind of making love and he felt the need to escalate her desire. Her breasts were small and he found the compact shape, the smoothness, erotic. His hand sailed over one breast and then the other. He moved his massage back down to her stomach. She continued.

"The doctors call the police and they take her away and before long she confesses. What she did was abduct another woman from off of the street, as she came out of her obstetrician's office, actually, and took her out to the West Mesa. The woman was very pregnant. I don't know how she did it, if she tied her down or what, but she proceeded to cut the baby out of her with a broken bottle. The lady died, of course, in the process, but the baby survived and she took it to the hospital saying it was hers. It turns out that she just wanted a baby really badly. That's what she told the police. She just wanted a baby.

"The woman's in jail and the baby's at the hospital. Eventually someone reports his wife missing, she went to the doctor and never came back, etcetera, etcetera, and the police put two and two together and they send him over to the hospital to pick up his baby. There are pictures of him all over the front page carrying this baby out of the hospital.

"What a way to start a life, huh? Can you imagine? What would you do? Would you tell the kid, when he grew up, what had happened? You're a dad, what would you do?"

Julia laughed in the demented way she had when she knew it wasn't funny but she couldn't help laughing anyway. Ray felt her stomach get tighter and tighter as she tried to stop. He decided to give up for now on making love and took his hand off her.

"Have you ever had an abortion?" Ray asked her, looking down at her large, smiling mouth.

"No," she said after digesting the question for a moment. "Why?"

"Just curious."

"I've never thought I could. So I've always been careful. I may not be careful about a lot of things, but I'm careful about that."

"Did you and Roget want to have children?"

"I guess we always thought that we would. I don't know. We never talked about it. He always meant home to me. All the crazy things I've done, the dozens of times I've left him, whenever I go back it's like going back to a dream of a husband, a house, a white picket fence, a dog. I guess children have always been a part of that dream. It's never lasted long enough to find out. After a week or two it's all in pieces again and we're ready to kill each other."

She became quiet. Ray kept looking at her as she drifted, like a shimmering wave, away into the heat of the sun. In the Caribbean near St. John the previous spring, on the deck of the forty-two-foot sloop they rented, Ray had looked down on Betsy in just this attitude.

"What about last spring?" Betsy had asked Ray that last night before he moved out, remembering the same moment.

"What about it?"

"At St. John?"

"Yes."

"It seemed special. You said you loved me. It seemed like there was a real connection, that we were finding something."

Ray had shaken his head and shrugged his shoulders. He did not remember telling her he loved her. It might have been in a moment such as this, in the sun, with her miles away in peace, just as Julia was now. Ray was tempted to tell Julia just that, that he loved her. Only the nagging doubt that there might be more to love than the warmth of the winter sun stopped him.

Not that Ray had any trouble believing that he had told Betsy that he loved her that spring in the Caribbean. He had told it to her often. When they went to bed, he always told her: "Good night. I love you." It was like a kiss on the cheek, like the squeeze of a hand. It was a language, a promise that there was more there than met the eye: more than the dinners with plates full of barbecued chicken and mounds of mashed potatoes served with peas so that Ray could mix them together as he loved to do as a child, dinners at which they read *TV Guide* and never spoke; more than the off to work in the morning and home late at night; more than the kitchen they remodeled with a black glass built-in oven. Something that "I love you" might bring to their lives, something more.

But there was no more, and the promises of "I love you" became empty behind the frightened and dulled routine of their daily life. Ray had been counting on "I love you" to come riding in like a late-charging cavalry and rescue them from themselves, had been waiting. Until he could wait no longer.

Ray winced at the "I love you's" of the Caribbean, the deep blue looks like the ocean that meant "Yes, I do love you, really." He wished that it would just all go away, that he had never been there.

Ray leaned over and kissed Julia on her wonderfully broad lips. He kissed her around her neck and then on her lips again. She resisted out of laziness, but then went with him and gave him her tongue. He was back to wanting to make love and pulled her shirt up to expose her breasts and began kissing them. Her skin was hot and sweat had collected between her breasts. He licked it. He could smell her armpits. He touched the hair there and it was wet. He rolled on top of her and they kissed with more passion. He pressed himself against her.

They made love. Julia was languid, half owned by the sun and the warmth. She crooked one arm around Ray's neck and held him tight. She braced herself against the earth with her other arm, laying it straight and hard away from her body. Ray knew that Julia was only his for that moment, that with her outstretched hand she was holding on to other worlds, other options, even other men. He would settle for the moment. It was healing. Love might have abandoned him with Betsy, but here, by the river, he could once more touch and feel it with Julia. And it felt alive and real; no longer some dusty and dim hope of what might have been.

"I would tell him," Ray said as they were getting dressed.

"Tell who? What?"

"The baby whose mom was murdered on the West Mesa. I would tell him. Kids understand these things."

"What do you mean?"

But Ray did not know exactly what he meant. He was feeling as if you could survive your worst nightmares, and thinking that the West Mesa baby might be able one day to step out into the world a well person. It seemed, at that moment, like a real possibility.

"He deserves a chance," Ray said. "He should know."

Weekend

Friday night Ray picked up Jesse and Zach for their first bachelor weekend. The new beds had arrived that afternoon; he had bought new sheets at J. C. Penney. Ray was ready.

He took them to Furr's cafeteria for dinner. Friday was a busy night at Furr's and the line snaked out the door. Ray stood in line as Jesse and Zach paraded in and out, through legs, under arms, up and down the hallways of the mall that housed the cafeteria.

When they got inside, properly in line, the two boys crawled up on the waist-high brick wall separating those headed down to the start of the cafeteria from those sliding their trays back up the counter. It was cold and everyone lugged heavy coats. Jesse ran four steps down the wall and stopped, his arms out like wings for balance. His hair was cut short and his eyes were concentrated on his game. His whole body was focused, like a high-wire artist. Zach followed behind, trying to imitate his brother. Zach's hair was longer and more unruly. His body teetered from side to side and his arms flailed; he was always just catching himself from disaster. Other children watched, envious, looking at their parents, hoping they would change their minds and let them play up and down the wall, as if Jesse and Zach's presence might somehow change the rules, but the other parents just watched disapprovingly. Zach slipped and fell on the back of a man reaching for a plate of roast beef. The man deftly caught him with a backhanded reach and perched him back up on the wall. There was a silent wave of amusement down the line. Zach looked at Ray, scared to have slipped, scared of the strange man who caught him, scared of Ray's opinion of it all. Ray smiled. Zach waved and Ray waved back; then Zach turned to see what new dance his older brother had started.

Ray shuffled forward bit by bit, looking over the shoulders of the line going the other direction to see what might look appealing. As if he didn't know what he was going to eat: broiled fish (they sometimes called it cod, sometimes perch, or flounder—it was always the same rectangular breaded fish plank), corn (swimming in buttery water), broccoli (as an example to the boys), and a muffin that he would smear with butter.

When he made the far turn and headed back with trays, Ray gathered Jesse and Zach to the business at hand. He put Zach in a high chair, where he stood like a naval captain on the prow of his ship, and as Ray gave the chair a nudge past the salad one of the wheels caught on an uneven tile and Zach did a back flip out. As the high chair caught, Ray felt Zach lose balance, and as he looked and reached, he realized with the instinct of an athlete that he would not catch Zach, and he stopped, frozen for a second, taking in the neat loop Zach made on his way to the floor, noticing Zach's back arch as his arms swung up above his head, his knees bent just so, his feet following in a fine arc. Zach would not do nearly as well learning a back dive off a diving board when the time came, if the time ever came. As Ray watched, he stooped to the floor, turning his own body so that Zach might put a little more bend in his flip, a little more twist to keep his head from a direct hit. Ray had Zach up in his arms before his legs had finished crumpling down around him. Zach held for a moment, stunned and disoriented, and then began crying lustily. Ray held Zach's head against his shoulder, not knowing yet if it were split in two. He thought the loud crying a good sign. He pulled the high chair and Jesse aside, against the wall, and let the line pass as he assessed the damage.

Zach stopped crying quickly, more frightened than hurt. What had, moments earlier, been the terror of death was now reduced to a few sniffles. With his pulse still racing and his cheeks hot, Ray pulled them all back into line. A matronly woman who looked at Jesse and Zach with nostalgia let them cut in front of her. She was, perhaps, a grandmother. They were all too hot in their coats, and Ray took them off and stuffed them around Zach in his high chair.

"Can I help you with a main course?" a small lady in a white dress and a hair net asked Ray flatly. She did not look at him, but past him.

"What do you want?" Ray asked the boys.

"What is there?" Jesse asked.

"There it all is," Ray said, pointing to the trays of food in front of them.

"Do they have fried chicken?"

"I don't see it. Why don't you ask?"

"Do you have fried chicken?" Jesse asked the lady timidly.

"No. We have the chicken and dumplings there"—she pointed with her tongs—"and we have chicken-fried steak."

"What's chicken-fried whatever she said?" Jesse asked Ray.

"It's not chicken. It's steak cooked like chicken."

"I don't get it," Jesse said.

They had used up their allotted time. The lady in the hair net asked the matronly woman next to them what she wanted. Ray felt the woman hesitate, still trying to be his ally, but then she gave in and ordered. The serving lady began spooning up food and sending the plates down to the vegetable crew. The line began filing around Ray and his boys.

"Well, it's steak," Ray told Jesse. "You know what steak is?" Jesse nodded his head. "Well, what they do is put flour on it, just like they do chicken, and then they fry it in a pan, just like they do chicken. Because they cook it just like they cook chicken, they call it chicken-fried steak."

Jesse looked at Ray, still confused. "Why didn't they just fry chicken?"

"I don't know, they just didn't."

Ray's explanation made him change his mind from fish to the chicken-fried steak with mashed potatoes, all swimming in brown gravy. Gravy came in two forms at Furr's: white and thick as paste or brown and thin.

"What's that?" Jesse asked pointing.

"It looks like some kind of enchilada."

"Does it have chile?"

"I don't know. Let's ask."

Ray caught the attention of the lady in the hair net and asked.

"I don't know," she said. "I'm sure they do."

Ray shrugged his shoulders at Jesse, who breathed loudly and looked back at the offerings.

"Do you know what you want, Zach?" Ray asked.

The current of people flowing around them was tugging at their collective ease.

"I want chicken," he said.

"Chicken and dumplings?" Ray asked.

"What's that?"

"Chicken in sauce, like stew."

Zach just looked at Ray.

"Right there," Ray pointed.

Zach stared but still said nothing.

"It's good, you'll like it," Ray told him.

"OK," Zach said, his eyes still swollen and red from crying.

"Jesse, have you decided what you want?"

"I want the enchiladas, if they don't have chile in them."

"But we don't know if they have chile. She didn't know."

"Well, that's what I want."

"Even if they do have chile?"

"No, I want them without chile."

"OK."

Ray went about trying to catch the attention of the lady in the hair net again.

"We're ready," he said when she stopped for him, "finally."

"Can I help you with a main course?" she asked.

"I'll have the chicken-fried steak," Ray said, "with mashed pota-toes and brown gravy."

She tonged a slab of breaded steak onto a plate and slid it down the stainless steel to the next lady in a hair net. "Mashed and brown," she yelled, much louder than she needed to, and then im-mediately looked back for the next order.

"And we want a child's plate of the enchiladas, but only if it doesn't have chile in it."

She fixed Ray with a stare and then banged her tongs down and walked back through the doors to the kitchen. Ray, Jesse, and Zach waited. The line congested behind them. Finally, she reappeared with a hard step back through the swinging doors.

"The enchiladas do not have chile in them. The chile you get on the side, with the vegetables."

"Good, then we'll have a child's plate of the enchiladas."

She slopped the dripping cheese and beans onto a plate and then looked past Ray for the next order.

"One more," Ray said as she began her "Can I help you . . ."

"We have one more order."

She did not answer but stood poised with her tongs.

"A child's plate of the chicken and dumplings," Ray ordered.

She picked up a plate and then stopped in mid-motion. "The chicken and dumplings don't come in a child's plate."

Ray looked at Zach, who was looking down the line at the desserts.

"They can't give you the chicken, Zach," Ray told him.

Zach looked at Ray. "Why?"

"How about some fish?" Ray suggested. "Fish is good."

Ray heard the hair-net lady asking someone else for their order. Jesse and Ray's plates were waiting down the assembly line for them.

"Why don't you go tell that lady what veggies you want," Ray told Jesse.

"I want fish," Zach said.

When Ray once more caught the lady's attention, she cut a piece of fish in two with a spatula and sent it down the line. Ray and Zach followed behind. Steam trays full of vegetables always reminded Ray of boarding school, and of all the vegetables, green beans stirred the memory the most. They were always limp and waxy, generically tasteless, awash in salty water with little pieces of ham. In boarding school, everyone thought they put saltpeter in the vegetables to keep the boys from getting erections, but at Furr's Ray had an insight about that theory. He still held that there was a conspiracy, but not just at his school, but behind all cafeteria vegetables. It was not just about sex, as they had thought, but about bad taste, or no taste, about food without flavor, sustenance without nurturing, cost without value, life without passion. It was just that at his all-boys boarding school, sex had been the only life subject with any meaning.

When they finally got arranged around a table and Ray transferred all their coats from Zach's high chair to another chair, their food was already cold. It didn't matter. One of the beauties of Furr's was that the food was just the same, hot or cold.

"I pooped," Zach said as Ray was sitting down.

"Really?"

Zach nodded without looking at his father. Ray paused for a moment, thinking. Then he got Jesse's food arranged in front of him. He looked around the tables—mostly old people and families. A man in a suit was playing an ornate version of "Some Enchanted Evening" on the piano in the corner. There was an odd-looking man in a booth against the wall, a bum perhaps. Hardly a threatening group, but there were so many stories of child-napping these days. Ray decided to take Zach, with the diaper bag, and leave Jesse with his food. He could already smell Zach's dirty diaper.

"Stay here," he told Jesse.

Jesse nodded absently. Ray thought he needed to impress on his son the importance of staying.

"Don't go anywhere. With anyone. Understand?"

Jesse looked at Ray and nodded again.

"OK. I'm going to take Zach to the bathroom."

"OK," Jesse said, looking back across the dining room at some children running around their table.

With the diaper bag strung across one shoulder and Zach held carefully in his other arm, Ray made a loping kind of dash for the bathroom. There was one urinal and two stalls. The place was empty. Ray was at a loss as to what to do next. He needed to lay Zach down, but nowhere did the tile floor seem anything but dirty, cold, and hard. He also needed access to the toilet paper. Feeling pressed, he made a quick decision to go ahead and use one of the stalls.

Ray put down the toilet seat and put his bag on top of it. He lay Zach on the floor with his head toward the door. He put a pad under Zach's bottom before beginning. There was no room left for Ray and he couldn't quite reach perched on the edge of the toilet, so he got on his knees, his back to the bowl and his feet extending behind him on either side. The last time he had been so intimate with a toilet was in college when he was drunk and he was passing out and throwing up all at once.

"Dad?" Ray heard Jesse outside the stall.

"Jesse, what's wrong?"

"I have to pee."

"I thought I told you not to leave."

"I have to pee."

"Well, go ahead."

"The thing's too high."

Ray bent his head to see if the other stall was empty. It was. "Use the one next to us."

Jesse pushed on the locked door of the stall Ray and Zach were in. "Are you in there?" he asked.

"Yes. Use the other one." Ray had Zach by his feet and his dirty bottom was hanging in midair.

"I can't undo the zipper," Jesse said.

"Well, you'll have to wait."

There was a short silence, then Jesse said, "I can't wait Dad. I have to pee bad."

Ray wiped at Zach's bottom the best he could with some toilet paper and then had to get the diaper bag off the toilet seat with his elbow so he could raise the seat to throw away the toilet paper. Houdini was never so challenged, he thought, sweat soaking into the armpits of his shirt.

"OK, just a second, Jesse," Ray said, working furiously. "Why didn't you tell me you had to pee?"

Ray could see Jesse's feet move up and down in the I've-gotta-pee dance. The toilet paper kept ripping off in small squares before he could gather enough to use. Finally he had Zach clean enough to let him back down on the pad. He leaned over and unlocked the stall door and opened it toward his face. It would not open all the way unless he moved, which he could not do, so he leaned around the door and unzipped Jesse's pants. Sweat was dripping off his forehead as he returned for the final cleanup on Zach. Jesse ran into the other stall.

Walking back from the bathroom with Zach in one arm, Ray wondered if their food would still be there, if, in fact, they had ever really ordered any food; it all seemed like a few lifetimes ago. It was still there, just as they had left it. Ray put Zach back in his high chair and reattached the tray.

"Let's eat," he said with a deep breath as he sat down.

By the end of dinner, which they ate in exhausted silence, Zach had scattered some portion of every part of his meal in a ten-foot radius from his tray and mouth. He was also rubbing his eyes with the back of his hand in a punching motion, as if there were something behind there that he was trying to get to. Ray felt his forehead and it was warm. Either he's caught spinal meningitis from the floor of the bathroom or his brain is hemorrhaging from his fall off the high chair, Ray thought. By the time they returned to the apartment, Zach was definitely sick. Ray carried him asleep from the car. He was hot and his sweaty head flopped against Ray's neck. He did not wake up when Ray laid him down and stripped him to his diaper. It was as if his consciousness had been stolen away, his body possessed. His eyeballs fluttered beneath his closed eyelids. His breathing was deep and labored.

Ray rummaged through the plastic bag of supplies he'd bought from Walgreen's until he found the thermometer. Betsy said once that if a temperature got up to 103, it was time for a sponge bath. Ray was not sure what a sponge bath was.

Ray put the thermometer under Zach's arm. His armpit was smooth and looked misshapen. It did not curve in like a channel but was lumpy with joints and connections. Ray laid his arm back down against his side; the thermometer protruding like a pop-up indicator on a Butterball turkey.

"I'm sleepy." Jesse was sitting on his bed, his head drooping and listless, his voice flat. There was something about the slope of his shoulders that reminded Ray of himself.

"Just a second."

Ray's eyes lingered on Zach, looking for a clue, a sign of life, that he would return sometime and be OK. By the time he turned to Jesse, Jesse had slumped over asleep, his feet planted on the floor and his head and mouth open to the sky. Ray took off Jesse's clothes slowly, one article at a time, and laid him under the covers. Jesse rolled over and pulled his pillow down under his shoulders, where he liked it.

Ray retrieved Zach's thermometer. His temperature was 102. He retreated to his room and sat in the director's chair for lack of anything else to do. His Civil War novel was open on the floor by his feet. The new phone looked out of place. Ray considered calling Julia. She had been a baby-sitter as a teenager; she had told Ray stories. She was even something like a nanny one summer for newborn twins. She would know what a sponge bath was. The awesome quiet from the next room would not bother her. But Ray did not move toward the phone; he continued sitting.

Zach's fever drew a curtain around their new apartment. The three of them were cut off, adrift. Ray felt responsible, as if he had done something wrong, like a boy who had run off with the circus and suddenly realized the grimness, the isolation, of what he had done.

Ray was used to being the spectator, the observer, just outside of the center. If a child was sick, Betsy took care of it. Even at work, Scott was the one who solved the problems, who made the lights come on no matter what. Sure, Ray was the boss, but he operated as a bridge between the general contractors, the plans, the contracts, and his workers. He was the grease that kept things moving, and the glue that held things together.

Ray remembered when Zach had been born. Betsy had invited her best friend, Janice, to participate. Ray sat by Betsy's head as the breathing coach, a rather unnecessary job, as Zach came so quickly into the world that the art of breathing was never needed. Janice stood shoulder to shoulder with the doctor, whooping, yelling encouragement, and announcing every new body part like a frenzied sportscaster.

In spite of his peripheral role, Ray became dizzy from hyperventilating as he tried to set the tempo of the breathing.

"A boy!" he heard Janice exclaim.

"Another boy," Betsy said laughing.

Ray was familiar with the ensuing routine. He switched his allegiance from Betsy's breathing to Zach, yet to be named, although "Zach" was a strong contender. Ray left the patching, repair, and recovery of Betsy to Janice and the doctor and padded, light-headed, behind the nurse carrying Zach to the nursery. Ray considered it his responsibility to make sure they put him in the right place with the right name. He was guarding against bureaucratic screwups like he'd seen in the movies.

First they put Zach on a stainless-steel tray underneath some heat lamps, as if he were a Big Mac. He cried lustily, which had no impact on the nurses. They measured and weighed him; they washed the vanilla film off him; they ran an ink roller across his feet and took his footprints; they made notes and told Ray, solicitously, that he was in the fortieth percentile, which sounded to Ray as if Zach had just failed his first test; they pricked his finger for blood which made him cry harder, and they smeared some yellow, pasty medicine across his eyes, which made him even more riotous.

"I'll get the doctor," the nurse finally said, and left Zach lying there crying, his fists spasmodically punching at the air. Under the lamp he looked like a plucked chicken.

The doctor pulled at Zach's legs and studied their recoil when he let go, and then did the same with his arms. Ray had to keep moving to see what was going on, peering over the doctor's and nurse's shoulders—the worst seat in the house.

"Good," the doctor said, and turned to Ray. "I need to see him in a week. Everything's fine."

He snapped off his gloves and left as if there were a phone call waiting for him.

The nurse put a Pamper on Zach and wrapped him in a flannel blanket. As soon as she picked him up, he stopped crying. His eyes were streaming tears mixed with yellow goo. Ray was grateful that he was finally quiet.

"Do you want to hold him?" the nurse asked Ray.

Ray was surprised and declined quickly. Zach was in better hands than his.

She walked with him through a room with four incubators, and Ray followed her. The air was moist and overly warm. Two of the incubators had naked babies lying in them. They were impossibly small, like baby mice. Tubes ran from their noses. Ray could not imagine that they could actually live and grow; it seemed too far to go. They passed into a nursery with two rows of clear plastic bassinets perched on top of miniature metal gurneys. The nurse laid Zach in one on top of a thin covered foam pad. When the time came, Zach would be wheeled down to Betsy's room in the entire arrangement. It was his temporary nest. On the shelf below him was an array of Pampers, blankets, and wipes, all included in the basic package of eleven hundred dollars.

Along one wall of the nursery, red curtains were drawn across the viewing windows. It made Ray feel as if he were backstage waiting for a play to begin. The nurse returned and slipped a white card in a slot in the front of Zach's plastic bin. On the top was written the date, and then Betsy and Ray's name. There was a place for a room number, which was still blank, and on the bottom line it said BREAST. The nurse attached a standard plastic hospital bracelet around Zach's wrist.

Zach was now sleeping. Except for the teary medicine smeared across his puffy cheeks he looked fresh and clean, ready for the world. There was a scattering of white dots clustered between his eyebrows, a remnant of some reptilian origin, no doubt. Ray was satisfied that Zach was now identified beyond reasonable potential for mistake. There were six or seven other babies scattered through the two rows of the nursery, all facing the covered window. Were they the audience or the actors? Ray wondered.

Suddenly Ray's shoulders and back were tired and he sat down on a gray metal chair in the corner. The fluorescent light was bright, but still there was a sweetness and warmth in the room. He had liked being there, in his green gown, mask, and booties, backstage, waiting for Act I to begin, waiting for the years to unfold, waiting alone with the babies.

Now, in this new place, in this new life, he was suddenly alone again, operating on his own this time. It felt dark and different. The urge to call Julia was strong, but it was complicated by the fact that she had not yet visited him here, at his new apartment. It kept him from reaching for the phone. He just sat, the ends of his fingers tingling as if he had hyperventilated once more and was once more floating down some hallway behind his children, waiting for he did not know what to begin.

When Ray woke in the morning, Zach was lying on his back. His eyes were open and he seemed to be staring at the ceiling. He moved his eyes to take in Ray, but he was otherwise quiet. Ray smiled at Zach and put his hand against his forehead. The fever had disappeared. He put his finger to his mouth for Zach to be quiet and pointed at Jesse, but just as he did, Jesse opened his eyes and stared at the two of them staring at him.

"Good morning, morning," Ray said cheerfully, wondering with some trepidation what might be next.

At six-thirty in the morning on Saturday, the weekend stretched out in front of Ray like a desert highway, without horizon. No matter what direction he headed, he felt he would be nowhere different from where he now was. Time did not exist. Yet he was not unfamiliar with things to do, ways of entertaining Jesse and Zach.

After Jesse was born, Betsy had carried an extra burden beyond the exhaustion of childbirth, intermittent sleep, and the mind-numbing routine of diapers, naps, and nursing: because of Sean's death she worried that, at any moment, Jesse might die.

When Jesse breathed, she breathed, and when his breath caught, her breath stopped on the edge of fear, gasping and calling out, riding off like the horseman of death, and when he breathed again, she breathed a sigh of relief and sat back half sick with the thought of it.

She was tired. Tired beyond a day's work, tired from the effort of helping Jesse breathe, of coaxing him past death. She slept whenever she could, and when she was not asleep, she was thinking about when she would once more be able to sleep. Sleep was her addiction; she could not get enough of it. She believed that there was an end, that one more hour would have been enough, that one good night would get her through a whole week of bad ones. Like the mythical character Tantalus, who, for sleeping with the wrong goddess, was forced to live out his life standing with water up to his neck and plump grapes hanging before his eyes; yet whenever he bent to take a drink or reached to take a bite, the water and grapes receded just beyond his reach. Like Tantalus, Betsy could not quite get what she needed. She saw rest and relaxation dangling in front of her; she concentrated on them, molded her life around this relief; yet the days, weeks, months went by, and still there it sat, just one good night away.

Ray, who thought of all problems as having solutions, decided that this was a fixable problem. So the summer after Jesse's first birthday, on Saturday mornings he got up with Jesse and fed him and dressed him. He packed the large brown diaper bag that went wherever Jesse went as if they were going camping for the weekend. He cinched him into his car seat and left with no particular direction, with only the intention of staying gone for as long as they could possibly manage. They left behind them, Ray had hoped, a house of sleep.

But the problem had never gotten better. Betsy frequently slept sixteen hours, but the weight of fatigue, of anxiety, never lightened. After Zach was born, it was as if a final lead weight had been attached; she went under. Ray continued his weekend sojourns, including Zach. They went to the race track to watch the early-morning workouts, to the dump to watch the remote-controlled airplanes, and to the park for the swings and the jungle gyms. One fall a house was being built near theirs and they hiked over every Saturday to inspect the progress. But he no longer held any hope that he was helping Betsy; one weekend somewhere back there in the midst of it all, without realizing it, he had given up on Betsy.

Ray had believed that they were on paths that would one day meet, that if he helped, if he worked hard, one day they might go to bed at the same time, get up at the same time, live the same life in the same hours. Not that they ever had, but the promise that they might had once been enough. But Ray had been no match against the pull of sleep. Even when she had been awake, Betsy weighed everything in energy units, using her precious daily allotment gingerly.

Looking back, Ray realized that it had not been Sean's death that had wasted her this way, nor Jesse's or Zach's birth, but that long before he had ever met her, something had ambushed Betsy along the trail and stolen a part of her life from her. Betsy's parents had been alcoholic. They had fought, thrown wild parties, ignored their children, or worse. And Betsy had had a string of bad luck and bad boyfriends. The last one, before Ray, had been a heroin addict and had broken the windshield on Ray's car when he had first dated Betsy. Although Betsy had told some of these stories from time to time, they had never discussed these experiences. Ray could see it all anyway; anyone could. It was in the hang of her head, the paleness of her skin, the lines between her eyebrows. Yet, somehow, that had appealed to Ray. He had thought that he might provide some proper environment in which such stolen things could grow back, but it had been a vain thought.

Ray was not yet able to see himself, his past life, or his relationship with Betsy in this clear a light. Their drama had been acted out in more intimate scenes: small angers, small resentments. Betsy might be upset because Ray worked late and didn't call; Ray might be upset because Betsy had forgotten to feed the dog. Yet all the time, nothing was ever said. Great, silent wars were being waged behind earnest smiles. While neither one of them could see through this screen of deference, Ray was beginning to realize that instead of Betsy rising up from her unhappiness, they were both being sucked in deeper.

Ray took Jesse and Zach to breakfast at one of their favorite old haunts, the Copper Kettle. They ate as if time did not exist. The booth behind them served an old couple who read the paper without talking, and then three teenage girls who gossiped in low voices, and then two men with baseball caps were just sitting down when Jesse asked, "Can we go, Dad?"

Bits of scrambled eggs and biscuits lay around Zach and his high chair like confetti, and Jesse's pancakes sat half-eaten on his plate. Had it not been for Jesse's sudden impatience, they might have sat there until dinner.

After they left the Copper Kettle they drove south to Arroyo Hondo to visit Dimitri. When they arrived, Dimitri was in the back room watching TV. He was wearing his white cotton bathrobe tied at the waist like an aging karate instructor. He wore slippers stepped down in the heel so they flopped along behind his every step. His hair, wispy and thinning, was in disarray and his eyelids looked heavy, as if he were angry or hung over.

"Where's Eleanor?" Ray asked, as he always did, just to see him snarl.

"In Mexico on her goddamn fishing trip," Dimitri answered sullenly.

Eleanor had forsaken Dimitri for the outdoors. Ray inspected the pictures of her, in her late fifties, scrambling over boulders on the rim of the Grand Canyon with a forty-five-pound pack on her back, or portaging her canoe through the boggy lowlands of Minnesota's boundary waters. She had short hair and rosy cheeks.

Dimitri was not a likely candidate to share her enthusiasm. His weekends were less grand, his interests more intimate. He liked building fireplaces, tiling showers, busting in a new window, installing solar water heaters, insulating the crawl space. His projects were perpetual. When Ray began his weekend visits, Dimitri was just finishing his most ambitious addition—a greenhouse with a bricked atrium connecting it to the house. Finishing for Dimitri was an open-ended phase, for nothing was ever done unless he just quit on it; then it was not so much finished as it was abandoned. Eleanor kept him from leaving the living room in a messy state of incompletion when he put the fireplace in, and pushed him all the way through the dining-room-window project until they were at least closed in, but she had no interest in the greenhouse. She could close the door between their bedroom and the new atrium and the whole mess just didn't exist. On his own timetable for the first time, he kept every portion of it in such a state of almost finished that bougainvilleas were growing in the planting beds before the skylights were installed and precipitous two-foot concrete drops down the middle of the greenhouse waited forever for some more manageable steps to join them.

"The bank won't give me the final five thousand dollars until the brick is all laid," Dimitri told Ray. "Sons of bitches."

"Awfully pushy of them."

"Bastards," Dimitri said, laughing.

It amazed Ray that the bank loaned Dimitri any money at all. He never had any plans that Ray ever knew of and he formulated his budget by asking Reynaldo, his assistant editor at work, how much he thought it would cost to put in a greenhouse.

It was only after Dimitri got his loan that the details of the project began to take shape. The block wall of the greenhouse needed to be filled in with more steel where it was underground, the mason told him; so he did that. The skylights need shades, his friend at the nursery told him; so he found some of those. The atrium floor came out twenty-six inches too low; so he added steps, and that inspired him to run a banco across the entire wall. He decided to build a large permanent fish pond of rock and discovered he needed a special neoprene membrane laid underneath the concrete to keep it from leaking. The water of the pond had to be circulated, so he devised a waterfall of seashells collected from the beaches of Florida.

"Put me a plug here," he told Ray when they were reviewing the electrical plan, "for the pump."

He decided to put in a half bath and a kitchenette on the back side of the bathroom wall, and then he had his grandest inspiration—a Jacuzzi bathtub. The idea became a fantasy; through all the hard, slow weekends of construction, of setting the timbers for the greenhouse, of cutting the bricks for the atrium floor, he began to imagine himself forever, always, floating in the froth of his new whirlpool.

Whenever Ray visited with Jesse and Zach, Dimitri was in or on his way to his tub. It was dark brown, deep, at least twenty-four inches deep, and long enough to truly lounge in. An array of potted plants formed a curtain around it, screening out the still unfinished kitchenette and the table saw in the middle of the room. Once the tub became operational, the whole project began to slow to where months went by without anything being done. Only the bank's refusal to release the last five thousand dollars of his loan kept it moving at all, and on most weekends, five thousand dollars just didn't seem worth it to Dimitri.

The first place Jesse and Zach wanted to go was the greenhouse. Dimitri let them feed the fish, warning them not to give them too much. Then they went to water the plants, spraying them with the trigger-action nozzle on his hose.

"Look for snails like these," Dimitri told them, picking a snail out of a dirt bed. "When you find them, put them on the concrete and step on them."

He dropped the snail on the step. "Step on it," he told Jesse.

Jesse looked at the snail without moving.

"It won't hurt you, go on," Dimitri prodded him. "I have my slippers on, I can't do it. You have those big shoes. Go on. Step on it. They're killing the plants."

Ray sat on the top step watching, leaning his head against a post and feeling the thick moisture. It was like suddenly being in the tropics, and he felt the exhaustion of constantly being with Jesse and Zach settle into his blood. A bougainvillea with orange flowers hung down next to his head. Jesse looked at Dimitri, still making no move to squash the snail.

"Go on, step on it. You don't want all my beautiful plants to die, do you?"

"Really?" Jesse asked.

"You think I would lie to you? You think I would tell you to step on the snail when I didn't mean it? They eat my plants. Look." Dimitri reached over and pulled a limp plant toward Jesse. "Snails have eaten at the stem of this plant. It will probably die."

"It's moving," Zach suddenly screamed, his eyes riveted on the snail.

"Get it, Zach, before it gets away," Dimitri told him.

Zach swiftly stomped on the snail, its shell cracking with a sharp snap.

"Good boy, Zach. See," Dimitri told Jesse, "your brother is not afraid of snails."

Zach lifted his foot, and he and Jesse both squatted down to examine the gooey stain on the step.

"Yuk," Jesse finally said.

Dimitri laughed loudly and went down the next giant step. He lifted Zach down next to him; Jesse stood for a moment staring after the two of them.

"Let me spray," Zach asked, following behind Dimitri.

Dimitri handed him the hose and whispered something in his ear. Zach looked up at Ray.

"Go on," Dimitri told him, looking up at Ray and laughing.

Ray got up and left the greenhouse with a smile at Zach.

"Look," Ray heard Dimitri tell Zach as he shut the door, "now he's gotten away."

Ray turned the water on in Dimitri's new whirlpool bathtub. He laid his clothes across the half wall, still not finished on the other side, which separated the head of the tub from the rest of the room. There was some bath oil in a bottle next to Ray, and after he had lowered himself in he poured in a capful and pushed the air switch in the tile to activate the jets. The motor kicked on with a high whine and the water began to suds up.

There had been a whirlpool in the locker room at Ray's Massachusetts boarding school, a stainless-steel cylindrical tub that looked clinical and dangerous, so Ray had never used it. His predominant memory of the school was of the locker room: sitting on a wooden bench too tired to pull off the sopping-wet practice shirt; pulling smelly, sweaty clothes out of the locker; the sharp crack of towels being flicked at bare butts; standing under one of the shower heads lined up in rows of eight per side, turning the water hotter and hotter by small degrees.

Ray turned the water running into the tub a little hotter; it was too hot by itself, but just right mixed in to the swirling, foaming tempest around him.

The headmaster at Ray's boarding school used to talk about such things as "the playing fields of life." When he spoke he conjured up images of good soldiers and good men. Ray's classmates were all fuck-offs: rich kids thrown out of other schools; kids who snuck out at night and got drunk; kids who cried because they were homesick; bullies who beat up the kids that cried; kids who were so smart they couldn't sleep; and kids so dumb they knew better than to care. And to them all the headmaster held up his cardboard cutouts and said, "You, each one of you, can be like this, can do this."

Ray was a believer. He wanted to become one of those cardboard cutouts, to live in grace. This was not well defined, but there was never any doubt in Ray's mind what it meant. He carried what it meant in pictures in his mind.

Stretches of mowed green fields brought up some of the pictures, for he could see himself, a small left fielder, poised in the center of such expanses, eager for the crack of the bat, the report of the starting gun, lost in the stretches of fecund New England beauty, pulling on the brim of his hat and waiting, waiting for the job to do, the ball to chase, waiting for whatever it was that would draw him to it, that would scribe his course across such fields. Waiting.

The far football field, the one reserved for games on Saturday,

with its more cared-for grass and a roll in the land that left an un-
noticeable ridge running diagonally across it, that was the playing
field.

"No one expected Ray Griffey to be the star of the football team
this year," the headmaster read to the entire school the dinner before Christmas break. "A steady safety, a defensive workhorse last
year, none of us saw him as anything more. He won a starting spot
as halfback, number 23 among more familiar numbers, and he began to roll, like a steam engine. By the end of the year he had
scored eighteen touchdowns, run over eight yards a carry, and
gained over nine hundred yards. Not to mention his record perfor-
mance on defense with seven interceptions and 'tackler of the
week' four out of ten weeks."

A yellow flower bloomed in the playing fields of life, an uncon-
scious act. There is no truth to the football you see on TV, Ray
thought, for in fact, when he ran with the ball, when he closed in
for a tackle, he saw nothing. Peripheral images, colors, floated all
around him and he floated with them, like air bubbles trapped in
thick liquid. There was none of the shock and clock of TV, none of
the calculation drawn by analysts and commentators, none of the
earth-slapping noise. To watch films of himself was to watch another person. He lived on the inside, and it was as slow and gentle
as a breath hung on the fall frost.

On the playing fields he learned to be soft steel, the last one to
fall, the last one to cry uncle, the last one to know. He wanted to
believe. When he got married it was an act of faith, another play up
the middle.

"No problem, coach," said the good soldier. "Up the middle."

"If the linebacker jumps between his guard and tackle, you're
going to have to adjust to the inside as soon as you get the ball."

"No problem, coach."

"Go for daylight."

Ray nodded his head. Go for daylight. Colors. Slow, thick liquid.
He became dumb with the dance of it.

Ray had liked the way he looked with black grease smeared under his eyes and he was never afraid. A fearless man at the altar,

saying, "I do." Down the aisle, up the middle. Go for daylight, through the heavy, tall oak doors with flashbulbs popping and Betsy's mother crying, telling stories about when she was a beautiful girl growing up in Georgia and her mama didn't approve of her first beau, who was the one she really should have married.

Ray lifted a handful of bubbles off the surface of the water and blew on them, hoping they would fly off and drift through the air, but they stubbornly hung together on his hand, only bending with his breath. He felt nostalgic for the locker rooms, for the playing fields of life, where all his reactions were the right ones. Lately, they always felt wrong. Something had gone wrong with the chemistry. He felt betrayed by the headmaster, his mother, Betsy, the wide, green fields, the swell of feeling, of goodness inside him. He had fallen from grace.

He sank his shoulders and head under water. The noise of the Jacuzzi motors sounded like giant propellers running over him and he allowed himself to be buffeted back and forth by the jets of water. When he was six, at Rehoboth Beach, there was a game he played with his brothers. They stood knee-deep in the surf at the spot where the waves broke and they would let the thundering breakers knock them down and kick them over and over in the fizzing, turbulent water. His brothers always quit long before he did; he loved it and went back again and again, his small red bathing suit full of sand, went back until it was time to leave, and then he begged to stay for just a couple more times. With each wave he never knew if he would survive, if the wave would let him go and he would find daylight before he ran out of breath. Each wave held his small, bony life in its hands, and each time that he came up alive, salt water stinging his eyes, sand in his teeth, he sang inside with his own excellent mortality.

When Ray came back up for air, Dimitri was towering over him with Jesse and Zach standing beside his legs.

"God damn it," Dimitri said, "did I say you could use my Jacuzzi?"

Jesse and Zach watched to see how their dad would handle being caught and scolded. Ray smiled and went back down into the warmth and turmoil of the whirlpool. When he reemerged he heard the three of them at the fish pool.

"Please, Dimitri, can we feed them?"

"Please?"

"You've already fed them."

"That was a long time ago."

"Fish can't eat too much. They die."

"Please," pleaded Jesse.

"All right, god damn it, get the food."

Ray heard Jesse and Zach racing back into the house, down the hallway to the laundry room to retrieve the food, elbowing and arguing over who was going to be first.

"Bastards," Dimitri said quietly, and laughed to himself.

"Don't swear so much around them," Ray yelled over the sound of the motors.

Dimitri laughed again, louder. "Get out of my goddamn tub, you son of a bitch," he said. "You're using all my hot water."

Dogs

Sunday evening the phone rang as Ray was packing Zach's diaper bag to return to Betsy. It was his first phone call and it startled him. Jesse and Zach were outside tramping through the dry leaves and getting to know the poodle that lived next door to them. Not knowing the poodle himself, Ray was trying to keep an eye on them through the window. The phone would take him out of eye contact. Call them in or take a chance?

He took a chance. "Hello."

It was Betsy.

"How did it go?" she asked.

Ray tried to detect if she had anything invested in his answer to that. Ray was not going to tell her how frazzled he felt, how grateful he was that the weekend was over. The thought of the night alone with his Civil War novel or, better yet, with Julia, seemed like a little bit of heaven.

"Fine," he told her. "A little short on supplies, but we're working that out."

"The reason I called. Can you come back tonight, after the boys are asleep? Something's come up that I'd like to talk with you about."

An unnamed dread rose up in Ray's throat, as if he had done something wrong and had just been caught, and he used a moment of silence to purge it from his voice. He thought of Jesse and Zach out in the yard with the dog. He could hear their voices and the leaves swishing as they ran about. What could she want to discuss? Did he sense a hint of threat in her voice? Suddenly he was angry—he was gone and that was that. How much more clear could things be? He took another moment to let the anger clear.

"OK," Ray finally said.

"Around eight?"

He had not yet arranged it but was hoping to call Julia and entice her over. After a weekend scattered on bits of tears, TV, and changes of clothes, Ray was hoping for a little conversation, some return to civilization, and, of course, a night, a full night, his first full night alone with her.

"OK, I'll be there at eight," he told Betsy.

When Ray hung up and looked out the window, he saw the poodle had knocked Zach down and was humping his leg. Zach, he could see, was moving from playing and laughter to horror and tears. Jesse was harmlessly whipping the poodle's rear end with a limp branch of dried, yellowed leaves. Ray ran outside and pulled the dog off just as Zach let out his first wail. Ray picked him up and carried him, crying against his shoulder, to sit on the steps leading to the yard.

"You have to be careful with dogs you don't know," Ray said, directing his comment more to Jesse than Zach.

"I didn't do anything," Jesse said.

Zach's crying filled the yard, expanding like a mist through the crisp fall afternoon, ballooning until it represented every fall and scrape, every loss and disappointment, every crass injustice in the world. Ray held him thinking that he should save him from such things and feeling guilty that he had not.

"You didn't have to be hitting the dog like that," Ray told Jesse, "it was just getting him more excited."

"I was trying to get him off Zach."

"I know, but you were just getting him more excited."

"Well, I was just trying to get him off."

Jesse looked at Ray. His lower lip crept out and then he too began to cry, not with the agony of Zach, but softly, from deep within, where his fear had caught up with him.

As best Ray could, he put his arm around Jesse and drew him under his other shoulder. They sniffled and smeared themselves all over Ray's shirt. Zach showed great endurance and kept his near howling going, pausing only to take deep breaths now and then. Ray wanted to tell him to shut up.

"I want to go to Mommy's," Jesse said just as Ray was thinking how nice it would be to take them back.

"I want to go to Mommy's," Zach took up.

Suddenly a spring in Ray released. He felt both relaxed and exhausted. The three of them became one body, knocked over and humped by poodles, scared and in need of a home. Ray looked at his watch: four-thirty. Half an hour until they were due back.

"Soon," Ray said, the sound like deep water. "Soon," he told them over and over, and their tears receded as the shadows quietly lengthened and darkness began to grow. They stayed sitting on the steps. Zach was still sniffling lightly, his body winding down slowly.

"I'm cold," Jesse finally said, and they went back inside and finished packing to leave.

Ray knocked loudly when he returned later that night. Betsy had disconnected the doorbell so that she wouldn't be awakened while she slept. She was wearing a loose turquoise sweater with white pants that disappeared stylishly into ankle-high gray slip-on boots. She looked dressed up, but her mouth was pinched and her face was red when she invited Ray in. It might have been Ray's imagination, but he thought she was angry.

"Just a second," she said as she fled back toward the bedrooms. "Jesse is just getting to sleep."

Dash, their dog, left behind like everything else in the house, shook himself loose from his place of permanent rest under the dining room table and came out to say hello. Only the stupid grin on his long white muzzle suggested that Ray still lived in his memory as someone other than the UPS man.

Dash kept himself sequestered under the dining-room table in order to stay clear of the imaginations of Jesse and Zach. If he was visible they inevitably found a role for him in their games. Zach, just after he had learned to walk, practiced back and forth across the living room in that stilted, jolting half-run that toddlers use at first, and on one lap he veered to the right and tramped right across Dash's back.

With the same casual stroke, Jesse regularly crashed his oversized red plastic baseball bat across the top of Dash's head as if it were a tent peg that hadn't quite been driven all the way down. One night on TV there had been a program about Australian sheepdogs working their sheep in the outback, ceaselessly running back and forth nipping at their heels.

"Those are hard-working dogs," Ray told Jesse.

"Is Dash a hard-working dog?" he asked.

Ray had looked at Dash fast asleep under the dining room table, living the life of an outlaw in hiding, never safe, never secure, never able to let go of the thought that at any unwary moment he might be found and called out to play.

"Yes," Ray told him. "Dash is a hard-working family dog."

Ray sat on the couch in his usual spot, at the far end. It put Ray in front of the blank, dull gray TV. He felt as if he had never left and then, just as strongly, as if he had never been there, as if he were a different person from the Ray who had lived there. That Ray had spent a lifetime on that couch, in front of that TV, drinking Budweiser and watching early-evening reruns of *Hogan's Heroes*, following the intricacies of *Hill Street Blues*, staying up late to watch *The Rockford Files* after Betsy had gone to bed. On Saturday afternoons he had liked to lie down and fall asleep in front of the Channel 4 Baseball Game of the Week, and Sundays he sometimes had friends over to watch the big football games. Betsy made a bowl of her guacamole dip, which they all scooped with tortilla chips. Then there had been the early mornings, when his back hurt, that he had watched the cable sports channel, his body frozen and twisted like a wild piñon tree. He realized, suddenly, that his back was no longer hurting him at night.

"Jesse's having problems falling asleep again," Betsy said. "I think he's down now."

Ray nodded. Betsy sat in the armchair at the end of the coffee table. It was her mother's overstuffed chair with winged arms. Betsy had reupholstered it in a muted yellow, almost tan, corduroy fabric. She looked harassed and nervous. Her nose and cheeks were flushed redder than her hair. She bit her lower lip and looked at Ray a second before speaking.

"Do you want something to drink? I think there still might be some Buds in the refrigerator."

Ray shook his head.

"How did it go this weekend with the boys? Were they OK?"

"Yes, fine. OK, yes. Zach woke up once in the middle of the night," Ray said, forgetting that Zach had been sick Friday night.

"He does over here, too. He always has."

"Yes."

"Roget called today," she said. "He was looking for Julia and he wanted your number." Betsy paused and looked down. "He told me, he said, 'Did you know they're living together?' I didn't know what to say. I mean, I told him no, I didn't know that. He was very angry. He was sort of yelling at me for being some sort of dummy for not knowing that."

She paused again. Betsy had never cried much; Ray couldn't see her face but thought she might be crying now. She lifted her head and looked at him and said, "I guess I feel like some sort of dummy. I mean, you told me you weren't leaving me for Julia. I believed you, and now you're living with her."

She wasn't crying, but she was having difficulty getting her words out.

It was a relief, it made Ray feel good to be able to say, "No, he's wrong. We're not living together." For clarification he added, "It's never crossed my mind. The last time I saw Julia was at work on Thursday."

It *had* crossed his mind. It was mystifying to him that he and Julia weren't spending more time together than they were, but he was grateful, just then, to say they weren't, as if it were part of a plan.

Betsy looked at Ray as if there was more to say.

"Roget's mad at Julia," Ray told her. "They've got their own stuff going on. It sounds like he's a little crazy."

"OK," she said finally, some of the tension gone from around her lips. "That's what I wanted to ask you. I felt like I needed to know."

"One more thing," Betsy added, stopping Ray from getting up. Her head dropped again and then she looked back up. "I guess I need to hear it again. I guess it's hard for me to believe or I don't understand. Do you really not love me anymore?"

Ray dropped his head. He was not good at this; he did not want to do it. He looked at her and tried to focus some intensity in his eyes.

"I don't love you anymore," he told her.

It was not so hard to say; it fell on the bottom of a long list of things he had said over the years: "I love you." "Will you marry me?" "I'm looking forward to growing old with you." "I don't love you anymore." A litany of lies, Ray supposed. When had they become lies? How had it all become a lie? Ray could not control it anymore. He did not know the truth. He only knew that he had to put aside Betsy, put her out of his life, whatever that might mean. There was a script for that too, just like all the other moments. He had to tell her he did not love her anymore. He spoke his line dutifully.

She heard him and sat staring for a moment. In spite of what Ray had said, Betsy did not feel so horrible. First, Ray had come when she had called. Then, Ray had quieted her greatest anxiety, which was about Julia. And then, even beneath his denial of his love, there had been further reassurance. Ray and Betsy had never been straight with each other, they had never fought. They had perfected a language that circled around things, that suggested anger without getting angry, that suggested hurt without tears. This obliqueness had been a part of their relationship. Her question had been, in part, an expression of her confusion and hurt, and even though Ray had told her that he no longer loved her, he had also kept faith with their indirect code of conversation. His answer had been a reflex, expedient. He had not addressed her feelings and he had not expressed his own. In a way that only a couple who have lived together for years can understand, Betsy had received Ray's negative answer in a positive light. She was not yet ready to give up on their relationship and she had heard nothing that night to make her.

"OK," Ray said getting up. There was a flurry of activity as Dash reemerged from under the dining room table, wagging his tail between Ray and Betsy at the front door.

"Just a second," Betsy said. "I almost forgot."

She ran back to the bedroom and came back with two huge shopping bags.

"I was in Albuquerque this weekend and saw these. I thought you might be able to use them."

Inside each bag were two large pillows and one smaller one. Ray and Julia had noticed them at American Furniture on Thursday. They were blue with small red and white designs spattered over them.

"Thanks," Ray said, hefting the bags beside him like birds shot in the early winter. "I need something over there."

Betsy opened the door and let Dash and Ray out.

"Thanks again," Ray told her.

Ray muscled the pillows into the backseat of the Toyota. Dash stood beside him wagging, waiting for the command to jump in. Ray stooped down and petted him around the ears and let him lick his nose once.

"Keep up the hard work," Ray told Dash, and left him standing on the sidewalk watching and wagging.

Part Two
Winter 1982

Trying to
Get
Through

It was late November. Two snowstorms had dropped on Santa Fe since the first. It was a month since Ray had moved out. When he got to the office, Scott was reading the results of a dirt-bike race in *The New Mexican*.

"Where are you going today?" Ray asked Scott. Ray had become more distracted, less sure of what was happening.

"Pedro and I are going to take care of that temporary service for Larry Robinson; then we're going out to the shopping center to hang some more lights with Jeff and Ricky."

Ray nodded. He knew they were behind at the shopping center and it made Scott nervous, but Scott was trying to keep the rest of their customers happy at the same time. A job like the new shopping center could swamp a company like Prime Time Electric. With six crews, they were one of the biggest nonunion shops in Santa Fe, but staying busy inevitably meant being too busy from time to time. This was one of those times. In the past, Ray might have strapped on his tools and helped. Those days were gone. Not that Ray was incapable; he had started the company with just himself and a helper in a dirty white service truck. As things grew, he quit working in the field, until eventually there was no place for him there. It was an unspoken thing, and Ray sometimes missed the old days. They seemed simpler.

After Scott left, Ray began on his stack of mail. He had sent out a notice changing his mailing address to work. There was a card about a group art show December 1 at the Santa Fe Fine Arts Museum. His friend Robin was one of the artists. Robin was Dimitri's stepdaughter, which was how Ray had met Dimitri the first time. Robin had scribbled a note across the bottom of the card urging Ray to come.

Julia came and stood beside Ray's desk looking, he thought, a little petulant.

"Noni called," she said drawing out the two beats of Noni's name in habituated sarcasm. "One of her kids is sick again, and she's going to be late."

"OK." She had done something to her hair that Ray could not quite figure out.

"I thought, if you wanted, if you're free"—she paused, looking up at Ray and smiling—"it's such a nice day and all, I thought it would be fun to drive down to the Jemez Hot Springs. There's never anyone there during the week—we'd have it all to ourselves, I'm sure. If you're free, after Noni comes in?"

Ray had to stop and think. There was something about the invitation that reminded him of boarding school; it smacked of breaking the rules.

"OK," Ray told Julia, "let's do it. What the hell. After lunch. I have lunch with Bud Jackson."

"Great," she said, smiling as if she were a child that had just been given a lollipop. "Can you come by my place and pick me up when you're ready?"

"OK."

She started to skip out of the room.

"Julia," Ray asked, stopping her, "have the gross receipts taxes been filed?"

"They're not due till Friday," she said cheerfully, and flew out the door.

Ray met Bud at Casa Isabel. Mrs. Flores, the owner, had a daughter named Isabel, and when she hired Prime Time Electric to add some lights and outlets in the old house she was making into her restaurant, Isabel and Roberto Baca, one of Ray's apprentice electricians, fell in love. Mrs. Flores was opposed to the romance; she thought apprentice electrician was not a promising position, and after she found out she called Ray and told him not to send Roberto over to her job. She asked him how much he made (Ray wouldn't tell) and how far he might go (Ray told her that he would go far). She complained to Ray about how hard the restaurant business was. He thought she was still talking about her daughter and didn't realize she was preparing him for not getting paid. Ray ended up with at least four or five years of free lunches at Casa Isabel, assuming both of them lasted that long, and whenever Ray ate there she greeted him like royalty. Royalty was her theme: she had decorated the place with plush red carpeting, high-backed, dark-stained chairs, and dim light.

Keeping him off the job had done nothing to deter Roberto's desire for Isabel, and they had gotten married. Isabel, with a belly at least seven months pregnant, served Ray and Bud iced tea. She was not yet twenty, as Mrs. Flores had told Ray frequently, and wore makeup to cover her acne. She was so nervous about spilling when she filled their glasses that it made Ray nervous and, inevitably, at some point during the meal, she did spill something.

"Do you have any soup?" Bud asked her.

"I'll have to find out," she said with a smile.

"Hello, Isabel."

"Hello, Mr. Griffey."

Mrs. Flores, a good six inches shorter than Isabel and with a stomach of her own, was soon upon them with her pad. Ray always wondered who did the cooking. Ray and Bud were the only ones there.

"Not many customers?" Ray asked her, concerned about all his unclaimed lunches.

"November is always a bad month, and Tuesdays are always slow," she said, the voice of time.

"Do you have any soup?" Bud asked her.

"Nope. Just the green chile stew. It's pretty watery, and hot. Or I can give you a big bowl of posole."

Bud ordered the green chile stew and Ray ordered a burrito with ground meat, forgetting until his first bite that she made them too salty.

"Are we doing Arby's?" Ray asked Bud.

"I think so. The guys in Chicago thought my price was too high, but they don't have time to get another, so they asked me to go back through my figures. I told them there was no point. I gave them a price, and that's my price. I don't make mistakes, not often anyway, and I'm never trying to screw anybody, no matter how much I don't like them." He laughed, but Ray didn't think he looked well.

"Have you been sick?" Ray asked him.

"I've had a flu or something for almost a month. It never quite goes away. Every time I think I'm better, it gets worse again."

"You should have a checkup."

Bud just looked at Ray and went on eating without answering.

"I don't need a doctor to tell me what's wrong," Bud finally said. "I've lost thirty pounds since the beginning of the year. It's all this business with Fran."

"What's going on?"

"I didn't tell you the latest?"

Ray shook his head, taking a bite of burrito.

"They moved out of town," he said.

"Who did?"

"Fran and the girls. About a month ago."

"Moved out?"

"Yep."

"To where?"

"Well, I don't know really. Probably to eastern Washington. She grew up there. Her mother lives in Spokane."

"Just moved out?"

"Just like that. One weekend. Packed up and gone. There was this note in my mailbox from Fran. 'We've moved,' it said. That was

it. And it had her mother's address on the bottom with 'in case you
want to reach me, a message with Gram will find me' written underneath it."

"You mean you didn't know they were moving?"

"Nope. Not till I got that note."

"And your daughters?"

"Gone. The whole lot of them. Gone without a word."

"Have you heard from them?"

"No. Her mother changed her phone number and got it un-
listed, so the only way I have to reach them is to write a letter. And
I don't know if they even get there."

"You're kidding."

"No."

"The girls haven't tried to reach you?"

"No. Not a word."

Ray didn't know what to say. He stared with his mouth open.
Ray knew Bud must feel awful but thought telling him so might
make him feel worse.

"She poisoned the girls against me," Bud said, spooning his
green chile stew without eating.

"Can she do that?" Ray asked. "Just leave like that?"

Bud shrugged his shoulders and then laughed. "She did.
They're gone."

Isabel poured them some more water, spilling an ice cube into
Bud's stew.

"I'll get you another bowl," she said desperately.

"It's OK," Bud said. "I'm done. You can take it away."

Isabel left without taking the bowl, returning with a towel, then,
realizing that there wasn't anything a towel could do, left again.

"What do you do?" Ray asked Bud. "How do you take it?"

"Well, there's a woman, Susan. Without her, I'm not sure I
would have made it this far. I'm not sure I could have made it at all.
She's been a godsend. She's really pulled me through. But
then . . ." he paused, picking the ice cube out of his stew with his
spoon. "I really don't have much left over to give to her. It's a problem."

Julia wanted to be an artist instead of a bookkeeper. She painted watercolors in fits and starts, on weekends. She had a canvas bag with her supplies that she kept in her car and she sometimes brought it with her like a purse, as if she might become suddenly inspired. The first time Ray ever saw her use it was at the Jemez Hot Springs that afternoon. She sat naked, with the water up to her waist, as if she were in a tub, and painted furiously for twenty minutes. She rested her back against one of the black lava rocks; the paints sat on another rock next to her, and she rinsed her brush in the water all around her. A light snow fell, the good weather of the morning giving way to dense colorless clouds. Her nipples became hard and erect from the cold and every now and then she held her pad high in one hand and slipped her whole body down under the water to warm up, the ends of her shoulder-length hair floating for a second around her, mixing with the swirl of colors.

She was not painting the landscape, because her head was not going up and down, from tree to paper. Her eyes were fixed on the picture, watching as some internal landscape came out. Ray asked to see it when she was done, and she reluctantly passed it to him. There was a realistic red armchair, twisted a little out of perspective, but the red was lush, like the carpet at Casa Isabel. The chair hung suspended in a deep wash of green-brown. There were so many shades to the background that it had texture and depth, as if you could live in it, breath it. In the top right corner was a small black telephone.

"What do you call it?" Ray asked.

"It's not very good. I don't have a name."

"How about 'Trying to Get Through'?" Ray suggested.

"It's not very good," she repeated as she plucked it from him, closed it, and laid it on the rocks next to the pool. She swam back to Ray like a giant snake, grinning.

"I like it. It's good," Ray told her.

"What do you know?"

She kissed him, delighted with something. Ray caught her around the waist and pulled her across to him. Her body was slippery and erotic, and when he pressed against her he felt the mineral in the water rubbing between them.

"Why don't you paint? Why don't you do it all the time?" Ray asked her.

She ducked her head all the way under the water and lay still as a log, her arms stretched out. When she reemerged Ray continued to press her.

"Really, why?"

"I've always been able to paint," she said dreamily. "I've always been able to make pictures. My uncle offered me a job once making pictures for greeting cards. He's some muckety-muck with Hallmark. He said I could make a lot of money." She stopped, as if that explained it.

"So?"

"So. It's just a talent I have. I'm not an artist and I don't want to make quaint Christmas cards of happy families with red cheeks for Hallmark."

"That's not a Christmas card," Ray said, nodding toward her pad on the rocks beside them.

"It's not art either."

"I think it's good."

"Artists work every day. They struggle to get things right. Like Robin. I admire Robin a lot, and her art, but she works every day at it. I toss something off once a month, when the mood hits, half an hour here, half an hour there. That's not art, that's doodling." She was getting angry.

"Well, if you did it every day, then you'd be an artist."

"No, I wouldn't," she snapped. "I'm too lazy. I could never do it every day. Besides, you know, I've got to make a living."

"You hate bookkeeping."

"Not as much as I hate waitressing."

"You could go to art school."

"With what money?"

"Ask your parents."

"I did."

"What did they say?"

"Same thing they always say."

"Which is?"

"Which is 'Fuck you!' " she screamed suddenly, like a blood vessel bursting. It bounced off the canyon walls around them and she cocked her head to listen to it. "Fuck you!" she screamed again, tilting her head back. "Fuck you!"

Ray slipped his head under the water, closing his eyes. The over-100-degree temperature was like a womb. There was no up or down, no in or out. There was no noise. He lay on the fine pebbles on the bottom as long as he could, feeling the skin on his fingers wrinkle.

"Sorry," Julia said when Ray resurfaced. She was contrite. "I go crazy sometimes." She slid closer to him.

"You're too good for me," she said. "I do bad things to people, to myself. You don't even know what bad is. You're just a babe."

"I don't know if I feel insulted or complimented," Ray told her.

"Neither. It's just true." She was now, again, rubbing against him.

"Have you ever made love in a hot tub?" Ray asked.

"It's no good in water. You'd think the water would, you know, lubricate or something. But it just makes you rub. It's never made sense to me, but it's true."

"You could be an artist."

"You could be a jerk."

"How much does art school cost anyway?"

"I don't know. How would I know?" Her temper was rising again.

"I thought you asked. Your parents?"

"I asked in theory, you know. I knew they weren't going to ask how much. Five cents would be too much for them."

Ray had an urge to send Julia to art school. She paddled away from him toward the small waterfall where the water tumbled out of the pool. The stones were covered with a slick yellow film of minerals like icing where the water had been running over them for years. Ray followed her, biting at her toes. When she climbed out, she stuck her butt in his face. He watched the dark, hairy folds between her legs, so incongruous with the smoothness of her skin. Of the naked women he'd seen, he thought that view of Julia at that moment was the most intimate. Because it was during the day, outdoors, with snow idly dropping on their shoulders; because it was so casual, a matter of movement rather than sex.

"I have to move out of my apartment the end of this month," Julia said when she had found a comfortable seat in the waterfall. "The landlord wants the place for his son."

"Why don't you move in with me?" Ray quickly volunteered. It was an impulse, out of his mouth before he knew it. He had not intended to ask her that. If she hadn't said anything about her apartment, he would not have invited her. He had moved like an athlete, an animal: a quick step and a leap.

Julia sat without answering, her eyes closed and her head back as if the sun was shining across her. At just that moment the sun did come out, making its way through a hole in the overcast sky, melting the snow flakes before they hit the ground, illuminating her wet, glossy skin.

"Maybe," Julia finally answered without opening her eyes.

Familiar faces were appearing in Ray's dreams. In one, Noni's daughter, Ashley, a redhead, was serving tea with a college girl-friend of Ray's named Margaret. Ashley had spent that day at work with Noni; she had been too sick for day care. Margaret and Ashley served Ray tea at a rickety old pink table. Margaret farted and they all were laughing and waving their hands to clear the air.

In another dream, a friend of Ray's whose picture had been in *The New Mexican* showed up with Curtis Ross from St. Stephen's School for Boys. A short note about Curtis had been in Ray's latest copy of the *Alumni Bulletin*. Curtis had just had his first child. "I never knew life could be so rich," he wrote for the *Bulletin*. In the dream, the three of them were talking about how to get to a restaurant in the hills. A TV was on, making noise and casting a strange white light over everything.

It was like that, night after night. Ray woke in the mornings feeling as if there were no filters between himself and the world. His old life mixed seamlessly with his new life. It was a vulnerable feeling and because he had no control over who or what might step into his dreams, he felt a little brave or bold. He liked it, and lay in bed each morning, quietly savoring the taste of it.

Ray thought about the dream with Curtis Ross. He had not been such a good friend of Curtis's, but Curtis had been the roommate of Justin Marks. Then he realized that even though Justin had not been in the dream, his presence had been strong. In fact, he further realized, the dream had really been about Justin. Justin had been Ray's best friend in boarding school. Maybe his best friend ever. Maybe, Ray thought, the only real friend he ever had. And suddenly Ray wanted to cry. For the first time since Sean died, Ray wanted to cry.

Where
Do I Sit?

Julia decided to accept Ray's offer and moved in December 1, the day of Robin's opening at the museum. All her clothes were in a hard-sided small tan suitcase with a red and green stripe running around one end. It had a worn leather handle and brass hinges. Ray thought that maybe it was her grandmother's.

She wasn't really moving in, she said. Just staying until her friend Reatta went to Albuquerque and she could stay in her place. It would help if she weren't paying any rent; she could save some money.

She took out some skirts and shirts and looked around for a place to put them.

"Where are your clothes?" she asked.

There were closets, but Ray had not yet bought any hangers. He pointed to the collection of three boxes in the corner that he used as drawers. It was a little makeshift, but he had developed a system. He explained it.

"I keep socks and underwear in this box. The socks I don't wear are on the bottom; the socks I do wear on the left, and underwear on the right. The middle box is shirts; they are also arranged, according to short sleeve and long sleeve. This box is pants. I know you think I only wear one pair of blue jeans all the time, but here is evidence that I own other pants as well, mostly more blue jeans, but here is a pair of corduroys that I never wear." He held up the corduroys for her to see.

"Which box is for skirts?" she asked.

"I'll get you one of your own, for female things."

"Forget it. I'll just use my suitcase. It's a box with a lid. A little higher class."

She dropped her skirts back in. The inside of her suitcase was lined with a dappled purple silk that hung loosely from the edges. She pulled out a poster from underneath her clothes and unfurled it. The poster was a jarring yellow-and-black print with violent lines and angles. It took Ray a while before he realized that woven in among the colors were images of a band, and their name was also part of the design: "Men at Work." She walked around the room, holding the poster against the wall in different places.

"Hold it here for me," she asked.

Ray pinned it up with his thumbs, and she stepped back across the bed to look at it.

"Good. What do you think? Do you have any tacks or pins?"

"I have some Scotch tape in the kitchen."

"No, I don't want to use any Scotch tape; it will rip the paper when I take it down."

Ray became disheartened whenever she mentioned leaving, which he thought she had already done too often.

"Look in the kitchen," he said, still holding the poster against the wall, "in the first drawer on the left."

She returned with a clear box full of stickpins and, after bending three, finally secured the poster. They both stepped back and looked. Ray hadn't realized until then how used to the emptiness he had become. The poster jumped and buzzed and made the room busy and small. The soft-edged, ill-defined white of the walls, like the inside of an egg, disappeared, and became background to Julia's poster.

Julia sensed Ray's uneasiness and put her arm around his shoulders like a father.

"I'll take it down if you don't like it. It's just that everything is so . . . so"—she swept the room with her free hand, looking for the right word—"bare. No offense, I mean it's nice. But so empty. You need a little color."

"No, it's fine," he said. "I like it."

She was probably right, he thought, it is time for a little color in my life, time to move ahead. He shrugged his shoulders.

"It's great," he repeated. "Welcome to Silver Street."

Ray turned to hold her, to give her a special embrace. She rested her elbows against his shoulders, keeping him from getting too close. She didn't like these moments foisted on her, these secret sentiments.

"Thanks for giving me a place to stay," she said, allowing him a kiss.

Wait until tonight, Ray thought, feeling something elusive even now, even as they took up living together. They had missed a step, he realized. Julia had moved in, yet she had still not spent a night with him in this new apartment. There were two things happening at once. Maybe too many things, Ray thought.

Ray dipped into his boxes and Julia into her suitcase to get dressed for Robin's opening.

Julia was stunning. She wore a simple black cotton dress that hung on her like a soft glove. She pulled it together with a bright silver Kmart concho belt buckled tightly around her waist. The dress was short, and she wore black stockings with silver hearts on them. Her shoes were red.

When they arrived at the museum, Dimitri spotted them immediately.

"Julia baby," he said, advancing on her, "if that son of a bitch can't make you happy, you call me." He hugged her with some pelvic thrust to drive home his message.

He looked at Ray and laughed. "You lucky dog. You sure know

how to pick them. Right away, leave the wife and kids at home and look what you've got. You think if I get divorced I can find something as nice as this?" He pulled Julia next to him.

"You're too old for that sort of thing," Julia kidded him.

"Try me, baby. Just try me."

When Robin and Jack arrived, they all went in to see the show. Besides Robin, three other artists were featured, one of them a friend of Robin's, a tall man named Luan. Robin hugged him as they said hello. They remained talking together and the rest of the group side-stepped around the show. Jack and Julia went in one direction and Dimitri and Ray in the other.

"What is this shit?" Dimitri asked in front of a large canvas of Luan's: a surreal green landscape, intricately painted. It looked something like a maze, an upside-down, floating English boxwood maze. All his paintings did.

Robin joined Ray and Dimitri.

"Luan wants us to join him for a drink after the opening," Robin said.

"Let's go now," Dimitri said.

"Stop it," Robin said, "you're so bad."

"Where?" Ray asked.

"How about Evangelos'?" Dimitri suggested.

"OK," Robin said, "I'll tell Luan."

Ray watched Robin leave. She was wearing a brown dress with a blurred print of stripes or zigzags or something. He had never seen her in a dress before and he was suddenly aware of how nervous she was. He looked at Julia across the room. She was so at home in her clothes, so eye-catching. Robin's dress made her look as if she wanted to blend in with the wallpaper. Jack and Julia laughed as they talked. Jack was more like Julia. He wore a leather jacket, tight brown Levi's, and boots. He looked like the artist. They both knew their bodies, their shapes, the way they appeared. They also shared ideas of themselves as artists.

"This isn't art," Dimitri complained in front of another of Luan's mazes.

Ray liked Robin's paintings of Jack better than the others. Robin didn't put faces on any of her figures, but Ray knew which ones were of Jack by the ease and power of the body. She painted that so well, he thought, that controlled, male kind of grace. An arm in one of her paintings reminded him of his own arm, muscular far beyond its function, simple and inert, slightly bent, as if you could hear the power in it like a heart beating.

On the way to Evangelos' Bar, Ray walked with Robin. They picked their way through the snow and slush. Ray had always been able to talk with Robin, as if their way of speaking and understanding had been made in the same factory.

"I liked your paintings," Ray told her.

"Thanks. It's always so amazing when they get hung like that. It's as if they're not mine anymore. As if I've lost them all of a sudden. I think I feel a little sad, but also relieved, because I can see them like you see them, just as paintings. I liked them too."

"I liked the ones of Jack. They are so distant, studied; at the same time, full of understanding, somehow."

"I liked those best too. I was a little surprised. I almost didn't include them."

Ray held poetry and art just outside his circle of interests, but because it was Robin's art, he found himself engaged in a way he had never been before.

Robin told Ray about Luan Peterson. He lived forty miles below Grants on a four-wheel-drive road. She told a story about visiting him in the winter and having to walk the last mile and when she finally arrived discovering that he lived in a trailer.

"How could anyone have gotten a trailer in there?" she wondered. "He converted the living room into a studio and had an outhouse because there was no septic system."

Ray sat at the red Formica table at Evangelos' between Robin and Luan. With the first round of ouzo, everyone toasted Luan, Robin, and the show. Luan was a tall man, over six feet, and thin. Ray thought how odd it must be for him in a trailer where everything is three-quarter size. He wore baggy, worn blue jeans and a plaid shirt with a leather vest. He had a rough beard with a lot of gray in it. Jack, Julia, and Luan's girlfriend, Lee, who was Japanese, were on the other side of the table, and the bar was too noisy for Ray to hear anything they said. There were booths along the walls partially hidden behind withered brown palm fronds. Dimitri was at the bar talking in Greek to the owner. Luan and Robin were talking about children.

"You have children, or a child, don't you?" Robin asked Luan.

"A son. He's sixteen. He came to stay with me last summer."

Luan did not look like a painter to Ray. He was too tall and rough, like an animal, like someone who lived outdoors all the time. He spoke slowly, as if he were always thinking.

"Where does he live?" Ray asked, interested in children who lived miles from their fathers.

"California."

"Does he come every summer?"

Luan smiled, almost laughing, and rocked back in his chair. "No, he doesn't, he definitely does not."

Ray waited for more, but Luan seemed absorbed in his own joke.

"When did you last see him?" Ray asked.

"Let's see. Kate and I split up in the late sixties, sixty-nine, I think. He must have been around four or so."

"You haven't seen him since then?"

"Oh yeah, once or twice. Sure. When I'm through California. He came two or three years ago and was going to stay the summer, but we got in a fight and he took off. You know, he was on the muscle, just coming into his nuts."

"Ray has two children," Robin told Luan. "Two boys. He's getting divorced right now."

"I'm afraid of not seeing them again," Ray said. "Like your son. I'm afraid they'll just disappear from my life."

Luan tipped his chair back again and smiled beneath his bushy beard.

"They come back," he said. "They always come back. Don't worry. Sooner or later, they come back."

Ray could hear the tires of the cars sloshing through the melted snow outside. Hot air from the overhead furnace blasted down on the group. The conversation between Robin and Luan spun off into galleries.

"Rachel used to run a shoe store, so you know where she's at," Robin said about her gallery owner.

The door opened and the cold touched Ray, making his shoulders and neck shudder involuntarily. He looked across at Julia. She and Lee were laughing and rocking back and forth in their chairs. Jack sat looking off at the bar absently. He had once told Ray that when he was a child he had spent hours watching the dust motes float in the sunlight coming in through the window. Someone put a Spanish love song on the jukebox and the romantic vowels and horns filled the room. Jack turned as Ray was looking at him and their eyes met. They both smiled. Ray thought that he did not want to go twelve years without seeing Jesse and Zach.

Ray got in bed with the smell of stale beer from Evangelos' still in his nostrils.

"Thanks," Julia said. "I really had a good time. Thanks a lot."

"I'm glad," Ray said. He knew what she meant; she had gotten outside of herself for the evening. He had not. Luan's story haunted him.

"I really liked Jack," she said. "We laughed a lot. I don't think I've laughed so much in years. Don't you love the way he laughs?"

Ray did not answer. He was beginning to prowl over Julia's body with his fingers.

"I needed that," Julia continued. "I didn't realize it but I think I was almost forgetting how to laugh. Everything has been so serious lately. Laughing tonight was like an oasis. Now I'm thirsty for more. We need to laugh more."

"How about sex?" Ray kneaded her breast.

After coming, after five minutes of delirious exhaustion, Ray was suddenly awake. Julia lay asleep with her back to him, her ass gently nudging his thigh. Nakedness, Ray thought. Wonderful nakedness. And sex as it had never been with Betsy. He wanted to shout about it, but everything was so quiet. The eerie, flat light from the street flooded through the uncurtained window. Julia's poster was glowing like something radioactive. Julia was so still he watched her back for signs of breathing. The warm smell of sex was trapped beneath the open sleeping bag they were using for a quilt. The world was asleep and Ray began to wish that he was, too, but something kept him awake. Julia had moved in; it was what he had wanted. Yet he lay awake and uneasy as the winter cold crept in on the light and inhabited the ghostly white walls and wood floors. This was not awake as it had been with Betsy, full of pain. This was different. His footing in life had turned liquid. Every lurch forward produced an uncertain result. Yet he sensed some definition, some meaning. As in a dream, he understood that somewhere behind the wacky reality some truths lay deeply hidden. That sense of things taunted him. He felt it without understanding it. He would be patient. Patience was his strong suit.

Ray held on through the long December weekends with Jesse and Zach. He felt every minute. Julia always had other plans, as if she were magnetically opposed to the presence of Jesse and Zach. Sometimes they visited Dimitri. Dimitri was becoming more and more unhappy with Eleanor and always wanted to talk about it. She was no longer sleeping with him. At lunch, during the week, Ray could keep up with Dimitri's frenetic monologues, but with Jesse and Zach on the weekend, he did not have the energy.

The three of them developed a new routine of going to Scott's house to watch the Sunday football games on TV. Jesse liked playing with Scott's baby. Zach and Ray let the endless football drivel wash over them like hypnosis. Zach liked to wedge himself behind Ray, propped up by Ray's shoulder and the couch corner, his plastic diaper crinkling whenever he moved.

"Look, he's holding my finger," Jesse called up to them from where he lay on the floor with the baby.

Ray and Zach looked, then returned to the game. Scott was more responsive. He lay down on the floor with Jesse and smiled at his baby, his big body stretched out. Scott was generally more animated, cheering for his teams, going back and forth to the kitchen for snacks, beers, and sodas. When the game became lop-sided, he went outside to tinker on his latest mechanical project for a while. Scott had a yard full of old Chevy Novas and motorcycles. He believed in Chevy Novas, that they were the soundest, most straightforward car ever made. The quintessential car. He bought all that he could, for parts, to save a dying breed.

When the baby needed changing, Jesse summoned Scott's wife, Glenda, from the back bedroom. She was a ghost in the house, al-ways hiding. Ray never knew what she did. When she picked up the baby, she jerked him off the floor, snapping his head back. Jesse did not like that and looked at Ray.

Ray thought Glenda did not like having them there. He stayed anyway, and kept coming back. He needed the corner of their couch. He needed the lost hours on those winter weekends.

Betsy called Ray at his office. She had taken to calling him there. She wanted to know if Ray had any plans for the boys over Christ-mas. He didn't. But he did not immediately say so. As with all his conversations with Betsy now, he felt compelled to weigh every thought, every statement, every word. Had it always been so calcu-lated?

Yes. He was slowly discovering it. Only before, his choice of tone had always been calculated to support her, encourage her, to love her. What he thought was love, anyway. Now it was more dif-ficult. He was in an opposite role. Before he had been the bright knight, and now, suddenly, he had become the single greatest cause of pain and suffering in her life. And while support and en-couragement had been easy for him, this new weave of coolness and rejection left him a little stupid.

He did not answer her questions right away. When he heard her voice on the phone, his "hello" was suddenly full of foreboding. Ju-lia had even mentioned it.

"I can always tell whenever it's Betsy on the phone. Just by the way you say 'hello.'"

Ray knew it was true. The trouble was, the Ray that had fallen in love with Betsy, married her, had children with her, and lived with her for so many years had not just disappeared. As much as Ray would have liked it, this was not a part of the body that could be so easily disconnected. It was not a part of the body at all, but a frieze of electronic impulses that, for better or for worse, also defined who he was.

So when Betsy mentioned Christmas, no matter how businesslike she was, he knew with all his body that she was in pain because he would not be going out with Butch to cut a tree from the Pecos Wilderness, because he and Betsy would not be setting the tree up in the corner on the stand on the small square of plywood stored in the shed with "Christmas Tree" written across it in indelible black ink, because they would not be hanging the special God's-eye ornament with Jesse and Zach, because the buying, wrapping, setting out, and opening of the presents was all just cruelly snatched away. Every fiber of his body knew that all he had to do was step in and it would happen once more, that he could return Christmas and once more be the hero. Instead, he had become the Grinch that stole it.

How many times had he been in that position? All his life. And he had stepped in every time, done the right thing whenever he saw it. Eased the pain wherever he saw it.

He had always confused doing the right thing with causing no pain. Now he was inextricably caught because leaving Betsy was, he knew, the right thing. Yet this was causing great pain—not just the discomfort of this Christmas conversation, but deep hurt for Betsy, Jesse, Zach. And for himself. And he knew that it would only get worse before it ever got better. For the first time, he could not merge his instinct to cause no pain and his instinct to do what was right. He had no resources for being torn in two this way.

On the phone with Betsy he struggled for words because he was looking for a way that could be different. He did not want to be the Grinch and he did not want to cause her pain. Yet he could find no other way.

"Why?" he asked her, still looking for some solution, not just to Christmas, but to the whole stinking mess.

"I thought of taking the boys to St. John in the Virgin Islands. For a month. A little getaway for us all."

She had money from her father. This would not be a problem. Was she trying to punish him by taking Jesse and Zach away? Probably. Maybe it was even a veiled threat that she might do something like this more permanently. Ray sensed, though, that it was not entirely that. Betsy was still holding on, still hoping. She was taking herself away so that hope could be more easily nurtured. She was going to a place that was their place; Ray and Betsy had been there for a vacation of their own. She was thinking that, given time, the direction of things might begin to reverse itself.

In spite of the sticky complication of this, Ray was actually relieved by her proposal. This trip might give Ray some respite from the swirling feelings and confusion that her presence caused.

"I have no plans," he told her. He did not add that he thought the trip was a good idea.

"So you don't mind if I take this trip?" she pressed him.

"No, I guess not. It sounds like it might be a good idea." Ray was aware of trying to sound disappointed.

As tightly and carefully as Ray tried to hold this conversation, he was really running wild, on instinct alone. He was crossing a raging river by jumping from one dry rock to another. He did not know, when he made a leap to the next rock, if there would be another after it that he could reach. He did not know if he could ever make it to the other side. Only two things drove him forward. The certain knowledge that he could not return, and the adrenaline of survival rushing through him from the fear of where he might end up if he ever fell in.

"Take these pills," Julia said, passing Ray a pill cap full of small white pills.

They were parked on the side of the dirt road by the cabin where he and Julia used to meet during the summer.

"What are they?"

"Homeopathy. They're for depression. Don't swallow them. You put them under your tongue and let them melt."

In spite of his lifelong resistance to drugs, especially alternative drugs, Ray took the capful of pills and poured them under his tongue. They were chalky, without taste.

"I bought some special tea, too," Julia said, pleased with her war against depression. "We'll have some when we get back."

They stood for a moment, looking across the wooden footbridge littered with dead leaves, and then they walked up the dirt road in the direction of Aspen Meadows and the ski basin. December was too late for color, and even on this mild day a touch of winter forced them to keep their jackets on. It had snowed two weeks earlier and the snow still lay on the north side of the trees. This was a reunion walk, a return to the scene where, on warmer days, months earlier, the two of them had walked and talked and fallen in love and then returned to the cabin to make love. Even in the heat of summer, the cabin had been cool and they had gotten in the habit of bringing a sleeping bag to lay over the rough mattress.

Walking up the road did not feel the same to Ray. His feet were cold and he did not want to linger and lounge along the side of the creek; he wanted to walk quickly to get warm. Where the water of the stream washed thinly over the rocks it was already frozen in a smooth, crystalline glaze. The dirt of the road, once muddy, was also frozen in ruts and puddles, as if time had stopped. Julia and Ray picked their way along, their hands shoved deep in their pockets, their collars turned up. Julia's nose began to run, and she dabbed at it with the back of her glove.

"Betsy's taking Jesse and Zach to St. John for Christmas," Ray said, "for over a month."

"That long?"

Ray nodded his head.

"Maybe we should take a trip," Ray suggested to Julia. "While the boys are gone. Let's go somewhere. Let's go to California where it's warm. Let's drive."

"What do you mean?"

"I mean go. For a few weeks, a month. I mean take off."

"We can't just take off like that."

"Why not? I'm the boss. The company will survive without us."

Or at least, he thought, things could not get much worse. Collecting on invoices, paying bills were constant problems.

"Well, I do have an old friend I could visit in San Francisco." Julia was warming to the idea.

"Exactly. What's San Francisco like in the winter?"

"Cold, I think."

"Ah well, to hell with it. We can go down to San Diego to get warm and then drive up Route 1 to San Francisco."

"You really think we can just leave, just like that?"

"Why not? What do you mean, 'just like that'?"

"I don't know. It seems so . . . so . . . so, well, it's your business, I guess."

"We can take the Toyota. It's got a trip left in it." Ray was already giving it a tune-up and oil change.

"When?"

"I don't know. New Year's. Maybe we should leave New Year's."

"We'll see."

"What do you mean 'we'll see'? What's wrong, Julia, don't you want to go?"

"We'll see. I don't know."

"Come on."

"You could go without me."

"I don't want to go without you. This is our trip, our chance to be together."

"We'll see," she repeated.

Ray was disappointed. "Come on," he pleaded.

"What do you think Betsy would say? How do you think she would feel?" Julia asked.

"Jesus, Julia, what does that have to do with it? She's going with Jesse and Zach to St. John. What does she care?"

"She cares. You know she cares."

"But what does that have to do with it? It's over. Good riddance; goodbye."

"How can it be over, just like that?"

"It was over years ago, not just like that. Just like that was only the end, the final note, the recognition. We stopped talking years ago, stopped having sex, stopped having fun. Years ago. Over. Done. End. End of marriage."

"Well, I don't know if I am," Julia said softly.

"What do you mean?"

"I don't know if I am. Done. With Roget."

"What?"

"I don't know. I'm not like you; I can't just wash my hands clean like that. I'm not sure that Roget and I are over."

Ray was silent. Roget and Julia had been finished a dozen times. For her, breaking up was just part of being together. He didn't understand it.

Ray had an idea about love: that it was like finding a bright coin on the sidewalk, that it was a special moment of fate. He thought it wrong, a perversity of nature, to pass it by. Some people were just too distracted to even notice, but to see it and not stop and understand that such moments are religious, are sacred, and not to stoop down and carefully pick it up, Ray could not understand that. Ray could not understand Julia's reluctance, the way she carried Roget around like a ball and chain.

"It's not so simple," Julia said.

"It is. You're wrong. It is simple. Love is simple."

They had turned around and were walking down the road now. It had not been, was not, simple with Betsy, Ray knew. Yet he still, desperately, wanted love to be easy. And in some primal, confident place in himself, he knew that he was right. He just had absolutely no idea how to get there.

"It is not," Julia said, stopping.

"Look," Ray said, stopping and facing her. "Look, let's just go to California. To give it time. To see about these things." He put his arms around her and pulled her closer. She avoided his eyes.

Ray thought of the times he and Julia had spent walking that road. He remembered in early October when the aspens were turning yellow and the entire panoramic spectacle of it had somehow hung on their words as they quickly, breathlessly talked of life and love, things bigger than themselves, and how the chemistry of the day and their words had created the feelings of understanding, of satisfaction. He remembered in August lying naked with Julia in the cabin, laughing spontaneously, freely, her large mouth stretched wide, her eyes clear. These were the times that made Ray a believer.

"OK," Julia said, "only . . ."

"Only what?"

"This doesn't mean that . . ."

"OK. OK. OK." Ray said, still holding her, granting her certain undefined rights of ambivalence. "Let's just go. It'll be fun. You'll see."

"OK."

Ray thought he felt Julia relax just a little.

Ray, Julia, and Dimitri went to Christmas Eve dinner together at Andrea and Mark's house in Pecos. They walked down the two-mile driveway which was, as it usually was in the winter, impassable. They carried shoes to wear once they arrived and a potato dish Dimitri had decided to make at the last minute.

Dimitri was still living with Eleanor, but it was clear that they were headed for a split. He talked about it constantly, about the five hundred ways Eleanor did not love him, about the five hundred ways in which she was able to daily mistreat him. He was explaining how Eleanor had gone to visit her relatives in Minnesota. Dimitri hated Minnesota because he hated the cold. And because her relatives were so boring and because, greatest sin of all, because they cooked strange food, like tuna-fish casseroles. Her trip to Minnesota was a betrayal. One more betrayal.

The ground was muddy underneath the snow and they slipped with every step they took. Ray was in charge of the potatoes, which were proving too hot to carry. Dimitri directed his slipping as much as he could in the direction of Julia, grabbing her arm and waist when he lost his balance. Her presence warmed Dimitri, reminded him that there were beautiful women waiting the other side of separation. Perhaps even Julia herself might be there for him. He would have denied such a thought, but Ray knew that it lurked in his Greek brain.

"You would never do such a thing?" Dimitri was fond of asking

Julia as punctuation to another grievance against Eleanor.

The moon was bright and reflected off the snow; it gave the night a glowing, gray color. It reminded Ray of cutting Christmas trees with Butch, stomping through the deep snow, and how, sometimes, they were caught out past sunset. In places, the mud and snow had already frozen and made walking even more difficult than the slush. The three of them lurched and slid in all directions, and the road seemed interminable.

Ray allowed some distance to develop between himself and Julia and Dimitri. Usually, listening to Dimitri's woes with Eleanor cheered him and created a comradeship between them. Tonight he felt tired of them. He was reluctant with his usual rejoinders about how he knew what Dimitri meant because Betsy this, that, or the other thing as well. He thought about Julia's little white pills for depression, several of which were currently under his tongue, now almost entirely dissolved. Julia had prescribed a double dose that day, since it was Christmas Eve. He shifted the potatoes to his other arm, pausing to widen the gap a little more between himself and the other two. Depression had become tangible to him lately. Julia had been teaching him about depression. Giving him lessons.

"I think we're too depressed to eat in," she said. "We need to go out."

Really, Ray had thought, we're depressed? This is it, huh? This sort of too quiet lounging around with a vague sense of unease is depression?

He was starting to define the unease. Something was missing. An expectation fired at no target, lost in its aimless trajectory. Betsy and his life with her had been cleared out with a backhanded swipe across the table. Only, what was left, what remained? What he imagined as a life with Julia, a love, a relationship. Only that had turned into this study in depression.

The little white pills did not help. Or at least, they did not make him feel any better. They did, though, provide some definition, and the truth was, Ray had to admit, having some definition lifted his spirits. Whatever ailed him, these organic herbs and minerals defined it, they embodied it. It was as if he could put his feelings into the pills and then swallow them. And then the problem lay outside. It was nobody's fault; it was a condition, like acne. The stars were out of alignment. He needed a little tune-up. He was depressed; it was a relief to know that. It was a gift from Julia, a Christmas present.

Andrea was a duchess or princess from Austria. She had blond hair, cut short, and a permanent, deep tan that confirmed for Ray her royal blood. Mark was a volatile architect who was always screaming at clients and contractors both. He was recognized as an architect with a genius for design, but Bud once told Ray that he would never work on any of his jobs because it wasn't worth the abuse it entailed. That, and Mark didn't know a thing about construction. He resented the responsibility of detailing. He thought builders should know how to build things properly. He only wanted to define how they should look.

In Ray's mind, Mark kept the gorgeous princess Andrea imprisoned at the end of this long dirt driveway outside Pecos. She cooked and tended to the garden and made a science out of composting scraps. She liked the animals they had: the fourteen rare hens that gave them eggs; the two goats they bred and from which they took milk; the two dogs, mongrels, one of which was black and white and had only three legs; and the calico cat named Monster by their son, Jody, who was in preschool with Jesse. Mark had an office in town, but he did most of his design work on the large drafting table in the corner of their living room. Andrea and Mark had met as undergraduates at the University of Virginia fourteen years earlier. Mark had gone to the University of Chicago School of Architecture and worked for six years at a firm in Chicago before moving the two of them to the edge of the Pecos Wilderness. Ray did not know them well enough to know why they moved, although Bud had heard a rumor that Mark was one of the architects involved in the collapse of the ramp at the new Hilton Hotel in Springfield, Illinois.

Their house had a large entry, where Ray, Julia, and Dimitri sat on a bench to change their shoes. The entry was all glass with a rounded glass roof. The floor curled up a slope like the shell of a snail, and inside the rooms climbed up to each other like stairs, with studies, bedrooms, and bathrooms shaped and hidden in a variety of ways. In all, it was not a large house, but was full of interest and light, a splendid and, it always seemed to Ray, fragile jewel lost in the rough of the piñon, pine, and rock canyons of Pecos. The first winter that Mark and Andrea lived in their new house, Jody was born, and the midwife had walked there just as Ray, Julia, and Dimitri had.

Dimitri had never met Mark and his family or been to their house. He was enchanted by it all, but most particularly by Andrea and Jody. Andrea provided him with a body on which he could temporarily transfer some of his fantasies about Julia. But Jody captured his imagination the most. To Dimitri, Jody was a wild child, running out in the snow in his bare feet and a T-shirt, speaking a language of his own with the three-legged dog, hanging by his feet through the hole in the loft over the dining room. Dimitri saw Jody as a human mountain goat, a mythological Greek figure hidden out in the rugged slopes and ravines of the wilderness. When he wasn't in the kitchen with Andrea, Dimitri followed Jody around, laughing at everything he said.

In three days, Ray and Julia were leaving for California. Ray watched her come to life talking to Gunther Richards and his wife, Hillary, two artist friends of Andrea's from Austria. It turned out that Andrea had once been an aspiring artist herself, ever since she was very young and in school in Austria with Hillary.

"I still plan to get back to it one day," Andrea said shyly when this information leaked out, "but Hillary and Gunther are both very good and quite well known."

Julia was enchanted and stared flushed and speechless at all three of them. "Really," she finally said. "Do you have anything here I could see?"

Hillary and Gunther did not, and if Andrea did she was not telling. Ray could tell that Julia wanted to say more, that she wanted to say "I, too, am an artist," but her life as a bookkeeper kept her from it. It did not, however, diminish her enthusiasm for talking with artists. Or maybe it was the white pills. Maybe they were working for her.

Ray admired Julia's ability to pick herself up that way. Ray felt he had been left behind. Julia had created this well-defined, depressed mood, and Ray had gotten stuck in it. Even Dimitri, who was in the lowest of spirits, was running around like Jody's playmate. Ray felt betrayed and confused. He had given in to misery and then been left there alone. He could not escape his resentment about all the different ways in which Julia would not have him. She kept Roget hanging out there as a place to go when Ray became too comfortable, too confident in their relationship.

Julia lived with being miserable much more easily than he, Ray thought. She took her pills and then moved on, and in this group of total strangers she was having the most fun of all.

Andrea served a turkey cooked in a wood stove, with both sweet and white mashed potatoes. The house was hot and Mark opened a window. Andrea, Hillary, and Julia shuttled food in from the kitchen, laughing and talking. Andrea and Hillary moved back and forth from English to German as if they did not know the difference. Dimitri was only half-listening to Gunther as he surveyed the spread on the table.

Ray watched Jody as he pulled out a chair and sat down. Suddenly he seemed to Ray more adult than child.

"Mark," Jody asked, calling his father by his first name, "should I sit here?"

Ray stood behind a chair, waiting for his seat assignment.

"Where do I sit?" Ray wanted to ask, but he caught himself. It was a question his mother might ask. In fact, as the words had formed in his mind, they had been in his mother's voice. At the dinner parties that she gave, there were cards with people's names set on top of each china plate. Everyone was told where to sit.

"It makes it so much easier," she explained to him once. "Don't you think? Then no one gets hurt feelings."

In boarding school, too, seating had always been assigned. His mother would have approved. They posted maps of the dining room on a large bulletin board with names typed in on every table. The list was changed every other Monday.

Mark was circling the table, pouring cold white wine. When he was done, as if on cue, all the guests made a circle around the table and held hands. Jody stood back up to join the circle. He stood next to Ray and his small, bony hand felt like Jesse's.

"Thank you," Andrea said with a heavy accent, "for this circle of friends at this moment in time. Thank you for the abundance of food."

She repeated it in German and then Dimitri said something in Greek. Ray recognized the sorrow in his voice. There was a pause to let anyone else speak who wanted to. No one did and they all sat down.

Not the
Bikini
Season

Ray and Julia waited on 4th Street through three changes of light before they finally moved across the bridge and on to Isleta Boulevard. It was the afternoon rush hour in Albuquerque. They followed the directions past the Pink Slipper, a bar with nude dancers, turned left on Esperanza, down two blocks to a dirt road, and another left to the last house on the dead end. Ray turned off the Toyota in the driveway. An old wooden garage in front of them leaned heavily to the right, the door jammed open and falling apart. The house, too, seemed to lean, although not so dramatically. The wood trim around the windows had recently been painted a bright blue. Tall, leafless cottonwood trees with deeply wrinkled bark like old elephant skin lined a ditch behind the house. The yard was a lifeless stubble of weeds. It was bright but cold, like fall.

They had begun their trip to California by driving one hour to Albuquerque's South Valley to visit Robin and Jack. Julia was happy, because she admired Robin's art and wanted to see her new work, and because she and Jack had developed an immediate rapport at the museum opening a month earlier. Ray, though, had

arranged this stop for other reasons, going back to the morning after Sean had died.

That early morning seven years earlier, the doctors and nurses
at the emergency room eventually all fell away from Ray and Betsy.
There was still a state policeman in the lobby, who talked with the
doctor and then left. Betsy was hysterical, crying and moaning into
the large crack in the earth that had unbelievably opened up at
their feet. The doctor prescribed some Valium.

"There's going to be an autopsy," he said, sitting in the lush,
gray, waiting room chair next to them. "It's routine in the case of a
sudden death like this."

Betsy cried louder. The doctor left. Ray sat back, numb. The
world turned: a knifing victim was wheeled in, a large red stain on
his white shirt; an old Pueblo Indian lady with no teeth sat across
from them without reading or moving, a picture of patience; the
admitting clerk talked quietly on the telephone, giggling. The fluorescent lights burned like a fire, searing the air with brightness.
Ray considered driving home but it did not seem right, as if they
had just been to a movie. There were people to notify, calls to
make. Betsy wailed, and he began to worry about her.

Then he decided to go to Betsy's mother's. Hand Betsy over,
hand the whole situation over. It was an effort to take himself to the
phone and call. He let it ring until she finally woke up and answered. Her voice was slurred and angry. Ray told her what had
happened. There was a long silence. Ray said he thought he should
bring Betsy over there.

"Of course," her mother finally said.

"That's her," Ray said, referring to the noise he was sure that she
could hear over the phone.

As they pulled up to her mother's house the sky was just turning
the first bland gray of morning. Her mother came out of the
kitchen in a blue bathrobe and held her daughter, and Betsy cried
on her shoulder. They walked inside together. It all seemed like
other people to Ray, like another life, and he listened and floated as
the word spread and a crowd began to gather at the house.

One of Betsy's sisters told him how tired he must be and how upset he must be, but she could not finish and broke down crying. Ray left her sitting on the bed with her head in her hands. He drifted out into the large hallway, the morning, bright and full, shining through the bank of skylights. Betsy's other sister had brought her laundry and was sorting whites from colors. Robin appeared from nowhere and grabbed his sleeve.

"Ray?"

He looked at her. Her eyes were dark and hard. Ray noticed that she had a green fleck in one of her brown irises. With a gentle pressure she pulled him into the TV room and after he sat down on the couch she went back and shut the door. She sat next to him and Ray suddenly felt at home. He leaned back, relaxing into the soft cushions. Robin did not hold his hand nor touch his knee. Maybe she said something. Robin had never seen Sean and did not know that he had blue eyes or that he was cute or any of the rest of it. In the nine days Sean had lived, Ray was not sure he knew any of that himself. What, after all, are nine days in a lifetime? What, after all, are nine days when they are a lifetime? Ray puzzled it over briefly and then let it go. What came in behind it was tears. He hung his head and cried for the first time since Sean had died, for the first time since he was eleven and his dog was run over on the street. Robin cried with him and they put their arms around each other and wept.

Since that morning, Robin had held some vague allure for him. She represented some opportunity for friendship, something so new and different that Ray had no name for it, and through the fog of his life since Sean had died, he had only dimly seen the possibilities. Now that he had left Betsy and definitions were crumbling around him like old statues, he was drawn back to Robin, sensing that in the architecture of living, she might know something.

Robin came out the kitchen door and down the three steps to greet them.

"Welcome to the South Valley," she said, giving Ray a hug. She seemed tight to Ray, tense inside. Her smile was shortened.

Robin had totally straight hair. She cut it short; she let it grow long. She had bangs halfway over her eyes, and then none. She had her hair pulled back in barrette, in a ponytail, and in braids. No matter what she did, it was always just straight hair. It was no longer blond, like in the picture in Dimitri's office, but plain brown, what Julia called "hair color."

Jack stood at the top of the steps holding open the screen door. In his spare time Jack was also an artist; most of the time he was studying at the University of New Mexico for an advanced degree in computer sciences. He too seemed distant to Ray.

"Is it all right that we stay?" Ray asked.

"Of course," Robin answered, "we invited you. We've just been fighting, is all."

She helped Julia with her bag. Ray was a little intimidated by the atmosphere as he walked in behind her.

Jack served beans, posole, and corn bread for dinner. He put out a plate of grated cheese mounded up like a small mountain. There was a tub of honey butter for the corn bread. The mood lightened as they ate. Jack told a story about a friend of his at the university who played the bass in a jazz band. They discussed jazz. Ray said he had never been able to understand or like it. Jack said he was learning to play the clarinet. Julia told a story about the time she had seen Thelonious Monk in a small pub in Paris.

After dinner, Jack and Julia went to the living room to play some songs on the record player. Robin and Ray stayed at the table talking.

"We were fighting about who's the better driver," Robin said, laughing. "It's amazing where these conversations can go. Jack scares me sometimes when he's driving. He doesn't seem to pay attention. I always find myself all tensed up when I'm in the passenger seat. He says it's me, that he's never had an accident and all that, that he's a good driver. But I can't help it; he gets to playing with the radio or even just talking and he's not paying attention. He sees other cars pulling out much later than I do; slams on his brakes when he didn't need to. So I always want to drive, but he doesn't like that. Today, he almost ran into an acequia coming down Esperanza because he didn't see this kid on a bicycle. That's what we were fighting about."

Ray remembered Dimitri's complaint. "That damn Robin," he said once, "she'll jump your ass for any goddamn thing."

Robin laughed again. "It can get so absurd. That's what so hard sometimes. Everyone is always saying, 'What's your problem? Everything seems OK to me,' and I'm the bad guy, saying 'No, there's a problem here.' Jack's better than most; he'll hang in there with me."

Loud music erupted abruptly from the next room as someone put the needle down in the middle of a song. It took a second before they found the volume knob and turned it down. Ray heard them giggling. He supposed that he fell into Robin's category of "everyone" who considered her extreme. He and Betsy had never fought, and just remembering the tenseness between Jack and Robin when they arrived made him nervous. He did not believe relationships had to be so hard, yet he was listening. His easy relationship with Betsy had not turned out to be so easy.

"How's Betsy?" Robin asked.

"OK. I don't see her much—when we swap the kids, that sort of thing."

"It was such a shock for me. You guys, you and Betsy, always seemed so real—having children, buying washers and dryers, owning your own home. I didn't realize it, but I was really wrapped up in that. Then when you called and—*boom!* it's all over, that's all, just over, no explanation or anything, just done. It was as if something had been stolen from me. I suddenly felt like my relationship with Jack was shaky, that it was nothing and might evaporate too. It's weird, and it's hard to explain, but it's like if Ray can just walk away, there's nothing solid anymore, no bedrock. Or that's how it felt. I've sort of gotten over it now, but it was a big deal for a while."

"Do you think I shouldn't have left?" Ray asked. He was picking up small pieces of corn bread from the table with the ends of his fingers. Jack was playing selections from different jazz records in the other room.

"I don't know about that. We do what we have to do. It doesn't seem right, though, running out and falling in love again right away. I think you've got to finish one thing before you start another."

Ray was hoping that this trip was the start of many things.

"It was over a long time ago with Betsy," he said. "Wrung out and hung out."

"Maybe."

"Are you angry with me?"

"A little, for wanting me to think everything you're doing is wonderful. It doesn't mean I don't love you, though." Robin smiled. "That I don't want us to be friends."

Ray was not used to having women friends, but he thought being friends with Robin would be a good start.

Robin got up and started clearing the table.

"I can't stand jazz," she said, laughing.

"Me either." Ray stood and helped her clean.

Ray liked the sound of Globe. He picked it for its name. In every other respect, it was just another small abandoned mining town east of Phoenix, where the hills sensually crowded around like so many bare shoulders. They had just come through the Salt River Canyon, and it was almost dark. They drove the main drag twice, looking for a hotel. The Silver Star advertised that it was American owned and proud of it.

"Gag me with a spoon," Julia commented.

Globe had a subdued, neon glow to it, like an empty room late at night with a dim lamp left burning in the corner. Julia was in a grumpy mood, as if she'd landed on the moon with no way home. Still picking by name, Ray pulled into the Mineshaft Motel.

"At least there's a sense of place," he said.

Julia sat in the car while he registered. The TV in a room behind the counter drowned out the bell on the door.

"Hello," Ray yelled into the hidden noise, "hello."

A fat lady dressed in yellow pants and a yellow turtleneck finally emerged full of apologies.

"My husband can't hear very well is why the TV is up so loud."

She had a mother's geniality and Ray felt as of he were the neighbor stopping by to borrow some flour.

Their room was made of exposed-block walls painted white, which radiated the cold of the night out into the room. Julia pulled her toilet kit out of her bag and disappeared into the plastic shower stall without a word. Ray turned up the heat and sat in the orange chair next to the round table, suddenly exhausted from the long drive. He thought of Jesse and Zach in St. John and wondered what he was doing here in the Mineshaft Motel in Globe, Arizona.

Julia emerged from the bathroom looking as if she was wondering the same thing. Her hair was plastered wet against her head and she was naked except for a pair of white cotton panties that came up to her waist. She lay on the bed across from where Ray sat and stared blankly at him.

Ray reached into his suitcase, pulled out his camera, and snapped her picture. The flash flooded the room and after his eyes readjusted the white walls and ceiling seemed a dingier shade of gray. Julia laughed.

"Recording our trip," Ray said, "for the photo album."

"Right," she said. "Are you going to show that one to Jesse and Zach?"

She pulled down the covers and rolled between them.

On the outskirts of Phoenix, as the hills began to level out, Ray and Julia began seeing the huge cacti called saguaros. Julia corrected Ray's pronunciation—"swarrow," like sorrow. They stopped at a diner called Jose's on the west end of town. On one side of the diner were booths for eating and on the other was a gift shop where they sold cowboy hats and black velour tapestries of women in bright-colored dresses. Ray bought a bolo tie with a copper armadillo clasp.

West of Phoenix they drove through incongruously green and lush fields of alfalfa that surrounded the dry, hot, dusty roads. The irrigation ended and they were soon once more surrounded by thick stands of saguaro sentinels. The heat in the car became heavy.

"Each of these saguaros is hundreds of years old," Julia announced reverently.

They stopped on the gravel shoulder of the highway and climbed through the tight barbed wire to visit some of the cacti. On closer inspection, and maybe because Julia had told him their age, they struck Ray as wounded veterans. Each one had a broken limb, a scarred trunk, or gashes where birds had made their nests. They were bent and with their arms askew looked like actors or mimes frozen in mid-motion. Julia kept pointing at different ones.

"Look, that one looks like St. Francis. You know, like one of the wooden statues by Ortega. And that one looks like my father." She laughed.

Ray told her to stand next to the one like her father and took her picture. The saguaro towered twenty feet beside her, a mute patriarch too concerned with enduring time to notice the small woman with a short dress and short, hennaed hair trying to put her arm around its trunk. Julia squinted and cocked her head. Cars zinged by on the highway and trucks shook the ground as they passed.

Seeking some relief from the heat and monotony of the desert, they exited at Quartzsite, just before the California border. Behind the predictable white Stuckey's stretched a road lined with an informal, open-air flea market. There were three-sided wooden booths and mobile homes lining the road on both sides. Mostly people sold rocks—quartzite, Ray assumed. Ray and Julia went into an old motor home. The shade was cool and welcome. The walls were lined with glass jars full of different rocks and minerals. A man in a white T-shirt, white shorts, and a safari hat sat in the captain's chair with a magazine in his lap. He swiveled toward Ray and Julia when they entered. His face was deeply lined and darkly tanned, as if he had spent his life scratching the desert surface for this rock collection.

"Jesse and Zach would love this," Ray whispered.

"Did you hear about the guy that bought a stone in a place like this and it turned out to be a perfect emerald, worth over a million dollars?" Julia said. "Evidently this guy was a geologist. He recognized the stone right away. Of course, he didn't know it was perfect or worth that much money right away. He just knew it might have an emerald in it, or however that works. So he asked the guy how much for the stone. First he plays it cool, he asks him about one worthless stone, then another: fifty cents, two dollars. Then he asks about the one he saw, the emerald. His heart is in his mouth. Can you imagine? The guy must have heard something in his voice because he paused a second, wondering how much this guy will go. 'Five dollars,' he says, thinking how outrageous that is. The geologist still plays it cool, pretends like that's a lot of money, looks at a few other stones, then decides to pay the five dollars. The radio interviewed the guy that sold it. He said that stone had been for sale for years. No one had ever even asked, 'How much?'"

Julia picked a jar off the shelf and held it toward the proprietor. "How much?"

"A million dollars." They both laughed.

"How about one?" Julia asked.

"Two."

"Fair enough."

She extracted two dollars from her purse and shook a deep-toned, striped brown rock from the jar.

"Look," Julia said, holding the rock in the light of the doorway. "Look at the stripes. Isn't it beautiful?"

They reached Palm Springs before dinner. Ray wanted to spend the night there, but all the hotels were full. They parked and ate dinner at a sidewalk cafe. Ray was interested in the wealth, the reputation, the opulence, the decadence, but it was hidden behind walls and gates. They could only see the red tile roofs tucked among the palm trees. The streets, cafes, and boutiques were the same as in Santa Fe.

So they left for Los Angeles as the sun was going down. The air cooled. They spread maps out, readying themselves to negotiate the myths of the L.A. freeways. Ray arbitrarily picked Pasadena as their destination, because of the Rose Bowl. He chose the third of five exits, turned left at the stop sign, and crossed back over the freeway.

The other side of the bridge, he turned left again. At the first motel he saw, the Red Coach, he turned in. In front of the office there was a courtyard of flowers, trees, and a fountain, all separated from the street by a white stucco wall and large, locked iron gates.

The flowers were beautiful, large red and orange hibiscus with broad, dark green leaves. Already Ray did not trust California. Nature is so easy here, he thought, that even the fleabag motels look nice.

Their room had a thin, slightly damp commercial carpet, stale air-conditioned air, and a dim bedside light. Ray pulled Julia onto the bed. They were both exhausted. He undressed her and they made love, but it was more like mouth-to-mouth resuscitation. It was after midnight and they lay awake next to each other.

"Where are we?" Julia asked.

"Pasadena, California," Ray told her.

"This sucks," Julia said.

Ray didn't answer. He sat up and used the remote control to turn on the TV. He flipped through channels, stopping at a soccer game in Spanish. Julia rolled toward him and started playing with his penis. She lifted it and let it flop back into place.

"Does it always bend to the right, no matter what?" she asked.

"Yes. But do you know why?"

Julia shook her head.

"Because we're north of the equator. If we were south of the equator, it would bend to the left. Like toilets flushing, north of the equator they swirl one way, and south of the equator they swirl the other."

Julia laughed. "Is that really true? About toilets, I mean."

Ray noticed that the commercial for the Veg-O-Matic knife was on. The same commercial he had seen so many times on those sleepless, late nights when he was still living with Betsy.

"Look," he said, pointing at the TV.

Julia looked. The ad was in Spanish but the video was the same.

"Get a pencil and paper, quick," he told Julia.

She grabbed the pad from beside the phone and fished out a pen from her purse. The 800 number flashed on the screen.

"Write it down," Ray said. "Write down the phone number. I want to order that damn knife."

Ray picked up the phone and started dialing. Julia gave him the number, but he realized that he knew it from memory.

Ray and Julia rented a room in one of the hotels on the main drag of La Jolla. They were led up some stairs with indoor-outdoor carpet and then down an exterior walkway covered by the same green carpet. In spite of its eternal nature, the carpet was evaporating at the edges, eaten away by time or mice, or both. Their room was on the corner, perched above the road, with windows in two walls. After they put down their suitcases, Julia wandered out on the balcony and sat on the railing looking over the road to the ocean. Ray pulled his camera out of his suitcase and snapped her picture from the door of their room. A study in melancholy, he thought.

La Jolla had the feel of the ocean. They had driven down that morning from L.A. through a heavy fog which had burned off just as they arrived.

"Let's go get a muffin or something," Ray suggested, concerned that Julia might turn to stone on her perch.

They found the Croissant Corner, a cafe that was started and owned by the same people who had started the Croissant Corner in Santa Fe. The waiters and waitresses all wore aprons that said the Croissant Corner in bright green, with La Jolla and Santa Fe written in smaller orange letters underneath.

"This one is doing much better than the one in Santa Fe," Ray commented as they sat down.

"This is California," Julia said.

They ordered.

"I have a friend, her name is Christina," Julia said. "She never saw the ocean, growing up. She grew up near Taos. She was fifteen the first time she saw the ocean. She told me the story once. It was really funny. Anyway, it was here, in La Jolla, where she first saw the ocean."

"Let's go to the ocean, for a walk," Ray said halfway through his avocado, cheese, and mushroom omelet. He, too, was getting anxious for the ocean.

"I think I'll go back to the hotel and sleep," Julia said. "I didn't get much sleep last night."

"What's wrong?" A walk was usually a sure hit with Julia.

"Nothing's wrong."

Ray didn't want to walk by himself, but he felt trapped into it. He felt gotten rid of. A few blocks south there was a sign that said BEACHES. As soon as he turned, the crush of the main street fell away and small houses and ordinary people began to present themselves.

The beach that Ray found was no beach at all. It was a shore of giant boulders smoothed by the waves. The coastline swept in an arc to the south, and in the distance it looked as if there might be some sand. He began hopping over the boulders. The strong wind made it cool, and Ray leaped from one rock to another with enough vigor to stay warm.

He observed the brown, sudsy remains of a higher tide: pieces of Clorox bottles, Pepsi cans, rubber tires, fish bones, Bic pens, old shirts, shoes, plywood, unknown organic substances, and unidentifiable inorganic ones. The ocean was neglected and abused. He remembered sailing and fishing on Cape Cod when he was a child.

Julia was reading *Moving On* by Larry McMurtry when Ray returned. She lay on the bed with plastic bags spilling clothes around her legs.

"Hello," Julia said cheerily.

"Hello."

"Look at what I bought. I went on a little shopping spree."

Julia stood up, stretched her arms out, and turned 360 degrees. She was wearing a new sleeveless top, a band of rainbow colors that stretched tightly around her chest and middle. It stopped short of her navel and ran in a straight line across the tops of her breasts.

"And this." She pulled a pair of bright yellow shorts from one of the bags and held them across her hips.

"And this." She discarded the shorts and extracted a pair of white leather sandals from another bag.

"And this." Still holding the sandals, she pulled out a long swath of light green which she shook until Ray could see it was a cotton skirt.

"What do you think?" she asked.

Ray smiled.

"Wait," she interrupted before he could say anything, "one more thing." And she found her new purple sunglasses and put them on.

"Not that I need another pair of sunglasses," she said.

"It's great," Ray said, clapping his hands. The elastic top flattened her breasts, but he found it sexy.

"No bathing suit?" he asked. Julia had mentioned a number of times that she wanted to buy a bikini in California.

"No bathing suit," she said, making a face of disappointment. "The next town."

"They're all these little whorish things or old lady's skirts like something my mother would wear. There's nothing in between. I want a bikini but with a wider hip on the bottom."

"There's no beach here," Ray announced. "As best I could tell, it's all boulders."

"Well, I don't want to swim. It's too cold anyway. I just want to get a bikini. This is Southern California, after all."

"Tomorrow we head north," Ray said. He hugged Julia and pressed his hand against her breast and was surprised at the rubber-band texture of her new top.

As they drove back up Route 5 toward Los Angeles, the clouds were low and thick and the wind was strong. Whenever the highway brought them close enough, Ray strained to see the ocean. Glimpses of it, flat and black beyond the sandy cliffs, reassured him. He longed to be out on it.

"I have a friend," Julia said, "who races solo across the Atlantic in a sailboat."

"They have races?"

"Yep. He does well. He won once, two years ago."

"That must be something."

"We grew up together, in Nebraska. He never was even on a sailboat until after high school."

"I'd like to do something like that."

"He's crazy, though. I think the only time he's happy is when he's out on the ocean alone. He can't handle anything else. When you talk to him, you can tell he's a little crazy. He doesn't really look at you and smiles all of a sudden, as if he's having a conversation you can't hear.

"He was my first boyfriend, junior year at high school, the first boy I ever slept with. He told me last Christmas that I'm the only person he's ever made love to. I didn't believe him, but somehow it seems possible. He's that out of it. He still lives at home with his mom. When he's not out on the ocean, that is."

"It must have been traumatic for him, breaking up with you."

Julia laughed. "Not that big a deal, really. I just went off to college; things fizzled out. He went to college too, back East; that's when he started sailing. I saw him sometimes on holidays. He got into drugs pretty heavy. We'd sneak off and do some acid, but we never slept together again."

Ray decided to get off the four-lane just as it turned inland south of Los Angeles, a few miles after San Clemente. He thought it would be more scenic, and the names of the beaches—Laguna, Newport, Huntington, Long Beach, Redondo, Hermosa, Manhattan, and at the end, Venice—read like a cultural history book, echoing in his memory like the names of shrines. He had never been to Los Angeles, but the names of these places were as familiar as rubbed stones.

He exited the highway following signs for Dana Point and Route 1. Here it began. If this trip was to anyplace in particular for Ray, Route 1 was it. Ray was in California to see Big Sur, Carmel, to look out over the ocean, to stand where Kerouac and Cassady had stood, where Henry Miller had stood, where a whole generation of America had stood, mouths agape.

Route 1 through southern Los Angeles, though, was a disappointing beginning. It was thick with traffic lights and clogged by slowly moving traffic that inched past derelict buildings.

The sun intermittently broke through the clouds, warming the air to a suffocating humidity. The ocean, on occasion just a stone's throw from the car, was a slab of concrete, still and oily, meeting the dirty shore without an edge.

They drove out of the city's sprawl on to flat, low land where oil drills pumped and a cyclone fence enclosed acres of storage for metal sheets, metal beams, metal posts, and spools of wire taller than their car. There was no horizon, only a dirty mist.

Ray pressed on in the Toyota, in and out of the congestion. It became hot and uncomfortable, and when they opened the windows it only got worse. As they drove past the airport, a 727 flew so close over their heads that they could not help but duck.

By the time they reached Santa Monica, it was after one and they were hungry. Still, Ray drove another thirty minutes, past Malibu, before he felt safely rid of the shoreside ghetto. Julia picked out a roadside fish joint and they stopped. The clouds had thickened, and it was drizzling and cold. They put on sweaters. There were no other cars in the parking lot and only occasionally did one drive by. The hills rose sharply up the inland side of the road forming an impenetrable barrier.

By the time they reached Santa Barbara, the rain was steady and the day was turning dark. Ray drove on. Stopping did not occur to him as a choice. Stopping meant giving in. He abandoned Route 1 for Route 101, a thicker blue line on the map. Julia listened to tapes and read, not involved in Ray's struggle with the weather and with the dark vortex that came with it.

Just south of San Luis Obispo the rain became torrential. The windshield wipers of the Toyota could not move fast enough. Ray now had to watch out for stopped cars. He pressed on slowly.

"Holy mother of God Jesus," was Julia's only comment, and she went back to her book.

When they finally reached San Luis Obispo, Ray stopped for gas. As he pumped it, he heard the thundering of the rain on the metal canopy of the gas station recede a decibel. He walked to the edge of the canopy's protection and looked hard. It was after four and should have been getting darker, yet it seemed to be getting lighter. For the first time that day since leaving Route 5 south of Los Angeles, his spirits lifted. He returned to the car and consulted the map. There at the south entrance of the true Route 1 was a town called Morro Bay, on the ocean. They would spend the night there. Things were, he had no doubt, on the improve.

As they crested a hill above Morro Bay, the rain stopped. The sun was visible out over the ocean. On the right, on the way into town, Ray saw a white sign with black letters that said ROUTE 1 NORTH OF SAN SIMEON CLOSED. He looked at Julia. She was still reading and had not seen the sign. He did not mention it to her. He did not wholly believe it. How could they close a road? he wondered. This is no dirt trail, no bike path, this is a road, a paved road. Route 1. A route. He would check in town before he would believe it.

Morro Bay sloped toward a broad ocean inlet. There was a winding road that followed the bay shore, and all the other roads went up the steep hill from it. Julia and Ray checked into a white motel and had to drive up a back alley to find room number 17. They unloaded their bags but did not unpack before walking down the hill to the first restaurant they could find, the Seaside. Julia ordered fish and Ray had a hamburger. Sitting in the red vinyl booth was too much like sitting in the Toyota again and they were restless and quiet while they ate. The sound of rain still drummed in Ray's ears. Julia pushed her food around the brown plastic plate without eating more than two or three bites.

"I'm going to wander around outside," Ray said as he got up. He laid a five-dollar bill on the table.

Julia looked at him angrily, as if he were condemning her to sit in the booth until he was done with his walk.

"Here's the key," he said, putting it beside the five dollars.

It was after six o'clock and still light. Behind the Seaside Restaurant was a concrete commercial dock with large shaped concrete pillars for tying up. Ray perched on one, like a bird, and stared out across the water. Rough-looking commercial fishing boats were scattered on buoys among speedboats and sailboats. The water made quiet lapping noises against the pier underneath him.

Soon a forty-foot fishing boat pulled up to the dock and a redheaded, freckled teenager stepped off to hook the bow and stern lines. Ray moved from the pillar he was on to one further down the row, reperched himself, and watched the crew of the fishing boat.

There were four men, all in yellow rain gear and rubber boots. The redheaded teenager had on yellow overalls but no jacket, just a plaid, long-sleeved shirt with the sleeves rolled up. Ray thought he must be cold. In spite of his winter jacket, Ray himself was cold. Another boy, older and clearly the brother of the redhead, even though his hair was brown, jumped onto the pier and began uncoiling a long water hose from a spigot near the back of the Seaside Restaurant. He was wearing a yellow jacket but no rain pants, just some brown corduroys tucked into his rubber boots, and he looked grouchy. A man that Ray took to be the father emerged from the cabin and unlatched the cover to the hold in the middle of the open stern area. Nets and ropes hung haphazardly from booms and poles that swayed as the boat rocked. There was one other man who came from the bow to help the father, a black man, bigger than any of the others.

They loaded a cart with fish and the younger son pulled it away, straining to get the large wheels rolling. The three remaining men coiled lines, stowed gaffs and small buoys, cleaned tools in a bucket. They continued to work without talking, as if they were each part of some larger body with one mind directing them in as kind and easy a rhythm as breathing itself. They all worked willingly, even the sullen older son. Maybe the father had unhappiness too, or the black man—perhaps he had once had a boat of his own but had lost it to the bank and now had to work for someone else.

Whatever their problems, there they were, working together, getting the job done. It made them whole. They came together over this task, this life.

Ray shivered and slipped off his cold concrete seat and moved his feet to warm them up. The younger son returned with a small load of block ice on his cart. He stepped on board and fell in beside the others. The black man dropped back down into the hold and the older brother began passing him the ice.

Suddenly, Ray had a picture of the mother of these two boys. She wore a yellow dress that came down to the middle of her calves. Her dirty-blond hair was cut short. She was stocky but not fat, except she had a large bottom. Unlike these silent males, she talked incessantly. Her chatter was light, warm, and friendly, and not above gossip. She worked for the principal at the high school and, as is often the case in those situations, she was the one who really ran the school. Like her husband, whom she had met at the same high school where she now worked, she had grown up in Morro Bay. There was a daughter too, in between the two sons, and she and her mother were best friends.

Ray walked back to the hotel, his feet numb and his knees aching. Julia was in bed reading, her hair wet from a shower. The room seemed as cold as the outside and Ray quickly got undressed and got into bed. He turned his back to Julia and pulled his knees up for warmth.

"What's wrong?" Julia asked.

"Nothing," Ray answered. "There were these fisherman down at the dock. This family. You know, a family operation."

Ray paused. That family had been like a river running by him. He had stood on the shore watching. That feeling of being a spectator was choking him. Morro Bay was a long way from anything he would call his own life; yet, when he considered it, Santa Fe was not any closer. He realized that he hated his new apartment on Silver Street. When he returned, he would move. The thought lifted him a little, but the feeling of being stuck on shore, watching, had him in a tight grip.

He had been a spectator for so much of his life. That's what

Justin, his old boarding-school friend, had tried to tell him for years. That was why he had always been drawn to friends like Justin, the ones that misbehaved. They played where he didn't dare; they took the chances he couldn't. Wasn't Julia in this group too?

He rolled over and put his arm across her waist, his cheek against her shoulder. She continued reading.

Betsy had been the opposite choice, the road of no risk. With her, he had opted for the safety, the status quo, of his own known self. It had been a hothouse marriage, rotting from its own limited temperature range. He had been right to leave it.

Yet, here was Julia, naked, next to him, on the remote coast of California, as he had wanted it. It had been his idea, a chance to take them, their relationship, away, to simplify their lives so that they could just be together. Yet it was not Julia that captured his attention, but an anonymous fishing family from Morro Bay.

Julia stretched her arm out and drew Ray's head into the soft spot between her shoulder and chest. She held her book with one hand. Ray tightened his arm around her waist. As close as she was, Ray felt her to be a great distance from him, like Justin, who had died so long ago. Her wild path through life left no place for a slow learner like himself to grab hold.

When Julia was done with her chapter, they made love. Ray marveled at the smoothness of the skin on her stomach, running his fingers across the thin patch of hair on her mound. She pulled him into her with her legs, arching up against him. They came together and she grabbed him tightly with both her legs and arms, raising herself up off the bed with the primitive instincts of a baby animal trying to hold on to the underside of its mother. She buried her face in Ray's neck. She felt light and Ray held her without effort. It was as if she would never let go.

When Ray woke in the morning his dreams were right in front of him, more real than the cold, dark motel room that he could not immediately recognize. In his dream he and his brother had been living in something like a villa near the Mediterranean. Dinner was being served to many people: Julia, his father, Betsy, everyone Ray knew. But Ray was concerned about something happening outside, up in the hills. Dash was up there barking, and he knew something was wrong, or something was about to be wrong. Something to do with children and fire.

Awake, he felt anxious. He tried to recall everyone back to his mind. He needed to know what was wrong. His dreams, and these stories he had been making up, were welling up inside him, pushing against him.

They returned to the Seaside for breakfast. Ray noticed that the boat was no longer tied at the dock. He scanned the harbor, trying to pick it out on a mooring somewhere. Finally he gave up, concluding that the two men and two boys had been up before sunrise and left already for another day of fishing.

"Route 1 is closed," Ray told Julia as she slopped down some puffy pancakes.

"What?"

"There was a sign by the road on the way in last night. It said that Route 1 is closed. I thought we should ask around. See if it's really true."

Just then the waitress approached to clear off their plates. "Is it true that Route 1 is closed?" Julia asked her.

"I don't know," she answered without looking at them. "I wouldn't be surprised. In the winter, it's closed a lot."

Julia grabbed her plate back from the waitress. She was not done.

"What are we going to do?" Julia asked.

Ray didn't answer.

Back outside, they walked over to the dock. The flat, gray sky of the previous day persisted. Looking out at the horizon, where the water blurred into the clouds, Ray longed to be out there, lost in the vastness and colorlessness of the ocean, where location is a mathematical equation and a small dot on a chart. He did not like being left behind, stuck on land. Roads, restaurants, relationships, all crowded together on shore in a confusing press of noise.

"You want to take a trip?" Julia asked.

"We're on a trip," Ray said.

"I mean away. A trip away, out there." She tilted her head toward the ocean and hooked his arm with hers.

Ray shrugged his shoulders, not ready to admit his longing, not really sure what to make of it.

"I do," Julia said when Ray did not answer. "It seems like I always want to go somewhere away. Sometimes it scares me. Sometimes I think away might mean for good, forever. You know, dead." She laughed weakly. "I don't have the guts for that, though, so I just move on to some other place, some other guy, whatever. It still scares me though, like something awful is going to happen to me."

Ray put his arm around her. He stifled the urge to comfort her, to tell her everything was OK. He sensed the emptiness of the words before he spoke them. Beneath his reflex to reassure her lurked his own longings, which understood what Julia meant, which embraced the simple, naked truth of what she had said. Julia leaned into him.

They walked across the street, arms around each other, to confirm at the post office what they both had come to believe was true, that Route 1 north of San Simeon was closed.

Ray was not to be denied. He was determined to find Route 1. His expectation of what he would find there had come to include peace, a break from the driving, a simple rest. Driving had become a state of tense inertia, a dull, unremitting fact. Ray imagined that arriving in Big Sur would be like breaking through the tape at a finish line; something would give way; the race would be over and the resting, the long drink of water, the happy recollection would begin.

A quick glance at the map showed Ray that it was less than twenty miles back to Route 101, and then it was around a hundred miles to Monterey, where they could rejoin Route 1 from the north and drive down, past Point Lobos (there was another name—had he heard of Point Lobos from his brother who had gone to Stanford, or had it been the title of a photographic exhibit he had once seen?), and from there down to Carmel and Big Sur.

Ray had no guarantee that Big Sur was accessible from the north. He had no idea which part of Route 1 was closed; it might all be closed. He was acting on faith. He wanted to believe that there was a small section of road just north of San Simeon that was washed out or being worked on. It was not his nature to assume that vast chunks of road, mile after mile, had just disappeared. Hurricanes, volcanoes, and tornadoes were not things he anticipated meeting up with in his life.

Being with Julia, Ray thought, made him vulnerable to natural disasters. He realized it as if it were a sudden epiphany. For the first time he felt vulnerable, as if something might happen to him, and it had to do with being with Julia.

Back on Route 101, it began to drizzle again. Ray drove on. The rain had to end somewhere, sometime. Being disheartened only made him more determined. They could not make the temperature in the car right. It was humid and uncomfortable, yet the outside air, when they opened the window, was cold.

When they reached Carmel, the rain had stopped and the sun was coming out in bits through the still heavy clouds. Ray parked at a meter across the street from the library and they prepared to walk around town. Still not sure if it was hot or cold, they both carried jackets. The library was a brick building with a fancy stainless steel and picture window entry. It looked new. People, residents, entered and exited. Life went on, Ray thought. Carmel did not hold their arrival in the same esteem that he held Carmel.

Julia and Ray strolled around the parking lot adjoining the docks. There were boutiques selling turtlenecks and T-shirts, jewelry, hand-tooled leather belts and bags, watercolors, gifts like prisms and glass vials full of colored water, cookies. They all lined the waterfront and were mostly closed.

"It's like Santa Fe," Julia observed, taking Ray's arm in an abstracted gesture of affection.

Ray was drawn to the water and led her out the municipal dock where two men, dressed all in green, as if they were hunters, were fishing with cane poles. Ray liked the feeling of being out over the water.

They decided not to eat lunch. Ray stopped at a convenience store and bought gas. When he was inside paying he bought some snacks: two Hostess chocolate cupcakes with cream filling, a Snickers bar, a bag of unsalted cashews, a small bag of barbecue potato chips, a large bag of popcorn, a box of miniature sugar donuts, a package of Twizzlers, and two Dr. Peppers. All the things that he would never buy for Jesse and Zach. At the counter he added two shiny red apples, for health. He put the brown bag in the backseat and they proceeded down Route 1 toward Big Sur. Just outside Carmel was another sign, simpler this time: ROUTE 1 CLOSED. Ray just drove on. The sun was out fully now, and the clouds had retreated to the mountains lining the inland side of the road. The coast was precipitous cliffs of rocks, and before long Ray could understand how large chunks of road might easily fall into the ocean below. With his new sense of vulnerability, Ray drove cautiously, expecting at any minute to come upon a large hole where the road had once been.

The coast was not exactly how Ray had imagined it; even so, he liked it. It was big and rough, even intimidating. The ocean beat noisily against the rocks below; seagulls floated on the air, squawking loudly; foliage spilled out of the mountains and creeks on their left. Nature felt aggressive and uncaring, domineering; even going so far as to push the road out into the ocean. Ray drove with his window down, feeling good. Julia, too, rolled her window down and let the chilly air blow back her hair.

They drove through Big Sur without knowing it. After they were over an hour from Carmel, Ray knew they had gone too far and turned around. Whatever Big Sur was (Ray had assumed it was a village of some kind), it was not something that clearly announced itself. On the way back there was a green-and-white sign: BIG SUR. Only there was nothing. Ray drove slowly. To the right, burrowed into the mountain, was a long, low building surrounded by smaller cabins, all of it looking old and run-down.

Then on the left, the ocean side, was a giant parking lot built out on a point of land. There were only three cars in it—two rental cars, both white, and an orange VW van. Ray pulled up next to the van and parked. When he and Julia got out they could see that the point continued out, sloping down, and into the rock were built sitting terraces with tables and chairs for eating. Following the contours of the land it was built into, and itself made out of the same rock, was a chain of buildings housing a kitchen, several indoor eating areas, and several serving counters, with large metal doors covering their openings. Everything was shut and empty, a carnival that had packed up and left. Julia and Ray wandered aimlessly around the tiers. There was no sign of any of the people from the other three cars.

Ray finally sat on a rock wall looking out over the ocean 100 feet below. This, he supposed, was it. They had arrived and, having arrived, had found everything just as impenetrable as it had ever been. He searched for some feeling of arrival, but there was none.

"Well," said Julia clapping her hands, "here we are."

She sat down next to Ray smiling and acting otherwise cheerful.

"Want a cupcake?" Ray asked, handing her one of the chocolate cupcakes from the package as he ate the other one.

"God, I can't remember when I last had one of these," Julia said smiling.

"They always look better than they taste," Ray said. "But still, you've got to keep checking it out."

Ray found a hotel, if that's what it was, the other side of town. It was high on the hill overlooking the ocean. The lobby was built of a wildly grainy wood panel broken by eight-foot-square picture windows with incredible views of the sea. The restaurant was closed.

"What are we meant to eat?" Julia asked the manager, a friendly blond girl who wore a thin white blouse with shoulders that puffed out like balloons.

"We have food," Ray said to Julia, bumping the brown bag of snacks with his hip.

"Most people that come this time of year are on retreat and bring whatever they need with them," the manager said soothingly.

The room was one hundred dollars for a night. Julia wanted to drive back to Monterey, but Ray insisted on staying and offered to pay the whole bill. He was not yet done with Big Sur.

The gravel path to their cabin was cut through thick brush and lined with rocks. Prayer flags hanging on wooden poles appeared suddenly along the way. The cabin had the same wildly grained wood on its walls. There was a large window looking out into the dense forest. There was a table with two chairs beneath the window. The wood floor had a small purple-and-black throw rug at the foot of the bed. Like all their previous rooms, this one was damp and cold.

Julia flopped back on the bed with a sigh, her legs dangling over the end. Ray took her shoes off deliberately; then peeled off her turquoise blue socks. He undid her belt and the buttons of her jeans and worked them down around her hips and then pulled them off one leg at a time. She lay passively. Ray kneeled down on the small rug at the foot of the bed and spread her legs. He leaned forward and lightly licked her crotch, brushing her pubic hair and the insides of her thighs with his tongue. Then, with a strong, flat tongue he parted her labia and like a dog lapped at her vagina and her clitoris. She still did not move. Ray kept up his wet caresses. She put her hand on his head and pushed him away as she sat up. She put her legs together and pulled them up next to her.

"I don't feel like that right now," she said.

"What's wrong?"

She did not answer. Ray asked again.

"I don't know," she finally said angrily. "Does there have to be something wrong always? I just don't feel like having you grazing around between my legs is all. Do I always have to be horny?"

Ray retreated to the chair by the large window, his half-aroused penis pressing against his pants.

"No," he said quietly as he sat down, more to himself than Julia, "no, not always."

The sunny respite had passed and it was again cloudy. Ray noticed water dripping off the eaves. He looked more closely. The rain was so light that he could not see it, but it was collecting on the roof and running off in small rivulets. He dumped the bag of snacks onto the table.

Ray looked back at the bed. Julia was lying with her back to him, her legs pulled up to her chest, her arms wrapped around her knees. Her bare bottom, smooth and large and ripe, was like a sculpture. A trace of fur like a wispy tail ran into the crack between her legs. Ray opened the bag of popcorn. He thought back to the first time he and Julia had made love.

It had happened easily, actually. Like dialing the phone. As simple as that. It was only after the connection was made that it had gotten more complicated. Ray and Julia had always communicated a level of sex between them, some particular polarization of the air molecules as they passed. It would have been impossible for them to say exactly when they became aware of that, or who had become aware of it first, or how it was that this feeling even existed. It might have been, for Julia, the way Ray walked, because she liked men with some body presence; or the way he talked to his workers, because he seemed gentle, quietly in charge, and she appreciated sensitivity in a man; or the way he laughed, because he liked to laugh and he had a sense of irony that rang true for her. For Ray, it might have been Julia's sharp tongue, because he liked a woman who spoke her mind; or her strong shoulders which she carried easily, because he found body strength and knowledge sexy; or her quick mind, frustrated and confused about where to land, because he sensed an echo of his own trapped self there.

These things and whatever else it took found expression one night after work. Julia and Ray had joined Scott, Roberto Torres, and a bricklayer from Nambe at the bowling alley. It was league night and no alleys were free, so they went in the bar and drank beers and played songs on the jukebox. The sound of rolling thunder and crashing wooden pins surrounded them as if they were under water. Scott started a game in which he held his ankle with one hand and, balancing on one foot, jumped through the hoop formed by his arm and leg and landed, without falling, back on his free leg, his hand and ankle now locked behind him. Scott had party experience in this game and was successful most of the time. Roberto tried, and fell every time.

"I can do that," Julia said with bravado.

"Yeah, let's see."

"Gimme another beer."

Julia, now standing, scooped a new glass off the table and drank it half down. When she picked up her foot, her tight skirt caught at her thigh and she hiked it up to just beneath her crotch. She wobbled and teetered and then put her second foot back down on solid floor.

"OK," she said, smiling and drinking again, "now I'm ready."

She rehiked her skirt deliberately, like a weight lifter squatting to lift his bar, and she slowly raised her foot. Waving her free arm for stability, she finally found a moment of balance and took the opportunity to bend low and leap up, drawing her knee through the loop and then getting so stuck and confused that she forgot, as the trick fell apart, to let go of her ankle and fell hard to the sawdust strewn floor in a heap of misdirected arms and legs. When Julia untangled herself and stood up her ankle was twisted and she limped back to the table wiping sawdust and dirt off clothes. Her face was bright red and, even though she was laughing, she lowered her head so people could not see her embarrassment.

"Piece of cake," she said as she sat down.

"Look," Scott said, back on his feet, "it's easy." He jumped through the loop of his leg and arm one more time and then jumped back again as an added show of dexterity.

Roberto and the bricklayer left early, and Ray, Scott, and Julia forgot about bowling; they drank beer, and kept putting quarters in the jukebox.

A Julio Iglesias slow ballad came on the jukebox. Ray picked up Julia's hand and led her out to a clear spot between the tables. He pulled her close to him and, since they had both, at one time in their lives, been to dancing school, they glided sinuously through the empty bar. Julia rested her head lightly against Ray's neck and kept the full length of her body, down through her thighs, pressed tightly against him.

When the song was over they were both sweating where the

skin of her cheek touched his neck and where their palms had been held together. There was a silence of recognition: that what they had just done was, if not sex, at least very sexy, and that there was now a deeper desire still unsatisfied. Another song started, but Ray and Julia went back to the table where Scott was busy watching a ten-year-old play a video game in the far corner.

"How about another beer?" Scott asked. Ray and Julia nodded without speaking, suddenly shy.

Scott offered them a ride back to their cars at the office, but Ray and Julia declined and walked the ten blocks. It was late August, cool for summer, and the dampness of his skin and clothes chilled Ray as they walked. On Cerrillos Road, where no one ever walked, they passed the Burger King, the Taco Bell, Midas Muffler, and the cars sped past them in a thick fog of noise, exhaust, and headlights. They discussed the movie *The Year of Living Dangerously*, which they had both seen. Julia liked Mel Gibson; Ray liked Sigourney Weaver; but they agreed that Linda Hunt as Billy Kwan stole the show.

"As if there's something smarter, or bigger, than just a boy and a girl, and love," Julia said.

When they reached the office Ray unlocked the door and they went in to get warm. Ray took Julia in his arms and kissed her. The lights were still off.

It was not so late, seven-thirty or eight. Neither one of them had eaten dinner and they were both a little drunk. Ray knew that Betsy would have dinner for him when he got home. They kissed with such hunger that Ray quickly had his hands under Julia's blouse and all over her breasts. They heaved and pressed against each other and then separated so that Ray could touch more of her and then heaved together again. Ray lifted Julia's skirt and ran his hand over her butt inside her panties. He dropped down on his knees and kissed her thighs and then pulled down her panties and kissed her pubic hair. She held his head back, trying to slow him down. Ray stood up again and pressed the bulge in his blue jeans against her naked crotch. He lifted her shirt and kissed her breasts.

Ray pulled her by the hand into his office. He did not want to take time to lock the door for fear that it all might disappear. They left Julia's panties on the floor of the reception room, next to Noni's desk. Ray knew that any of the eight to twelve people that had keys to the office might show up at any moment. It was not uncommon for Butch Davis, the general contractor that shared the office, the phones, and Noni's services, to come down after dinner and work on an estimate or a pay request. All the journeymen who worked for Ray had keys and sometimes came by to borrow a tool. Scott used the typewriter to write letters to his mother in Minnesota. Ray knew, but he did not care. It would have been unbearably awkward to be caught half naked with Julia, but he did not care.

He kissed her again, leaning her against the side of his desk, and then they slumped to the floor, her hands undoing his belt and fumbling at the buttons on his fly. He popped the buttons himself and pulled his pants and underwear down to his knees. He pulled off her blouse, the slip-over-the-head kind, and lay on top of her, wondering at the newness, at the excitement, of her breasts. He kneeled and undid his shirt, lying back down flesh against flesh, chest against chest. They kissed wildly, licking and sucking on each other and sticking their tongues deep into each other's mouth. Ray's penis slipped into Julia's vagina and she pressed up with her hips and he was seated like a precision tool. It grabbed his whole body to be so deep in her and he groaned.

Ray came in seconds, the frenzied passion of their kissing and touching shooting out of him with excruciating intensity. Ray was breathing too hard to talk. He rolled off Julia and lay on the industrial indoor-outdoor carpet next to her. He felt the dirt and grit against his back and thought of the heavy boots that constantly walked over this carpet and then thought of Noni always pestering Butch and himself to hire a cleaning agency. She was right. The rug was filthy. From where he lay, he could see the bottom of the middle drawer of his desk, the smooth wooden guides which it rode on. He felt his wet penis against his stomach, shrinking. Julia ran her first two fingers through the sweat between her breasts. She drew small circles.

"By the way," Julia said, propping herself up on her elbow next to Ray, "what's your name?"

They laughed. Ray pulled her head down onto his shoulder and they lay quietly. He wondered about birth control but let it go. It was done. Right or wrong, whatever it meant, whatever might happen, it was done. Life for Ray had deflected. Like some planet floating through space, he had been hit by a meteor, a dull, unnoticed thud in his vast and cratered expanses, but his course, his orbit, had been altered. It was not an impact that the scientists noticed, since it was a common occurrence in the thick soup of space, a typical collision, but the great, lumbering planet had changed its path: where it had been headed would never be reached and where it was now headed could not yet be calculated, but for certain, its course had shifted.

Julia still lay half naked on the bed, so quiet Ray thought she might have fallen asleep. Everything in the room felt frozen.

"Do you want to go for a walk?" Ray asked.

Julia did not move right away, but eventually sat up and put her clothes on, tying her shoes with two loops, the same way that Jesse was learning.

"Let's go," she said, throwing a scarf around her neck and over one shoulder.

They followed a trail leading out from the compound of cabins. As they walked, they slowly became drenched by the misty rain.

"I'm sorry," Julia said. "Sometimes you just want so much."

"I'm sorry too," Ray said. "I just can't seem to get enough of you."

"It feels as if you're putting a pillow over my face."

"I'm sorry. Sometimes I think that if you were all there, if it weren't for Roget, if it weren't for your ambivalence, I wouldn't be that way."

"I am all here. I'm in California, with no one but you."

"I know. But that's not what I mean. I mean, what about in a month, in three months?"

"How can we know these things? You had that with Betsy, and you left."

"It's true. If nothing else, she was there. But it was as if she didn't have a choice, as if neither one of us did. As if we were chained down."

They climbed a steep hill, breathing hard and sweating. Their hair was matted from the rain and a small stream ran down Ray's back. By the time they reached the top, Ray no longer felt bad.

On the way into San Francisco, Julia was restless and fiddled with the radio. Percy Sledge was singing "When a Man Loves a Woman" on one station. She leaned back and smiled. She picked up singing on the refrain, her clear, high voice blending perfectly with Percy Sledge's smoky blues tone. As she warmed up she sang louder, tapping the beat out on her knee with her fingers. She closed her eyes.

Ray joined in as they sang "When a man loves a woman . . ." one last time. The Toyota was full of the noise, puffed out with it, like a balloon.

When the song was over, Julia quickly turned the radio down and leaned back, savoring the contentment.

"It's so great to be in a real city," she said, "a city with soul."

Ray felt that he was at the wheel of a dirigible, high above the other traffic, floating out of harm's way. He zipped in and out, effortlessly weaving between cars at eighty. Traffic was thicker. They were floating into town, being pulled by the magnet of the city.

Aretha Franklin came on the radio singing "Respect" and Julia turned it back up, louder than before. Her fingers bounced on her thigh and instead of singing along she silently mouthed the words, letting Aretha have center stage to herself.

"Pull over, over here," Julia said suddenly, "over there, just for a second, quick."

Ray jerked the car over to the shoulder. Julia turned up the radio a touch more, opened the door, and jumped out next to the car and started dancing. It was a running in place kind of dance, her knees coming up high in front of her as she did a little skip step to the beat. Her arms were pumping back and forth. She hung her head as if to hear better the song as it came out her open door.

When it was over, she jumped back in and turned down the radio.

"Thanks, I needed that," she said, looking at Ray and laughing.

Sweat was beaded up on her forehead and chest, as if she had been working out at the gym. She laughed again, a giddy, happy laugh, and wiped herself off with an extra shirt from the backseat.

Julia insisted on finding her friend Jane's house from memory. The address and directions were in a suitcase in the trunk. They circled a ten-block area of yellow townhouses near the Presidio, all of which looked the same to Ray.

"Maybe it's that one. I know it had a garage."

Julia hit it on the third try. Jane was a lawyer with long black hair. She was short, around five feet. She and Julia hugged each other and then she introduced her boyfriend, Peter. He had a beard and his handshake was limp. Their apartment was small, tidy, sparsely furnished, and cold. The floors were polished maple, and Jane asked Julia and Ray to take off their shoes when they entered. The living room had one chair, with a lamp, and a cluster of pillows grouped in front of the radiator guard. It was two in the afternoon and the sun shone in through the tall, double-hung windows and made perfect, crisp squares on the shiny floor.

Julia and Jane were all hugs and old stories, so Ray tried to engage Peter as a fellow comrade, as another outsider, but Peter wasn't interested and soon said he had a class and left. Ray retreated to the small room off the kitchen where he and Julia were sleeping. A mattress had been thrown on the floor and made with flannel sheets for them. Ray laid his head on the pillow and closed his eyes to nap. It was too cold to fall asleep. He pulled his jacket out of the suitcase, put it on, and began reading *Tinker, Tailor, Soldier, Spy.* Ray loved John le Carré.

In the middle of his third chapter, Julia opened the door and laughed at him sitting in his coat. She sat next to him on the bed and looked at the book in his hand.

"Men all like le Carré," she said. "I don't know any women that do."

She laid her head on his shoulder affectionately, content with silence. Ray continued reading. Finally Julia spoke.

"Jane knows a great restaurant in Chinatown. I told her we'd love to go. Isn't it great being in a real city?"

Ray was not aware of much more of San Francisco than the cold room he was in now, which was far from great in his mind, but he nodded in agreement.

"Also," Julia said, her voice becoming tentative, "I realize, seeing Jane, that we have so much to catch up on. I thought, if you don't mind, that maybe instead of driving up the coast north with you, I'd stay here with Jane and just let you do that part yourself. Would you mind?"

Ray shook his head. "That makes sense. I don't mind."

But Ray suddenly had no desire to go north; yet there was no reason to stay either. He saw that he had no option but to keep moving.

"I'll leave in the morning," he said. He was reminded of his weekends with his children, where some other force seemed to be dictating his schedule. He was not yet aware of how despondent and rejected her request made him feel.

That night, as they left the restaurant, Ray noticed a large glass jar on the counter by the cash register. There was a note taped to the front and written in black magic marker which read:

> One of our cooks RAY has to have immediate emergency brain surgery. Your contributions will help.

Ray took out a quarter and let it fall into the jar on behalf of his namesake.

When they were in bed, Julia sucked on Ray's penis until it was hard, and then she licked and stroked him until he came. It made Ray feel luxurious, blessed with a sensual wealth; still, the days ahead haunted him with a cold emptiness.

• • •

In the morning Ray was aware of Julia getting out of bed, and heard through a dim consciousness voices in the kitchen, plates, silverware; sensed Julia return and dress and leave again; realized the return of an empty quiet to the apartment. Once or twice he tried to wake himself, to shake himself out of his stupor as a drunk might try to shake off the wobbles, but he was too tightly gripped and his eyes would never open, his mind would not clear, and he fell back into heavy sleep troubled by startling dreams that ran through his mind like movies. When he finally woke, at ten-thirty, he couldn't remember any of his dreams, but he could feel the impact of them in the middle of his chest. He lay in bed for a long time, happy to be alive.

When he finally got out of bed and wandered into the living room, Peter was the only one in. He sat in the lone chair reading a book.

"Julia and Jane have gone shopping," Peter announced.

Ray stood at the window in his socks, his shoes sitting over by the front door, thinking that even though the clouds had returned, it looked warmer outside than it felt inside. He turned around and looked at Peter, expecting him to be reading in heavy sweaters and gloves. The only thing of that sort he wore was fur-lined slippers. Ray wanted them. Peter looked up from his book at Ray.

"Do you live here?" Ray asked him; Peter had not gone to dinner with them the night before.

Peter thought before answering. "Yes, sort of. I'm looking for an apartment, because I lost mine; so I'm living here for now."

Ray had assumed that Jane and Peter were lovers, but he was no longer sure. It occurred to Ray that Peter did not like him.

"Is the heat broken?" Ray asked.

"It's the old radiator kind. It doesn't work too well, but we like it chilly."

Ray backed up to the radiator in case any heat was coming out of it.

"If you want any breakfast, help yourself," Peter motioned to the kitchen. "I'm afraid that I need to stay with my studying."

Ray was not hungry. He was high from his sleep and had not returned to a sense of mortality or hunger. He also, suddenly, did not want to spend any more time in that apartment.

"No, thanks, I think I'll just go."

"Julia left a message for you on the counter in the kitchen," Peter said without looking up from his book.

A purple piece of paper, folded in thirds and stuck with a dinosaur sticker, sat in front of the toaster with his name written on it. Ray wondered where Julia had found a dinosaur sticker. Just like her, he thought, purple paper and a dinosaur sticker, a designer note.

Ray sat on the edge of their bed on the floor, his suitcase open in front of his crossed legs. He laid the purple note on top of his randomly folded blue socks. He was aware of some tension about reading it. He closed the suitcase on the note, still not read.

He had forgotten about Peter and was surprised to hear him say goodbye as he was half out the door.

"Goodbye," Ray answered, pausing. He looked at Peter in his chair and suddenly wished they were friends. "Goodbye," he repeated.

Driving up a steep hill and then lurching over the crest and braking down the other side toward the main road to the Golden Gate Bridge, Ray was without destination. He was in San Francisco, headed north, without any reason. His sense of having been thrown out was complete, and he knew no words to describe the desolation he felt. Perhaps this is what is known as miserable, he thought, as he followed the ramp up to the bridge.

On the other side of the Golden Gate Bridge he followed signs for Sausalito. Sausalito. There was a name, like so many others for Ray, reverberating out of the mythology of songs and idle conversation. It was one of those places where people lived and met, gathering in cafes, shaping new ideas and drinking espresso. Ray did not know what it was, exactly, that drew him to these places, but they had all, one after another, let him down. He parked at a meter and went looking. None of the restaurants interested him; he was still not hungry. He stopped at a toy store and went in.

The air in the store was stale and hot. Ray took off his jacket. He was the only one in the store. The cash register attendant was in the back moving boxes. He stuck his head out of the double doors and told Ray to call him if he needed help. Ray nodded. The store reminded Ray of the nursery they had set up first for Jesse, then Zach. That room, too, had always been hot, as if that were the only atmosphere that was safe for babies. Ray had assembled and disassembled their crib many times. A white crib with a side that could be lowered by releasing the catch with your foot. As these things went, the crib had not been difficult to put together, not nearly as difficult as the storage shelves in the garage. Cribs were made to be put together and taken apart; their usefulness came and went. Storage shelves were more permanent.

Ray read the directions on some board games, looking for one that wasn't too old for Zach or too young for Jesse. He moved on to the books, reading a few that had golden award stars on their covers. He liked one about a train with a friendly face and put it on the counter to buy. He looked over the boxes of Duplo toys, mostly figures. He picked out a collection of cavalry people for Zach and doctors and nurses for Jesse. Zach was someone who might tame the Wild West, or make it wilder. Jesse was more serious; he might be interested in a career one day.

Ray did not want to carry his packages, so he returned to the Toyota to put them in the trunk. When he got there, he decided that he was done with Sausalito and drove out of town back toward Route 101 north, headed, once more, for Route 1.

As soon as Route 1 began to twist and turn, rising up over the hills toward the ocean, Ray felt himself relax. On the ocean side the trees disappeared and a V in the green hills opened up to the flat, gray sea. A small stream of water ran down next to the road. One slope was covered in the small pink flowers of chamomile bushes.

The road along the coast was narrow and hugged escarpments, bending in and out, steeply up and down. Ray drove mindlessly through Stinson Beach, past the surf shops, the beach-side cafes, the ducks swimming in the lagoons.

The road went inland and Ray slipped into a stupor. With one hand lightly on the wheel, he drove through thickets of eucalyptus trees, through a place called Dogtown, past ranches with corrals full of horses. Then he suddenly caught himself and realized that he needed to be back by the ocean. He had no idea how far he had come.

In Oleana, he turned left at a sign for Point Reyes. The road followed a canal of dirty water, passed through a village, Inverness, with a row of large wooden piers. He followed signs for Drake's Lighthouse, driving quickly, accelerating on the turns. Suddenly, once more, the landscape dramatically went naked. The road snaked through lush, rolling pastures. Fjords of water inched in on Ray's left. He always chose the turn for the lighthouse.

He rattled over cattle guards, past the Historic A Ranch and the Historic B Ranch. He crossed lands as green and treeless as he had ever seen. There was now water on both sides, signs for beaches. He climbed toward the lighthouse point. Signs warned of dangerous cliffs. The grass gave way to more rugged ice plants.

Ray parked in the lighthouse lot and walked to the edge. The wind was strong and cold, whipping around Ray and pulling at his clothes. He zipped his jacket and started down a slippery dirt trail toward a lookout. A foghorn bleated in the distance every thirty seconds, sounding like a lost, wounded animal. Ray's forehead and face were quickly wet. He could not tell if it was raining or if the moisture was just so thick it condensed in the wind. When he reached the small dirt platform, he sat on the only bench. He looked out over the white-capped sea far below.

He had not thought of Jesse and Zach much this trip, he realized. He pictured them in St. John, on the edge of a much different ocean from the one in front of him. Their ocean was blue to turquoise, like the New Mexican sky, and their surf was benevolent, regular, full of inflated inner tubes and Styrofoam swim boards. The shore that they sat on was of sand, and they were probably building castles with moats that filled with water as each wave ran up the beach.

The ocean that Ray looked over put him in mind of evil mythological birds that grabbed babies in their claws and flew out over the sea and dropped them. In an ocean such as this, Ray thought, a baby would disappear in seconds, would not even leave a trace. Babies could do that, could disappear, just like that. People were different; people had lives, histories. Babies were nothing, a few snapshots maybe; that's it. When they went down, they did not even make a ripple in the water. Ray had known of just such a thing. It had happened with Sean and he had been there to see it.

Because it had been so long since he had cried, Ray did not at first recognize the tightening in his chest and the jerking of his shoulders. It was as if some demon were trying to escape his body, and he took a deep breath and held it, trying to hold back the force of escape. Tears ran out of his eyes and he let loose of his hold on himself and sobbed, making loud noises that were lost in the din of wind and waves around him. His body seemed to gain force and shook harder and harder with each breath, until he had to grab himself around his knees for fear of tumbling off the cliff. He pressed his cheek to his thigh and screamed as loud as he could, trying to purge himself of his tears. They would not, though, be rushed.

Finally his crying abated and, soaked through, Ray returned to himself and began to regain a sense of where he was and how he was. He was cold and tired. The wind continued to drum against him. Thick clouds rolled by just above him. He noticed a pattern to some of the waves offshore and studied them a moment before he realized that they were whales, slipping in and out of sight. Two of them blew water at the same time. They were headed south. Ray watched, forgetting the cold. The whales moved slowly. Suddenly, he imagined Sean down in the water with them, shepherded by their benign and immortal bulk. In their ponderous, steady migration, Ray imagined they were carrying not just Sean, but many lost souls. For a moment, his own aching self longed to be rolling through the surf with them as well, impervious to the torments of the landlocked. He watched reverently until he could no longer see them. Then, quietly, he whispered, "Goodbye."

• • •

There was a white clapboard motor inn in Inverness. It was a re-stored house, and the massive square roof beams were no higher than six feet. In his room was a sagging bed thick with quilts and a large polished wooden headboard. There was an oak chest of drawers with a white porcelain bowl and pitcher on top of it. In the corner was a stiff-backed wooden chair with a cane seat. Ray thought his room more closely resembled a prison than a hotel room. Tomorrow, he thought, maybe I'll take the boat trip to Alca-traz. He had not eaten all day.

Ray lay down on the quilts. He tried to pull one around him. He was cold. He had been cold for as long as he could remember. He had not ever been so cold in New England. He looked around the room but saw no sign of heat. It was turning dark outside. He opened his suitcase to get a sweater. Julia's purple note was on top, still unopened. It seemed a long time ago that he had left the apart-ment in San Francisco.

Ray stood and stripped off his wet clothes, throwing them on the chair. He picked up the note and got in bed, pulling all the cov-ers up over himself. The sheets were cold, and he lay motionless until everything began to warm. When he was comfortable he rolled over and clicked on the bedside lamp. The urgency and im-portance he had felt earlier were gone, left by the side of the road. He read the note quickly, as he might a letter sent from another time and place, disconnected from himself.

Dear Ray,

I've checked on you a few times to see if you were awake, and I even thought about waking you, but you seem to be in the grip of a sleep more powerful than anything we might say to each other just now.

I know you are mad at me about this. I'm not sure I understand myself, for this morning over breakfast I have already begun to tire of Jane and to wonder what made me think I needed this so much.

Except for the shopping. It sounds stupid, I know, but I am excited to go shopping here. It is something I definitely could not have done with you. So let's keep it that simple. Let's keep it about shopping.

Have fun. You are getting the best deal. You have all that magnifi-
cent country and I will probably still not be able to find a bikini that I
like.

Julia

Ray felt a hundred arguments, a swell of objections, rise up in
him, but he let them go in a second. Maybe, he thought, as he
turned out the light, it is that simple.

In spite of how hungry he was, Ray ordered just fruit and yogurt
for breakfast. While he waited for his food, he studied a tourist
brochure and decided to visit John Muir State Park. If nothing
else, he thought, I will see some legendary redwoods.

When Ray parked at the state park, it was raining lightly. Very
little of the rain made it all the way through the heavy tree cover,
so he walked without a poncho. The asphalt trails were moss-cov-
ered and slippery. Elephantine tree trunks shot up to branches
heavy with moisture. The redwoods were too large to put his arms
around. Moss and vines hung from everything, and everything
dripped water.

The woods imparted a feeling of privacy, of secrecy. He passed
by a woman in a wheelchair staring across the rail fence at the
stream. After an hour of walking, his hair was wet and water ran
down around his temples. The shoulders of his shirt were soaked.
He was hot and sweaty and looped back toward the parking lot on
a new trail.

He stopped at a bench to rest, and as he sat had the urge to
strike out across the fallen tree in front of him and become lost in
the forest, to leave the trail. The thickness of the underbrush con-
vinced him that he would surely get lost. How bad could it be?
Probably, he thought, if I walk in any direction for half an hour I
would come out on a shopping mall. It's not really possible to get
lost anymore, is it?

Yet Ray felt utterly lost. Caught, like one of those young orphans
in old novels on a ship bound for unknown worlds, realizing for the

first time that he had truly moved out of sight of land and there was no certainty that he would ever touch the earth again. There was a reflex in Ray to run, to bolt, to resist, but he continued sitting on the bench and began to realize that behind his reflexes lay a deep tranquillity. In spite of feeling lost and scared, Ray had with him everything he needed for his journey, wherever he might be going. He realized that his life was not the line that charted his successes and failures from the day he was born to the present, nor was it that imaginary line into the future that was meant to rise in a confident, positive slope. Rather, he was a simple pencil dot, a moment, slouched on a bench in John Muir State Park, engulfed by the incredible indifference of redwoods and rain. The realization satisfied him, gave him a sense of contentment that lay beneath happiness and unhappiness.

A resolve formed in Ray like a stone. He and Jesse and Zach were the survivors. They had lives to lead, however mundane, and they were inextricably bound to each other, like "buddies" in rock climbing, tied together at the waist. With Betsy, though, the connection was broken. The pain and suffering of that tear did not blur the finality of it. As it had been with their son Sean, the end had come long before any understanding of the mystery and meaning of its life was understood.

And Julia? The thought of her flashed in the periphery of his mind like a darting bird. He smiled as he remembered her dance by the side of the highway two days ago. He had not found what he had been looking for with her in California. They had rubbed and pushed against each other enough for Ray to feel close to Julia and, at the same time, to realize that being with her was a state of emotional chaos and not, as he had hoped, the beginning of something new.

Ray followed the trail back to the Toyota in the parking lot. A patch of sun filtered through the lacy, high cover of leaves, shone on the asphalt, and where it hit, steam rose like dry ice vapors.

There was a pay phone in a pedestal in front of the Toyota. Ray fished Jane's number out of his wallet and dialed it.

"Julia, this is Ray. How are you?"

"Fine." There was a touch of whining in her voice.

"Did you find a bikini?"

"It's not the bikini season. Nothing even to look at."

"Too bad."

"Yeah."

"Julia, listen. I'm ready to go back to Santa Fe."

"That suits me just fine," she answered without hesitation.

Ray started the Toyota. The little bit of sun had run the humidity up to unbearable. He pulled out of the entrance to the park and headed south for San Francisco.

Part Three
Winter/Spring
1983

The
Magician
of the Real

An envelope, addressed in Betsy's handwriting, was in the giant stack of mail waiting for Ray on his desk. Inside were two letters, one from Jesse and one from Zach. He flattened them both and leaned back to read them. They had both been dictated and Ray had a hard time putting his children's voices to Betsy's familiar script. They were written on the blue stationary of a hotel. He read Zach's first:

> Dear Daddy,
>
> I am in St. John. Yesterday I saw three fish. One of them was black with yellow rings and a wave knocked me over and I cried but I am OK.
>
> Zach

Jesse's was a little longer:

> Dear Dad,
>
> I went scuba diving and saw lots of fish, pretty fish, of lots of different colors. You can really see in the water here if you wear a mask.

But I like the swimming pool better and Janet is teaching me to swim but I am still not very good yet. How are you? I love you.

Jesse

Ray slowly stuffed the letters back in the envelope. The noise of the office in the morning swirled around him like wind, tugging at him. He held on to the calm of the two letters. Jesse and Zach would be back in a few days. He was going to pick them up Friday evening. Over the weekend he had rented a larger place, with a fenced yard, that they could move into in a few weeks. It was not as if he had a lot to move, but the idea of moving seemed overwhelming nonetheless. More space meant exactly that—more space. What would he fill it with?

He pictured his new apartment: cold, white walls, a long living room with gray carpet, red linoleum in the kitchen, a dishwasher. Then he imagined Jesse and Zach into it and the image began to blur. The apartment was suddenly full, not of furniture, but of them. Too full. How could such small bodies have such a large presence? Maybe he had rented a place too small? How could that be when it was at least twice as big as the one he had now and they had gotten by with that space easily? Something was wrong.

Julia was moving with them, but she had renewed her search for her own place. Staying with Ray, she reminded him, was only temporary. While Ray had continued to try to persuade her to give up and stay, he did so now more out of habit than desire. He felt compelled to fight Julia's resistance even as he was developing ambivalence of his own.

"Ray." Noni was speaking to him from the doorway. She laughed when he jerked his head, jolted back into the present. "Joe Steppe is on the phone."

Ray nodded his head. This was a must-take phone call. The first thing Noni had told him when he walked in was that the check from Joe Steppe had not come while he was gone. Joe had promised to pay an overdue bill on the Rodgers job before Ray left, and they had counted on it to pay some bills and meet the payrolls. Noni had squirmed, deferred, and just plain not paid people to get by, but the squeeze was tight.

"Ray," Joe said in his loud, good-buddy voice, "how are you? Your secretary, I can never remember her name, what's her name?"

"Noni."

"Noni told me you've been vacationing. It must be nice."

"It was, until I came back."

"Listen, buddy, I know I promised you a check, but Rankin is getting weird. She hasn't paid me. She called a meeting for today at one. I think you should be there."

In the world of general contractors, Ray gave Joe credit for acknowledging that he had not done something that he had said that he would do.

"Are we going to get paid?" Ray asked.

"I've been on her pretty hard. I told her we all need the money. You know, Rankin is as rich as they come. Furniture money, from the Midwest. She's definitely good for it. Can you make the meeting?"

"I guess so." Ray did not see that he had a choice.

Meetings, money—Ray was not ready for it. Scott, sensing that Ray was not all there, had organized the crews and sent them on their way. He sat in the tall chair in front of the drafting table across from his desk. Ray gave him an exasperated look.

"Rankin has called a meeting after lunch," he said.

"How was your trip?" Scott asked.

Ray looked at him a moment. "I don't know," he finally answered. "It rained the whole time. And it's gone, as if it were last year, as if it never happened."

"Vacations are like that," Scott answered, flatly philosophical. "They always end."

Ray smiled. He did not add that it felt as if his vacation had never begun.

Rankin Rodgers's house was south of Santa Fe in La Cienega. The site of her new house, as well as her existing house (which was to become the guest house) looked out over a pond ringed by tall, wide cottonwood trees, and beyond that over the graceful, flat stretches of land that had been plowed and planted for over a century. The land ended at a fence just short of the precipitous arroyo that had once been, and still was, when it rained in the spring, the Cienega River. Since Rankin had bought the twenty-five acres in the mid-seventies, the land had not been worked except to be occasionally irrigated and mowed in order to maintain an aesthetic carpet for her visual pleasure. Rankin was from Santa Barbara and had moved to Santa Fe when her husband, an executive with the Electronics Division of Raytheon, died seven months after suffering a stroke. They had traveled frequently because of his job, mostly to the Orient, and had lived in Japan for almost four years in the early sixties, but Rankin remembered most vividly, passionately, the Christmas they had spent in Santa Fe, and once she made up her mind to sell their house and move, Santa Fe had been an easy choice for her.

Ray did the electrical work for Rankin when she remodeled the small existing farmhouse (she preferred to call it a ranch house) on the property. Joe Steppe had been the contractor, but Rankin liked to deal directly with the subcontractors. Joe encouraged that sort of relationship, unlike Bud Jackson, who didn't like his subs talking to the owners. Early in the job, Joe agreed that Rankin could deal directly with Ray and the other subcontractors on all change orders. That was the kind of contractor Joe was; he negotiated and tried to make things better for his clients; he made concessions that weren't usual; he provided them with subcontractors like Ray, a different breed who could understand what his clients wanted, a Brown graduate, after all. In Rankin's case, Joe's sympathetic style made the escalation of her remodeling job from a $125,000 contract to an eventual bill of $242,683 a little more palatable. Six years later, when Rankin decided to build the house of her dreams on the hill over looking the pond, she once more called Joe Steppe and asked him to bring in as many of the old crews as possible; they had become, after all, family.

Turning on the dirt road that ran behind the racetrack to La Cienega, Ray thought about Rankin. The new house was almost complete. His crews had been installing switches and plugs, but the light fixtures had not yet arrived. They had been delayed by a last-minute total change in the lighting schedule. Ray was relieved that the job was almost over and he felt anxious about this meeting with Rankin.

Ray realized that Rankin and people like her were probably his most natural clients; their jobs were the kind he did best. Commercial jobs, like the shopping center, were an anomaly for his company. And he vaguely understood why. Ray could take care of the Rankins of the world, just as he was on his way to doing now. He was comfortable with them, and understood their needs, which made them comfortable, and then he could zip-zip the electricity to make it do what they wanted. For Rankin, he was a bridge; he spanned the enormous gulf between the indirect mood lighting of a June sunset and the generators, kilovolts, transformers, meters, and circuit breakers that made it all happen. He was a magician of the real. Ray made the world turn for Rankin, and he did it in such a way that she never knew it was happening. It made her feel good that everything was in order, in place, in tune, and that she did not have to feel displaced to have it that way. When she wrote checks to Ray, that was what she was paying for. Contractors on commercial jobs and their high-finance owners did not need that service of illusion.

When it came to paying the bills, though, the whole cozy relationship began to fray. Hard things, like money, did not seem to fit the formula. Emotions suddenly built up like late-afternoon rain clouds. Rankin got weird, as Joe had described it. Everyone ran for cover. This was not the first time Ray felt left alone in the rain.

Ray drove by the half-plastered adobe house north of Rankin's. The front yard was littered with abandoned cars and on the other side of the driveway was a horse corral made of rough-sawed lumber. The top rail had been chewed to the point of breaking by the small, uncombed, skinny horse penned up there. All the times Ray had driven by that house, he had never seen a person, had never seen even a car that he thought would run. Yet the toys in the yard were always in a different place, the pile of wood stacked by the aluminum screen door changed sizes, and every now and then a few more square feet of cement plaster were added on to what was there.

Joe Steppe was outside inspecting the meter and bank of disconnects Ray's men had installed when Ray drove up.

"This is incredible," Joe said, even though he was more than familiar with the main distribution system for the property. "I've never seen anything like this for a house."

"Remember," Ray said, "it has room to add on a conference center with a kitchen."

When Rankin had disclosed plans for one day putting in a conference center where symposiums and workshops about growth and healing could take place, Ray had hired an engineer to design the power distribution.

"I know, I know," Joe said, wondering how it had all gotten so out of hand. "She's upset about money today. I don't know, Ray. I think she has an uncle in Minneapolis that has some control over her money, her family money. Whenever she talks to him, she gets upset about money.

"Don't worry, buddy, she'll pay. She always does," Joe added as consolation. "Let's go inside; they're waiting."

"They?"

"Bryan's here too."

Bryan was the architect. As they entered under the newly plastered arched adobe gate, down the flagstone walk, Ray felt guilty before the first word was said. It was little consolation to him that he never took advantage of Rankin, that he never took any of a number of opportunities to mark her work up more or add extra material to the bills. On the contrary, when he figured the price for her main distribution system as designed by the engineer he was so appalled he used an 8 percent markup, smaller even than his commercial markup. Still, the price for wiring her house had risen to over fifty thousand dollars and for that he felt guilty. It seemed wrong to spend so much on a house, and Ray could not escape the sense that he was a co-conspirator.

Rankin was standing with Bryan next to the grand hunting-lodge-style fireplace. She had one cowboy boot perched on the hearth with her arm extended stiffly to her hand resting on her raised knee. She wore a long blue denim skirt, buttoned tightly around her thin waist, and a turquoise-inlaid concho belt hung loosely around her hips. Her simple white blouse was sleeveless, showing off her unusually thin, firm arms. Silver-and-turquoise bracelets ran up and down her forearms like bangles, and her hair, jet black in spite of her age, was pulled back tightly and pinned behind her neck.

"Hello, Ray," Rankin said, moving only her head to address him and arching her neck like a horse under tight rein.

Ray nodded as he approached. He noted in Rankin what he had seen in many older women of northern New Mexico: a tightening of the face. The dry air took its toll over the years, and even in the time Ray had known her, Rankin's skin had dried and wrinkled and become tight. It made her look hardened and leathery. It was, to Ray, an attractive pioneer look, a look perhaps expressing some fantasy Rankin had about herself.

"Bryan," she said, "will you conduct this meeting? There are some phone calls I need to make."

Bryan nodded, although he was surprised by the request, and Rankin loudly stomped her cowboy boot to the floor from the hearth and clicked her way across the newly finished bare brick floor.

"Ray," she said, leaning theatrically back in the door, "there are some things I need to go over with you before you leave. Can you look me up when you're done here?"

Bryan, Joe, and Ray were left standing around the hearth of the yet unused fireplace. Bryan was a tall, youngish-looking architect who was quite wealthy in his own right and who, at moments like this, must have wondered why he ever practiced architecture. He let the silence of Rankin's departure linger until her presence had fully left.

"Well," he began in a voice as close to stern as he could muster, "Rankin feels this project is way over budget. She feels hurt, frankly, taken advantage of."

"Bryan," Joe interrupted, "maybe she needs some therapy to

make her feel better. She's asked for all these changes and most of them, most of the big ones, we priced out for her before we ever began them. Give me a break. I mean, she wants a big enough electrical service to run a conference center. Now who's out of line here?"

"I know, I know," Bryan said, slipping out of his patriarchal role. "She made some financial miscalculations of her own, I think. You guys could have done better, but you've kept up with your paper work pretty well. I've seen a lot worse." He shrugged his shoulders.

It was clear to Ray that Bryan's job in this meeting was to give them a spanking on Rankin's behalf, but he wasn't quite up to it. Bryan opened a set of plans across the hearth and began explaining some of the cost-saving cuts he had figured out with Rankin. They were token; the house was virtually done.

Ray wondered why Dickie Lopez, the plumber, was not at this meeting, but even as he wondered he knew the answer. Dickie liked beer and bowling. He worked his jobs himself and had little time for meetings and conversation. He installed plumbing; he did not create it. Except for the addition of the Jacuzzi, few changes had been made to his work. Ray knew that Rankin did not think of him as part of her construction family. After all, he spoke Spanish most of the time. Ray wished that he had created for himself the same immunity as Dickie Lopez. Dickie was probably not waiting for his money.

"When are we getting paid?" Ray asked, interrupting Bryan and Joe's careful analysis of a pocket door.

"She said next week," Bryan answered.

Next week was not soon enough, and he knew that next week meant in two weeks, but there was little that Ray could do about it. Rankin held all the cards. He would file a lien, just in case, but that would do nothing to speed up delivery of his money; in fact, it would probably slow it down. Maybe he would wait to file.

"See you guys," Ray said, and left to find Rankin. He was angry at her and felt used.

Rankin was in the "Jacuzzi room" when he walked down the

five stone steps and pushed open the hand-carved, narrow door.

"Ray," Rankin said cheerily, as if there had been no thought of spanking ten minutes earlier. "Look, I want you to see this."

She crossed to the light dimmer next to Ray and turned it on. Ray looked at the light. They stood side by side, looking at the light. In a minute, it began flickering, getting dimmer and then brighter. Ray turned the dimmer all the way up and the flickering stopped, and then when he turned it back down, it began to flicker again.

Bad dimmer, Ray thought, and started to say that he would have it replaced, when Rankin interrupted him.

"Isn't that marvelous," she said. "When it started a few days ago, I was over there, working on the planters, and I thought some aliens or something had tuned into my brain waves, because it dimmed and brightened in synchrony with my thoughts. It was magical. I don't know how you made that happen, but I'd like the same thing in my bedroom and in the library. I think not in the dining room; I'm not sure everyone would understand."

Ray was speechless. What were his chances of getting three dimmers, all defective in the same way, all defective in tune with Rankin's brain? He looked at Rankin, expressionless. I won't say anything, he decided. I'll take this straight to Joe, I'll ignore it, I'll tell Joe I can't do it, but I won't tell her.

"Tell me, Ray," Rankin said, suddenly back on earth, "did you have to go to Brown to learn how to be an electrician?"

Ray shrugged his shoulders. "I studied English literature. I don't suppose they're very related."

After work on Friday, Ray went to pick up Jesse and Zach for the first time since their return. The evening was clear and bitterly cold. He wished that they had already moved to their new apartment because, if nothing else, it at least appeared to be modern enough to be kept warm on a cold night. That was not the case for the apartment on Silver Street, which was like a refrigerator; the walls radiated the cold.

On the way to Betsy's house, his old house, he stopped at J. C. Penney in the DeVargas Mall and bought two wool blankets. They were dark blue with a faint red plaid and had annoying wool stringlets bordering the top and bottom, which, under other circumstances, would have made Ray pass them up. That night, he only wondered if two were going to be enough. To the west, over the Jemez Mountains, the sun burned a diffused orange, waning like a candle flame, as the moon, cold and white and bright as if it were lit from within, rose up in the east over the Sangre de Cristo Mountains.

When he knocked, Ray heard first Jesse and then Zach call out, "Dad," and, yelling it over and over and over, scramble through the house to open the front door. They jumped at him like puppies as he leaned over to scoop them up, one in each arm. Jesse threw his arms around Ray's neck and quietly pressed his head against Ray's shoulder. Zach, still yelling, "Daddy, Daddy, Daddy," leaned back in Ray's left arm, wildly throwing his hands as if he wanted to get down. Ray tried to contain Zach as he leaned his head over against Jesse's. In that moment, all his apprehensions about this reunion, about being a father, all his ambivalence and doubt, were shattered like thin wood into so much kindling.

Ray knelt down to put Jesse and Zach back on the floor. Zach immediately ran off to find whatever he had been so desperately needing. Jesse looked after him, looked back at Ray, and then ran after his brother. If they had not been all over him like young cubs, if they had not named him their "dad," Ray would not have recognized these two boys as his children. Their hair had been buzz cut, smooth as peaches, and they were deeply tanned, as if they were of another race. Jesse in particular had a particularly haunting look of anonymity, as if he were any five-year-old on any block in the country. Ray suddenly understood how children could disappear; his had disappeared in a month.

"The haircuts were their ideas—actually, Zach's idea," Betsy said, laughing.

Ray was too stunned to even think of objecting, too disoriented to consider having an opinion.

"How was your trip?" he asked.

Betsy checked herself, thinking for a moment before answering. "It was mixed. It was OK. They missed you, as you can see."

Ray had been overwhelmed by the energy of his children. Now he became aware of Betsy. They looked at each other. In the sun her freckles had expanded into a tan of sorts. The atmosphere, stirred to such a high pitch by Jesse and Zach, suddenly deadened.

"It was OK," Betsy repeated. "We're still feeling a little dazed, a little unsure."

Ray wanted to give her the certainty of separation, but it was not what she had in mind. He felt once more returned to his double bind with Betsy, with no way out. He realized how relaxed he had been when she was gone. He simply nodded his head.

Jesse and Zach reappeared, still frantically running like slapstick comedians. Jesse reached his father first and held up to him a present crudely wrapped in newspaper. Ray thanked him and opened it carefully. It was a fish made of small shells glued together, a gift-shop memento. Ray thanked him profusely and hugged him.

Then Zach presented his gift, unwrapped. It was a small box, another gift-shop memento, probably the same gift shop, of black enamel. "St. John" was written in blue across the top of it.

"It says 'St. John,' " Zach informed Ray, looking at his mother for verification.

Inside the box was a personal collection of shells and beach pebbles. Zach hung his head when Ray thanked him, embarrassed that his gift was not as elaborate as his brother's.

"Thank you, Zach. Thank you both," Ray said, and gave them both a hug as he knelt. "Are you ready to go?"

Jesse nodded. Zach shouted, "Let's go," as he jumped, throwing two fists in the air.

"I've got presents for you, too," Ray told them. He was not proud of the things he had bought in Sausalito, but he was glad to have something.

Ray had invited Dimitri over for dinner as both guest and chef. The prospect of his presence had alleviated some of Ray's anxiety about this first night of reunion with his children and about preparing a meal. Also, Dimitri had become a more frequent visitor as his marriage to Eleanor became more and more embattled. Julia had made plans to have dinner with her friend Christina. This, like so much between them lately, had been a source of unspoken frustration for Ray.

"Why do you go, tonight? Why don't you stay?" Ray had asked.

"Can't I have my own friends?" Julia had countered.

Julia had an interior world into which Ray had no access. He could only observe the movement of it; he could only feel the wind that it produced. He kept trying to slip in, to understand, but his efforts, like those of a child trying to jump on a wildly turning platform in the park, only served to throw him off onto the ground. With each try he grew more moody himself, and with each new skinned knee and bleeding elbow, he became more reluctant to try again. That she so fervently guarded this interior world of hers was a constant affront to him, a daily reminder of the distance between them.

From that, a new fear had grown in Ray. He began to worry that they might, by force of will and through their passions, form a union, an assumed togetherness, without ever breaking this hard shell of Julia's interior world. For the first time, he found himself agreeing with her agitated ambivalence, her profound distrust of any appearance, any suggestion of coupleness. He was giving in to it, accepting it, even as it tortured him.

In an odd way it reminded him of life with Betsy. He realized that he had always believed that if he waited long enough, patiently enough, Betsy would one day come to him whole, like one of those paintings of a naked woman with long hair on a scallop shell, emerging from innocence. Julia was nothing like Betsy, but Ray found he was cutting himself off and waiting for Julia in the same way.

This similarity touched him, in a moment of recognition, as he drove toward his Silver Street apartment with Jesse and Zach in the back of his Toyota; it touched him deeply, utterly, like a stone hitting the bottom of the ocean, there forever.

The smell and the sound of food rushed at them from the

kitchen door of the apartment. Dimitri was bent over, peering into the stove, a belt of skin showing between his pants, low on his butt, and his shirt.

"Dimitri!" the boys began to shout, repeating a more reserved version of the greeting they had given Ray.

"Hello, you little fuckers," Dimitri said good-naturedly. "You've been off in the sun, swimming, having fun, while the rest of us are back here freezing our asses off."

Everyone laughed. Dimitri began pulling out the various plates he had prepared, a feast far larger than the four of them could eat.

"You don't have any pots, pans, plates. Nothing," Dimitri complained. "How do you expect me to cook when there's nothing to cook with? It's pitiful."

He set a roast chicken with potatoes out on the coffee table Ray used for eating. He put down a plate of vegetables—squash and corn and cauliflower. He had made a salad in a glass meat-loaf dish. He laid out heated French bread in aluminum foil.

"I had to wash your goddamn plates," he continued to grumble as he handed out Ray's four plates.

"Thanks, Dimitri," Ray, Jesse, and Zach all kept saying, trying to appease him.

Dimitri had inherited from his mother the belief that good food was the ultimate medicine in life, and over dinner that night Ray understood and became a believer himself. Where Julia's little white pills had never made a difference, Dimitri's feast assuaged his pain. Food, as Dimitri presented it, was a nurturing experience, a force of life. They all ate too much, as Dimitri extracted stories about St. John from Zach and Jesse. Ray listened and watched, slowly identifying, from gestures and a close examination of their eyes, the two small children across from him as his.

After dinner Dimitri lay on Jesse's bed, holding his stomach, well fed and exhausted. Ray cleared the dishes and cleaned the kitchen. Every plate, pot, and pan, such as there were, had been used. The counters were littered, a gastronomic still life. Ray scraped and scrubbed happily.

Jesse and Zach climbed over and sat on Dimitri as his conversation turned from phrases to noises. When Jesse and Zach went to bed, Ray and Dimitri moved to Ray's bedroom. Dimitri resumed his posture of convalescence on Ray's bed and Ray sat in the director's chair next to it.

"I'm leaving Eleanor," Dimitri said after a while. "I wrote her a letter." He pulled a letter from his back pocket. "Do you want to hear?"

Ray nodded his head; a small sense of dread caught in his throat.

"It was my birthday Tuesday," Dimitri explained as he unfolded the letter.

"I didn't know. Happy birthday."

"Fifty-four, not a big one. Except that next year I can retire. We had a party Sunday evening. Gretchen was there, and Elena. We had a pork roast, crispy skin. The house smelled wonderful for two days. And I made some dolmas."

For Dimitri, the menu was always the guest of honor.

"We sat in the living room afterward, we made a fire, and I opened some presents. Gretchen gave me a beautiful Acoma pot." Gretchen was their youngest daughter, a sophomore at UNM in Albuquerque.

"After everyone left I told Eleanor I had a present for her. And I read her this letter:

> Dear Eleanor,
>
> You have given me many wonderful presents on my birthday and on many birthdays in the past. We have shared many years. In those years, there have been many happy times. We have built our family and our house, and we have worked hard, and on many nights we have shared our love for each other. Do you remember how we used to take off for the weekend and drive to Juarez and stay at the Jefferson Hotel and make wild love? It is not the same place now; they have fixed it all up fancy and rooms are over $100 a night. Pablo no longer works there. He has probably died.
>
> Our relationship is like that, a memory of a good time we once had. Everything has changed. So I want to give you on my birthday what you have been wanting for many years now. I give you a divorce

and we go our separate ways. In truth, we have not been together for
a long time.

Your loving husband,
Dimitri"

Dimitri began crying. The letter dropped out of his hand to the
bed. His shoulders heaved as he cried. Ray remembered when
Dimitri had cried at Sean's funeral.

Ray was surprised at the way Dimitri had written that he was
giving Eleanor the divorce that she wanted. Ray had been listening to Dimitri's complaints for so long that he had never considered that Eleanor, too, must have been complaining just as
vociferously to her friends, that she, in fact, might be even more
discontent that Dimitri.

"What did Eleanor say? I mean, when you read this letter, what
did she say?" Ray could not believe the drama of it, reading a letter
as if it were a literary event.

Dimitri had stopped crying. "She said nothing. I cried, like now.
I gave her the letter, but she just set it on the couch and walked out
of the room."

"So, this is it?"

Dimitri nodded his head, squinting back more tears. To Ray, it
was as if he were watching a play. It didn't seem quite real.

"Really?" he asked.

"Really. What do you think, I do this every day for my health?"

"Are you going to move out? Where will you live?"

"We have not discussed it. I am going to move out, I think."

"Why don't you move in with us?" Ray suggested, the idea coming to him in a flash. "We're moving into our new apartment next
weekend. The boys and I can share a bedroom; you can have the
other one."

Ray realized immediately that he had just painted a picture
without Julia. If she moved with them, then there would be no
room for Dimitri. Ray did not retract his offer. Time would tell.

"You are a good friend, Ray. You are good to put up with my
hysteria, It is a great Greek tragedy, isn't it?"

Ray and Dimitri hugged before Dimitri left. As Ray prepared for bed he thought about Dimitri's story. They had talked forever, it seemed, about their marriages, their problems. They had consoled each other, not with advice, but simply by listening. This dramatic request for a divorce by Dimitri caught Ray by surprise. Maybe because of the twenty-year difference in their ages he had assumed that between the two of them it had been Ray's path to get divorced and Dimitri's path to stay married. Suddenly Dimitri had stumbled into Ray's room like a hotel guest hopelessly lost.

When Julia returned, Ray was nearly asleep.

"It smells great in here," Julia said to him as she pressed her naked body against his back.

"Dimitri cooked chicken," Ray mumbled. "How was Christina?"

"We had a lot of fun," Julia answered, laughing. "She cooked her spinach lasagna and we talked. After dinner she took out all these clothes and we played dress-up."

Ray held himself back a moment from falling asleep. By the differences in their evenings he realized what different worlds they lived in.

"You know," Julia said quietly, "I've only just now realized. I wanted to kiss her. I've never kissed a woman before."

Julia
Wears a
Bra

It was the Thursday night before the weekend of moving. Ray was watching Julia undress as he lay in bed. When she took off her shirt, Ray saw that she was wearing a bra. It was, as far as he knew, her only bra. She wore it so infrequently that Ray liked the novelty of it. It was lingerie. He liked the word. It was the kind of bra that buckled in the front, between the cups. Ray liked that about it too. Julia complained about bras. Her chest was broad and her breasts were small. Bras always felt too tight, she said.

Bras for her were like neckties for him. They were leashes. Ray stayed with the thought a second. He would never have considered that he and Julia were alike in any way, but he considered that they just might feel the same way about clothes. It was true that Julia was much more serious about fashion than he was, but underneath the color and style, maybe they agreed that clothes should be loose, that they should not grab like a mother's grip on your wrist, should not clutch like a possessive lover around your chest.

Julia took off her bra as Ray watched. He liked the broad, flat expanse of her throat and chest. She tossed the bra away toward the chair where she had laid her folded shirt, clearly glad to be rid of it. There was a line in her skin under her breasts where the band had pressed. She wiggled her hips to slip her pants and underpants over them.

She walked awkwardly around the bed to get in next to Ray, her shoulders hunched slightly, her back bent, as if she were cold. She always got in next to him as if sleeping naked with a naked man were as commonplace as brushing your teeth. It was not like that for Ray. For him, this nakedness had an undying excitement to it. In fact, the more he got of it, the more exciting it became. He could not believe that there would ever be a night that Julia would get into bed naked and he would not want to make love to her.

In the brief time they had been sleeping together, though, Julia had turned him away more than once. Not because of her pe-riod—she liked making love when she was bleeding—but because she was not in the mood. It was a mystery to Ray. Nakedness gen-erated in him a response that was beyond mood. It was religious. It was what he was supposed to feel when he went to church but never had. In church you knelt and prayed, giving yourself over to the greater power of God. Ray felt the same solemn awe in the presence of Julia's naked body. Julia was more secular about nakedness, more casual, as if it didn't have to do with sex.

Ray tried to temper his more missionary zeal to accommodate Julia's less spiritual attitude.

"We have something in common," he told her as he threw his right leg across her legs and pressed himself against her side.

"What's that?"

"We both like loose clothes. Neither one of us like things to be tight."

As he said it, Ray realized that even this was true only on the most basic of levels. Julia actually wore clothes that were snug, that might, by a neutral observer, be called tight. Ray generally wore clothes that the same observer might call baggy.

"Well," Ray began to explain, suddenly losing his grasp on what he meant, "you don't like tight bras and I don't like to button the top button of my shirts because they're too tight."

"I suppose so," Julia answered.

"Why were you wearing a bra anyway?"

Ray's penis was getting hard, jamming itself against Julia's leg as it tried to rise. Ray shifted to free its ascent.

"Sometimes I just like to," Julia said.

"What?"

"Ray, I'm quitting Prime Time Electric," she answered.

"What?"

"I'm leaving. I'm thinking of going to school next semester. Whether I do or not, though, I'm leaving."

Ray did not want to talk about work. He ignored her and pressed himself harder against her side.

"I can't stand it there anymore," Julia persisted. "One of these days I'm going to strangle Noni, and more and more I just feel so angry and upset. I don't even know why sometimes."

"It's because you want to be an artist."

Ray felt his penis shrinking. He loosened his embrace of Julia and rolled onto his back, giving in to Julia's conversation.

"Don't be so smart," Julia scolded him.

"Maybe, since we're sleeping together, you can't stand working with me now."

"I've had this feeling in other jobs. In all my jobs. It doesn't have to do with you."

"Were you sleeping with your bosses at your other jobs?"

"No," she said vehemently, poking him with her elbow.

Ray took a deep breath.

"What am I going to do for a bookkeeper?" he finally asked. As problematic as Julia was, she was good at what she did, and Ray was no longer sure he understood all of what she did.

"It's up to you, but I asked my friend Mary Ann if she were interested and she said yes. I could train her."

Ray was relieved. He had never met Mary Ann, but he was grateful that Julia had at least considered this problem in her escape plans and was glad for a concrete alternative.

"How are we going to take afternoons off together?" Ray asked. He suddenly felt a desperate sense of abandonment and rolled back toward Julia, laying his arm across her waist.

"We'll have to be more organized about it, I guess," Julia said. "I'm thinking of going to school, though, and it might be more difficult."

"You're leaving," Ray said softly.

"Going to school is not leaving. It's going to school."

"You're leaving," Ray repeated and rolled away again onto his back. "You're moving to Albuquerque." He put his hands behind his head.

Julia said nothing.

"How do you think we can be together when you live in a different city?" Ray asked.

"I don't know," Julia said. Her voice sounded far off. "I just know I've got to do something. I thought maybe I could go to art school. I don't have the money. I haven't applied. I don't know how I could live. I just thought I might go to art school."

Ray turned his back to her.

"You're the one, after all, who's been encouraging me to be an artist," Julia said.

She was right. But Ray was still unhappy. He felt betrayed and abandoned. He didn't know how to object without sounding petty and jealous, without being the possessive, smothering lover that Julia already thought he was. Yet the whole thing about moving *was* a betrayal.

This was a familiar dilemma for Ray. He did not know how to say how he felt without sounding demanding and unreasonable. He wanted Julia to get what she wanted, but why had it worked out that it could only come at his expense? He felt stupid, too slow to understand the simplest of things.

Ray lay still as his thoughts and feelings tossed and turned. He stared into the darkness, wide awake, wondering and then losing track of what it was that he wondered about. After some time he realized that Julia had fallen asleep. He got up and put on a shirt and a pair of sweatpants. He walked into the living room, turned on the light, and got a pen and a pad of paper from his briefcase. He sat on the floor at the table and began to write. As his hand moved across the page, the feelings dammed up in him spilled out.

... you refuse to recognize the larger meaning of these little things you do. You want to go to school. That is not bad. But what does it mean? For us. For our love for each other ...

Love was an idea he kept muted during the daylight hours. Love was a bird with a broken wing. He had told Betsy he loved her too many times. Yet here it came, that word.

... you will sleep with me, but you have slept with a lot of men; you will move in with me, sort of; you will rest in the serenity of our laughter, but not call it happiness; you will think of me late, when the day has released you, but you will not call. ...

The more he wrote, the more he ached. Page after page, he folded the yellow sheets over as he finished them. Finally, he began to feel less angry; he began to calm. Yet what he wanted to say still eluded him and he wrote on in pursuit of it.

... I look into you as into a pool and see the depth of your waters and I step in to bathe and the bottom is only three inches beneath the surface and I can not get myself entirely wet, as if your depth is a trick of mirrors. You live in many different directions, all of them canceling each other out. ...

It was a dissertation: a style borrowed from his college days. But it was all he could find to express what he felt. He knew that it was overly abstract in its images, perhaps a little grand, a leaky vessel for the maiden voyage of his feelings, but he was proud anyway. Glad he had written it.

He wound down like a top, suddenly spent, as if they had made love after all. He set down the pen without conclusion. He thought for a moment, looking for some ending, some finish to what he had written. Finally, exhausted, he gave up and set the pad in the middle of the table with the first page, "Dear Julia," lying on top. He got into bed without taking off his sweats and fell asleep immediately.

• • •

In the morning Ray left before Julia was awake. He debated briefly taking the letter and hiding it. The sun shone brightly across the table and the simple morning made his torment of the night seem like a fevered delirium. It had been, really. He recognized that. But why should he hide it, why always take his fevers, like leprosy, and hide them in caves? Julia never did that. In the end, after his cereal, he decided to leave his letter out.

Julia arrived at work around ten. He searched her face, her movements, for some acknowledgment. She was a blank. Her face was puffy, as if she were the one who had not slept. At last she came into his office and stood next to his desk. The workers were all gone; Noni was on the phone. They could talk. He looked up into her face.

"Are you interested in interviewing Mary Ann?" Julia asked. "If you want, I could just start training her, or you could forget her and look for someone else."

"Did you see the letter?" Ray asked her, feeling as if he had left something very precious in her hands.

"Yes."

"Well?"

Julia dropped her eyes. "I don't want to talk about it right now."

"Are you upset? Can we have lunch?"

"No."

Ray was confused. He opened his hands, palms up, as if to say "What then?"

"What do you want to do about Mary Ann? I'm trying to help here, if you want."

"I guess I'd like to meet her before we hire her," Ray finally said.

Ray felt incomplete carrying two suitcases into his new apartment, as if he were checking into a hotel. Everything he owned fit into two suitcases and three cardboard boxes. Scott was bringing over the mattresses in one of the pickups from work.

Jesse and Zach ran around the empty living room trying to give it some function. Ray put his suitcases down and watched. The living room most closely resembled a gym. A gym with no hoops, no wooden seats accordioned out from the wall, no echo. A gym with a carpet. He remembered in the wrestling tournaments how the referee's whistle had resonated in the cavernous gym, as if the school alarm system was going off. There was no cheering, no crowd. No one ever came to watch wrestling; it was somehow too close to sex, two boys grabbing each other all over, burying their faces in each other's armpits. Being a wrestler was like being part of a cult: practicing in small, hot rooms, wearing two or three layers of sweats (depending on how much weight you needed to lose), sitting together, at a table of their own, for dinner, drinking water, and sucking on lemons. Ray had loved wrestling, had loved being hungry all the time.

Jesse and Zach ran to the back, flushing toilets as they found them. They quickly returned and asked which bedroom was theirs.

"Which do you want?" Ray asked.

"The one with the glass of milk on the floor," Jesse said.

"Glass of milk?"

They pulled at his hand as they walked down the hallway. Dead center was a shaped glass, the kind they used to have at soda fountains, full of milk. Next to it was a small loaf of bread.

"Sorry, guys," Ray said, "this room is mine. Where did the milk come from?"

"Can we drink it?" Zach asked.

"No."

Jesse went and picked up the glass.

"Pour it down the sink," Ray told him.

Jesse carried it down the hall as if it were a bomb about to explode. Ray picked up the loaf of bread and smelled it. It seemed fresh.

"Me smell," Zach asked, and Ray gave him the loaf. Zach didn't quite know how to operate his nose for smelling; he snorted and breathed around the bread for a minute and then handed it back.

"Who put that stuff here?" Jesse asked when he returned.

Ray shrugged his shoulders. Julia, he thought, except she did not have a key yet and she was camping near Tucson with Christina for the weekend. The landlady maybe, but that was a little strange.

Ray unpacked the video camera he had taken in exchange for wiring the video store on Rodeo Road. He mounted it on the tripod that the woman had thrown in on the deal when Ray complained that he had put in more lights than the camera was worth. She also gave him three long batteries and ten blank tapes and Ray had said OK, even though he felt that it was still a bad deal. He didn't know what more there was about video cameras that she could offer. She had made it clear that there was no money for him.

He set the camera against one wall of the living room about three feet above the floor. He plugged in the pack that held the video tape and started reading directions.

"What's that?" Zach asked.

"A video camera, for making tapes that you can show on TV."

"We don't have a TV," Jesse said.

"I know."

"So how can we watch the tapes?"

"Maybe we will get a TV. You can also replay the tape and watch it through the little window in the camera."

Jesse and Zach pushed each other around to try to grab a peek through the viewfinder.

"It's just black," Jesse said when he had finally asserted his authority as the older.

"I know, it has to be turned on. I'm reading about it."

Ray felt this video camera was the first real possession of his new life. Mattresses, sheets, pillows, and clothes didn't count. He was ambivalent about it. Owning nothing was like the hunger when he wrestled. It was spare and therefore essential; it was trim, ready for a fight, even a little on edge, looking for a fight; it was personal, outside of what other people knew or could do to him, inside and whole; it was hard, like a knot on a rope.

Yet, there was some relief in this first possession, a sense of belonging, as if he could now step into the world with everyone else. The knot in his stomach loosened; the edginess of life softened.

Things were by degrees not so difficult. He recognized vaguely that he could not have it both ways: he could not be both the vigilant sentry, sitting alone in the cold, high on a rock, and back at the campfire at the same time warming himself and telling stories with his buddies. With this video camera he was edging back toward the warmth of the fire.

Ray figured out the viewfinder. With some masking tape on the carpet, he marked the space along the opposite wall that was inside the scope of the camera.

"Stand inside those two pieces of tape," Ray told Jesse and Zach, "and you'll be on camera. First, to start it, you have to push the orange button there, on the front. When you're done, you push the orange button again, and it stops. Simple enough?"

Jesse and Zach just stared at the camera.

"Try it," Ray urged. "Go on."

After some hesitation, Jesse went over and pushed the orange button and then went and stood against the wall with his arms straight down at his side, his back straight.

"Come on, Zach," Jesse said in a voice too low, he hoped, for the camera to pick up.

Zach went and stood next to his brother in a much more casual attitude. They both stared at the camera.

"Say something," Ray said.

"Like what?" Jesse asked using his stage whisper.

"Say what's going on, about moving."

Jesse thought for a moment before speaking.

"This is our new house," he said, moving his hand from one side to the other to demonstrate. "We're moving in here today. Tonight we're going to spend the night here. Our beds aren't here yet. Scott's bringing them in my Dad's company's truck. That's it. We don't have much stuff yet, like tables or chairs, because this is a new house."

Jesse was done. The two of them continued staring at the camera. Jesse elbowed Zach and whispered something to him. Zach suddenly came to life as if he were a toy.

"That room mine," he said, pointing. "Mine and Jesse. We sharing. My room crib. Jesse room big bed. Dash bites me. I booboo crying. No more booboo. Booboo all gone." Zach stuck out his foot and pulled up the leg of his light blue corduroy pants to show, presumably, where he had been bitten. Then he continued.

"Angelo biting. Big dog. Angelo go hospital. Angelo got one, two, three, four, six stitches. Daddy biting too. Cat biting Daddy. On farm. Daddy got shots. Stomach shots. One, two, three, six shots. Daddy not dying. Big shots. No more doctors, Daddy."

Again, Zach pulled up the leg of his pants, more, this time, for his own inspection than for the benefit of the camera. Kneeling on his other knee, he ran his finger over the spot and then kissed it gently.

"Zach," Jesse, still standing at attention, hissed at his brother. "They don't want to hear all that stuff."

Zach stood, confused, and looked back at the camera.

"Tell them what you did at Christmas," Ray suggested.

"Christmas coming. Me get big bear. Spider! We go swimming. Big waves." He made a scared face. "I scared big waves. We go store. Mommy leaving me. I scared. Mommy scared too."

Zach was suddenly done. Jesse and Ray both leaned into the silence he left, expecting more. Jesse looked at his father.

"If you're done, push the orange button to turn it off," Ray said.

Jesse walked to the side, outside of the masking tape, and circled around to the camera and shut it off. It made some mechanical thumps and whirrs.

"Fun," Zach said. "Again."

"Zach," Jesse said reprovingly, "we just finished."

"Anytime you want," Ray said, "now you know how to do it. I'll leave it on, so all you have to do is push the orange button to make it work. If you feel like saying something, just do it. We've got plenty of tapes." Ray held up the ten six-hour tapes.

Ray lay in bed, exhausted but not sleepy. Zach was crying and had been for over an hour.

"Can you tell Zach to stop crying?" Jesse asked him sleepily. "He's keeping me awake."

"I wish I could and it could make a difference," Ray told Jesse. "If you want, I'll lay you out some pillows to fall asleep on in the living room."

"That's all right," Jesse said, shaking his head.

As Ray listened to his wailing, he could picture Zach in his diapers and plastic pants standing up in his crib, holding the white wooden slats like a prison inmate. He had visited him a few times and held him until he stopped and then laid him down, and each time Zach had started crying again. He knew that if he put Zach in bed with him, the problem would be solved, but he resisted the idea. That space was Julia's.

Zach's crying created a small hell. With time, it became unreal and Ray was transported to the depths of Zach's despair. Time, he thought, children have time, and with that they control the world. They don't have to be anywhere, do anything, even think anything. They are in charge of time. They can stop it, move it around, take you places where you are no longer human, where you only know the utter, unbearable moment of now.

Finally Ray relented and picked Zach up to bring him into bed with him.

"Just this once," he told Zach as he laid him down in the large space, but Zach was instantly asleep, burrowing his hands beneath the pillow like an animal.

Ray gently lowered himself next to Zach. He put his hands behind his head. What had Zach meant when he said, "Mommy leaving me"? What the fuck was that? Obviously he hadn't been left permanently, because Zach was right here next to him. But there was a ring of truth to it, something that was just possible with Betsy. What had he done, letting her loose in the world with two small children? His children.

Ray felt an enormous emptiness in his silent bedroom. If he had a TV, he would have turned it on. Then he thought of his video camera. In his underwear he walked out to the living room. He turned on the overhead light. Probably not enough light, he thought, but pushed the orange button anyway. He sat on the carpet between the pieces of tape.

"This is our new home," he said, looking at the camera, repeating with his hand the gesture that Jesse had made earlier.

That was it. No more words came to him. He stared at the camera, listening to the whirr of the tape. Julia was sleeping with Christina. Having sex with her. Nothing had been said, but he knew it was true. As he sat there, it was happening.

Christ in
the
Desert

"What are those pictures of?" Julia asked, looking at two photographs Ray had hung on the wall. "Are those of your dad or something?"

"Yes." Ray came up behind her and looked over her shoulder. "See if you can pick him out." Ray's father had died the same year as Sean.

Both pictures were formal team portraits. The top one was of a swimming team, three rows deep. They all wore tank tops and trunks, more of a wrestling uniform, to Ray's mind, than a swimming suit.

The second picture was of a football team lined up in two rows in front of an ivy-covered wall. Their shoulder pads more closely resembled what women now wore as fashion than what NFL linemen wore for protection.

Ray had found the pictures, which he had never seen before, in an old box sent to him by his mother. It had surfaced during his move away from Betsy. He knew that both pictures were from the military boarding school his father had attended, but the faces in

them were deceptively old. With the exception of one or two people, they could have been pictures of college teams. Ray's father in
particular looked to him old and serious. He was big and sturdy,
and in the swimming picture he looked muscular and athletic. His
collarbone drew a sharp line beneath his neck, and his chest filled
out the tank top.

"Is that him?" Julia asked, picking him out on the first try.

Ray nodded. "How did you know?"

"He's so serious. And you've got the same eyes."

Julia was scanning the football photo for the same person. Ray
looked at his father's eyes. His father was looking at the camera in-
tently, with his eyes wide open. It was a stare. Of all the swimmers
in the group, he was the only one who seemed to be really looking
at the camera, looking into the camera, even through it, as if he
wanted to get into the mind of the person holding it.

Ray looked at the football photo just as Julia picked his father
once more. His eyes were not so clear there. His eyebrows and
forehead protruded and shaded them. Ray looked closer. Still, he
found the same intensity, as if his father had some great clarity of
purpose, some unusual understanding of the world.

"I didn't know your dad was an athlete," Julia said, pleased to
have done so well picking him out.

"I didn't either. That's why I hung these pictures up when I
found them. The whole time I played football, he never mentioned
that he had too."

"You mean he never told you how to pass and catch and zip this
way and that? I didn't think fathers could resist those things."

"He never said a thing. Never passed a ball with us. Never told
us stories. Like the war, as if those times were too painful to speak
of.

"I remember once," Ray continued, "when I was a junior at
boarding school. It was my first game on the varsity. We traveled
about two hours by bus to another cow field somewhere in Massachusetts. I was playing corner back. In the middle of the game, just
before the start of a play, I looked up and there was my father
standing on the sidelines. I couldn't believe it was true. There was

no crowd or stands, nothing like that. About five yards from the out of bounds was a red snow fence, and he was standing all alone behind it. He was wearing his business suit, a tie, a heavy overcoat, and his hat, one of those business hats that everybody used to wear. As if he had just walked in the front door from work. I looked twice. I missed the play, I was so dumbfounded. I mean, in the middle of nowhere in Massachusetts, I don't think a UFO would have surprised me as much.

"He was a lawyer in Philadelphia. It was Friday afternoon. He laughed when I missed the play, staring at him, and when I saw him laugh, that was when I first knew for sure that it was him. I laughed and waved. He tilted his chin out at me, saying hello and get back to work in the same motion.

"When the game was over, I walked all around looking for him, but I couldn't find him anywhere. He had disappeared. I thought maybe he'd gone to the bathroom or something and I even made the bus wait until the coach said we couldn't wait any more, and we left. As we drove back through all those bright New England colors I started to think that he hadn't really been there, that maybe I'd made it up."

Julia had sat on the edge of the bed. "So, was he really there or not?"

"I guess I decided that he was, but, you know, we never talked about it. I never asked him, time went by, and in boarding school it's a long time between conversations with your parents. I probably just forgot about it. He never said anything either. Never mentioned it."

"Maybe it was a vision. You know, get one for the gipper or something like that, to get you all pumped up. Maybe you got hit over the head too hard, and your mind hallucinated your dad standing over there."

"I don't think so. I never had any other hallucinations in my life. I think he was there. He just had a plane to catch or something."

"A plane? You said you were in the middle of nowhere. What plane would he catch? How could he have ever gotten there in the first place? And even if he did get out there, I mean for real, why would he turn around and leave so quickly? It doesn't make sense."

Ray laughed and shook his head. "It doesn't really matter, does it? I mean, whether he was really there or not. I know I really saw him, so it doesn't matter if he was really there or not, does it?"

Ray knew that his father had been there that day. It had made him feel proud. No one else's father had found his way to the middle of Massachusetts to watch that game. Ray understood it. Even though his father had always worked late and on weekends, even though he had not been around very much, Ray had always felt his presence. His mother was the field lieutenant, and his father was the general, always aware of everything.

Ray lay next to Julia on the bed. The sun was streaming in the window.

"I don't know," Ray said. "It's all so strange."

"I think you had a vision," Julia said, half teasing. She giggled.

"Not that," Ray said laughing. "I mean life in general. Look at my dad there in the picture of the football team. The whole time I played football, I thought I was it, the first in my family. All my brothers played soccer. Not that I thought about it much. I never really cared. I guess I'm just amazed that there's my dad and he did it just like I did, and I never knew it."

"*Plus ça change . . .*" Julia said in her impeccable French—the more things change, the more they stay the same.

"But I've never thought of myself as anything like my father," Ray protested.

"Of course not." Julia was having a lot of fun.

Ray turned toward her on the bed, pressing himself against her side. "What are you smiling about?"

Julia laughed, her wide mouth showing full banks of southeastern Nebraska teeth. Ray tickled her, grabbing her waist so that she couldn't get away.

"Stop that," she scolded, still laughing.

Ray stopped and rolled away onto his back. The slanting sun was shining on the lower halves of their bodies and Ray's jeans were beginning to warm up. His feet were hot. He looked back at the photographs.

"Did your father play sports?" Ray asked Julia.

"My father was a thug." Julia's mood immediately dropped.

"What kind of thug?"

"He still is a thug. And thugs don't play sports. That's too refined for them. A thug gets in fights in back alleys and marries a woman that always wanted to move to New York to be a dancer. Then he never takes her anywhere."

"I thought your father was a businessman?"

"He is. He doesn't get dirt under his fingernails anymore, but he's still a thug. Not like a mafioso or someone with no values. You know, he grew up poor; hardworking, alcoholic mother because she couldn't stand eight kids and total poverty; father with a back as strong as Nebraska that never gave up; by rights, nowhere to go, but he worked his way up in the grain business, so on and so on. That kind of thug."

"A great American success story."

"Yes, he is that." Julia's tone turned wistful, bordering on the edge of respect. Ray could imagine her calling her father "sir" and being afraid of him.

"Did he beat you?" Ray asked.

"No, not but once or twice. But he whipped on JB plenty. JB sure got beat on." Her accent was suddenly 100 percent Nebraska.

"How did he treat you?"

"Like a daddy treats his little girl. Mostly, he loved me to death until I was around twelve, then he pretended not to know me, now that I had my period and was growing breasts. When I went away to college, I think he wrote me off for good. All he tells me anymore is how ugly my hair is."

Ray thought about his own father. He got up and looked into the eyes in the photo.

"I wonder what position he played," Ray asked softly of no one in particular.

Julia had a friend, Petra, who retreated to a Jesuit monastery every winter for three weeks. Ray and Julia went together to pick her up. It was twelve miles over a muddy road along the river. The rest of

New Mexico still had piles of snow hiding on the north side of the piñons, but the land along the Chama was breaking loose from winter. It was warm and windless when they stopped for a picnic. New grass was coming up through the tight clumps of dried grama. They ate bread and chunks of cheese.

"How much weight have you lost since fall?" Julia asked Ray.

"I don't know. I never weigh myself."

"Just now, as you were walking over here, I noticed how thin you've become."

Ray shrugged his shoulders. He was no longer drinking beer, but he wasn't working on losing weight.

"I think I've been good for you," Julia said, smiling.

Ray nodded and smiled back. He had to agree, but he found the comment ironic. She might be good *for* him, but he did not think it was a particular priority of hers to be good *to* him.

Julia took off her shirt and lay on it in the sun. Ray, who was always turned on by the nonchalance of her nakedness, resisted touching her and went for a walk along the riverbank.

The water was low; the runoff had yet to begin in earnest. Ray climbed over a fallen cottonwood, uprooted by the erosion of the river. The bark was thick and rough and hard. There was a song running through Ray's mind. It was "The Rose" by Bette Midler, a song about love. Julia had played it over and over between Espanola and Abiquiu on the tape player in the Toyota. As they crested the ridge below Abiquiu Lake and started toward the red cliffs behind Ghost Ranch, she had started to cry and turned it off abruptly. She had sat with her head tilted back against the head rest and tears streaming down her cheeks.

Ray thought about what to do with Julia. What to make of her. Being with her was alternately wonderful and terrible. As with the song in the car—at first she loved it, she was passionate and sexy with it, singing and moving and closing her eyes; and then, then came tears and—*zap!* off went the music. Back and forth, in and out, up and down, like a yo-yo. There was laughter and happiness; then there was pain. Ray remembered the homeopathic pills Julia had bought before Christmas. They were for depression. They were meant to take care of the pain. Ray had never believed in the pills, but he wanted the pain to go away. It didn't. There it was, at a moment's notice; there were the tears. It was infectious, because Ray was starting to feel it himself.

Ray remembered the weekend Julia had spent with Christina. They had kissed, Julia had told him, and held each other naked. That was all. She had told him without apology. Ray had not felt judgmental, but he had not felt good either. He fought against the bad feelings. He tried to will them away, but his will was weakening. Julia was a black cloud. She danced with this pain as easily as she made love. But this was a new dance for Ray, and he was not comfortable with its wildness, with its lack of definition. It seemed to Ray that once it started, the music to this dance never stopped; it only grew louder and more insistent. It was like *The Blob*, a movie he had seen when he was nine. Ray had hidden behind a thick pillar in the movie theater and he had never been to another horror movie since. Such unknown things, which grew uncontrollably, geometrically, frightened him. The only way Ray knew of to avoid being over run by the Blob was to circumvent it when it was just a small dab of strawberry Jell-O, no bigger than a robin's egg. He knew for a fact that if you humored it, fed it an insect or two, touched it, the next thing you'd know, it would be rolling over and eating you, your house, your town, and eventually, the entire world.

Ray heard Julia calling his name. He had walked in a circle and was near where they had picnicked. Julia had walked down through the shrubbery to the river. He looked down on her from the high bank above.

"What?" he asked.

She looked up at him, squinting and wrinkling her nose. "Look," she called, and started working her feet up and down in the mud. "Come here and look." She had put her blouse back on and she was holding the hem of her skirt around her thighs. Her bare feet disappeared into the thick mud.

Ray walked down a small trail through a cut in the bank.

"Take your shoes off and come on. It's elephant hide," Julia called to him.

"It's what?"

"It's elephant hide. It's this kind of mud. It feels amazing. Come try it."

Julia began working her feet again, and with every motion she sank slightly deeper into the elephant hide. Ray did not want to do it, but he took off his socks and shoes and rolled up his blue jeans. He tiptoed around the sharp stones and out onto the mud bank on the side of the river.

"It's cold," he said.

"Come over here. Get behind me and put your arms around my waist."

Ray did as she directed. Her feet were ankle deep in the slime.

"Now," Julia said, "step when I do. Don't lift your feet, just knead them, like bread dough."

Ray and Julia pushed and pulled in unison. Soon, Ray felt his feet attach to the mud, and they became heavy and hard to move. He began to sink.

"Is this dangerous?" he asked.

"No, it's not quicksand or anything."

They moved together and Ray began to feel attached to the earth. Julia leaned back into his arms; they kept their feet moving and Ray began to feel as if he and Julia were one person, one set of legs. His feet were cold and too numb to feel. He only felt the force of her legs, dull through the mud, pushing and pulling like his, caught and yet alive with the sensation of it. He felt her body in his arms, twisting and straining with each step. The mud became gentle and reassuring. Julia began to laugh and Ray joined in, laughing and kneading and losing control until he could no longer hold her and they both fell backward on the mud. They were sunk to just below their knees.

When they recovered from laughing, they began to extricate their legs. Ray discovered that if he stood up and very slowly, patiently, pulled up on one leg, it would come out. Back on the hard slab of rock, Julia and Ray surveyed themselves. Ray's pants and Julia's skirt were dirty and wet, and their legs were coated and browned by a fine, dusty plaster. They waded in the freezing water of the river to get clean and when Ray finally emerged his feet and legs were pink and sore from the cold. As he warmed in the sun, they began to hurt.

Christ in the Desert Monastery was next to the Chama River at the dead end of the dirt road. A gently sloping meadow full of wildflowers separated the monastery from the river. A sign directed Ray to park in a small visitors' lot before the monastery, and he and Julia walked down toward the small complex of buildings. There was a gift shop that sold postcards, carvings, and weavings made by the monks. There was no one inside.

Behind and attached to the gift shop were guest quarters where Petra had been staying for the last three weeks. Down the road a short walk they visited the chapel, built against the dramatic, multicolored cliffs of the canyon. It had been designed by George Nakashima, a furniture maker from Pennsylvania. Ray had heard of him, from his father. The main tower rose high from the center of the chapel to glass panels looking up at the cliffs. Ray noticed a large white cross on the highest ridge and pointed it out to Julia. They spoke in whispers and walked reverently on the packed dirt floors around the small wooden chairs. Some candles burned in a trough of sand.

When Ray pushed open the large, carved wooden door and stepped back outside, the sun made him squint and sneeze. There was a large bell with a sign that read, "If you want to speak to a member of the community, please ring the bell." Before Ray realized what she was doing, Julia had grabbed the string underneath and given the bell three loud clangs. The noise made Ray jump and seemed out of place in such a tranquil setting. Julia looked at him with wide eyes and shrugged her shoulders.

"I didn't know it would be so loud," she said, laughing.

After five minutes or so, a small, stout man with a full, white beard came through the gate next to the chapel. He was dressed in clothes made of rough blue cloth and wore a straw hat with a wide brim. Looped over his head and tied behind his back was a dirty white nail apron with a hammer hanging from the side.

"Hello," he said, extending his hands to both Ray and Julia, "I am Brother Aaron."

"Hello," they said back.

"How can I help you?"

Ray looked at Julia; she had rung the bell.

"Some questions, if you don't mind?"

Brother Aaron gave his head one quick nod.

"How many monks live here?" Julia asked.

"In the winter, there are three or four members of our permanent community; in the summer, maybe twice as many."

"I can see why," Ray said, meaning that he wouldn't mind spending a summer in quiet meditation in this remote and idyllic spot.

"How long have you lived here?" Julia asked.

"For twelve years."

Ray thought he seemed more friendly and happy, like an elf, than he seemed wise and serious. The three of them stood amid the sage looking at each other for a moment.

"Can I ask you a favor?" Brother Aaron said.

"Sure."

"Could you take some mail for me when you leave?"

"Yeah, sure."

"I was in town yesterday, but I forgot to take the mail."

"No problem."

"Thank you. I'll go get it now. I'll be right back."

"We came to pick up Petra," Julia said to him as he turned away.

"Petra?" he asked, stopping and turning back.

"She's been here for the last three weeks."

"Oh yes, Petra. Of course. I'm sorry. Yes, Petra. I hope she enjoyed her stay. I will get the mail now."

"What a nice little man," Julia said when he had disappeared. She took Ray's arm and they ambled down the path, waiting for Brother Aaron to return.

"What a nice place," Ray said, breathing in deeply, as if the scent of the sage, the sweep of the meadow, the tranquillity of the river could all be saved deep in his lungs.

"I'd like to stay up here for a while," Julia said. "Flush out my brain."

"It's beautiful," Ray agreed, thinking that he, too, or some part of him anyway, belonged in a place like this—far away and alone and full of peace. There would be peace out here, he figured. Peace came to quiet places. Places without other people.

Julia and Ray walked to the south side of the chapel. There was a hidden small side yard with a wooden bench against the chapel wall. They sat down. The warmth of the sun was deep in the adobe. In the corner, so that Ray had not at first noticed, were two crosses at the end of two humped graves. Ray got up to look at them. Each wooden cross had a sign hanging from it like a necklace. One grave was for Brother Richard, the founder of the monastery, and the other was for a Daniel Weller, who, according to the memorial, died climbing the cliffs while he was on retreat. Ray calculated Daniel's age from the dates; he had died when he was twenty-six. The graves were private to the point of being forgotten. Ray thought about Sean's grave, also forgotten.

Brother Aaron came in through the gate with one hand holding his straw hat against the wind, even though there was no wind blowing, and his other holding the mail. Julia had disappeared into one of her sun stupors, her face lifted and her eyes closed, so Ray walked over and took the mail from him.

"How often do you get to town?" Ray asked.

"When I am the monk in charge, about once a week. It alternates, being in charge. And yesterday we needed milk, so I went yesterday."

"I'll take your mail."

"Thank you. You know, the road can get so bad."

"Yes. Thanks for talking to us."

"Oh, no problem. I enjoy it."

Brother Aaron returned to his work. Ray read the addresses on the letters he was holding. There was a business envelope to Cook's Hardware in Espanola, a postcard, written in a childish script, to Thomas someone in Greece, and a letter to Elizabeth Jenkins in Teaneck, New Jersey. Ray wondered how to begin looking for Petra.

• • •

"I've got a job for you," Bud said over the telephone, "if you want it."

"Is there any reason I shouldn't?" Ray asked.

"No. I don't guess so. It's sort of a strange deal, but they pay their bills."

"Sounds good so far."

"Well, they call themselves the Blue Sky Ranch. It's up north of Ojo, built into the mountains there. You wouldn't be working for me. I'm not the general. We're just doing some concrete work for them. But the foreman up there asked for some recommendations on electrical work. I told him I'd give you a call."

"I appreciate it."

Ray jotted down the name and number of the foreman at the Blue Sky Ranch. He heard Noni and Julia in the front office talking to each other testily. It was Julia's last week of work. Noni spoke flatly and openly, raising her voice as her feelings rose. Julia spoke with more guile, attacking and retreating, angry and then hurt. Ray could not at first figure out what they were talking about.

". . . it won't work that way," Julia said. "That way I have to wait for up to a week before I get the information, and then it's not always right."

"It just seemed to me," Noni defended, her voice cracking, "that it would be better to just do it. I didn't know about the general ledger stuff you do."

"Well, I don't know why not. I mean, it's really stupid to send that out. I mean, you get the receipts anyway and then give them to me. It's obvious I should get them."

Ray winced and hung his head. He did not want this to go on but did not know how to stop it. Wasn't there something he could say to interrupt?

"Julia," he called to the outer office, trying to sound as if he was not hearing what they were saying. Julia walked in. Her shoulders were tensed and her face and chest, just above her shirt, were mottled red. That happened to her when she got angry and also when she had sex.

"Julia," Ray said, still keeping up his pretense of ignorance, "have we managed to pay our bill to New Mexico Electric yet?"

Julia put her hands on his desk and leaned her face close to his. "That bitch," she whispered, "is the most ignorant person I've ever met."

She bit off her last word and stared at Ray for a moment. Ray leaned back, smiling stupidly and feeling stupid for smiling. Julia straightened up suddenly and stomped back to her desk. She thrashed some papers around on her desk and then walked out of the office, slamming the door behind her. From his window, Ray saw her yank open the door of her car, throw her jacket across the front seat, and drive off, lurching forward with every change of gear.

Oh shit, Ray thought, and leaned forward, his head in his hands. The phone rang and Noni answered it in her calmest secretarial manner.

Ray took two deep breaths, leaned back in his chair, and threw his pencil against the phone. There was a knot in his stomach and he wanted to jump up and pursue Julia. He took two more deep breaths and willed himself to stay put. He was glad no one else was there. He wondered if Noni was getting ready to march in and quit. Probably not. Noni needed the job; the tile-setting work her husband did was erratic. Julia too needed the job. But there was a difference between them: Julia was more willing to spit on things she thought deserved it, regardless of how badly she might need them. Noni was more respectful, more anxious to please. Noni had worked for Ray for over two years. She was loyal and tolerated Julia as an eccentric deviation of Ray's, a temporary misery. Ray knew, though, that she would have a breaking point somewhere in this whole business.

"It's Betsy on the phone," Noni called to him from the front office.

Ray punched the blinking light. "Hello."

"Ray, this is Betsy. I'm calling about this weekend."

"Yes."

"Can you take the boys Friday afternoon a little early?"

Ray hesitated. It could be a trick.

"OK," he finally said, unable to imagine what kind of trick it might be. "Can you bring them by the office?"

"Sure." She hesitated. "Do you know what day it is Friday?" she asked.

"February twenty-fifth," Ray answered looking at the calendar-blotter on his desk.

There was a silence on the phone. Ray knew he was missing something.

"That's the day Sean died," Betsy said.

"Oh, yeah."

There was another long silence.

"Do you remember what that counselor said?" Betsy asked. "Couples that suffer the death of an infant get divorced seventy-five percent of the time."

"Really?" Ray remembered the counselor and her dreary den of an office, but not that statistic.

"I guess it makes sense," she said.

Ray saw Scott drive up and pop out of his Datsun pickup with the spring of a boxer.

"I've got to go," Ray said. "I'll see you Friday afternoon here at the office."

"OK. It will be around three. Thanks. Goodbye."

"Where's Julia?" Scott asked as he walked into Ray's office.

"Gone," Ray answered vaguely with a sweeping motion of his hands.

"For good?"

Ray thought for a moment. Possibly she was gone for good.

"What are you doing?" he asked Scott.

"Just checking in. I got Roberto and them squared away at the mall. I need to get them the bender from out of the back."

"Wait a second. Let me call this Blue Sky Ranch. If we can go up there this afternoon, we should go together."

Rick Mendoza of the Blue Sky Ranch was anxious for them to come as quickly as possible and gave Ray directions. It was eighteen miles off the paved road with a number of turns and Y's. Ray hung up and arranged to meet Scott back at the shop at one-thirty.

"I'll be back after lunch," he told Noni quickly as he left the office. He looked back at her as he grabbed the doorknob, thinking she might say something.

"OK," she said smiling, letting him know by her smile that it was all OK with her, that he needn't worry.

Ray drove home. Julia's car was in the driveway and his stomach began to flutter again. He could hear music from outside, but he was not prepared for the volume of it when he opened the door. He stopped for a minute, as if he were entering a mine shaft supported by rotten timbers, about to collapse. The music was so loud that he could not at first recognize it. He made out that it was Bette Midler singing a rock-and-roll cut from *The Rose.* Her voice was as aggressive and steeled as Janis Joplin's had been, every note sung with the passion of the last, of the end. The living room was bursting, bleeding, from the intensity of it. Ray spotted Julia sitting outside on some pillows, sunning herself in her underwear and a tank top. He went to the open patio door and looked down on her from behind. She could not see him and the music was so loud she had not heard him. Ray could see tears on her face.

He stood for minutes, looking at her, delaying his entrance. He looked at her legs. She had beautiful legs.

Ray was stuck. He couldn't figure out how to announce himself. In spite of the noise, or perhaps because of it, he felt the moment was private for Julia, that she had wrapped the music around her for protection. He considered leaving. The idea was immediately attractive, but he resisted it. Finally, he went and sat on the flagstone next to where Julia lay. He pulled his knees up to his chest and sat staring ahead.

Julia's eyes were closed, but she felt Ray's shadow as he came up next to her. She jerked up, startled, and looked at him for a long second, and then lay back down, closing her eyes again.

Neither of them spoke. Nothing they might have said could have been heard over the music. The last song of the album began, the signature song, "The Rose." Bette Midler, or the character she played, had died in the movie just then. Actually, she had died before then, on stage, of a drug overdose, and "The Rose" played as the credits ran across the screen.

The record clicked off. The silence that was left was enormous. Ray looked at Julia. Her eyes were tearing more than before, and were still closed. Ray was angry with her for the scene at the office, and now, perversely, for her tears. She was messing everything up. Making it messy. He was running around always trying to patch up after her. She was like a cyclone. He resented doing all the work, keeping the peace. He had, in his marriage, kept the peace. Peace had been kept at all cost. Peace had ruled with an iron hand.

"What's wrong, Julia?" Ray asked, taking a deep breath.

"You think I like it, don't you?" she said angrily, her face turning red. "You think I do it on purpose, don't you? You think I like flipping out."

That was exactly what Ray thought, but he was taken aback at being told so. He did not answer.

Julia continued. "That bitch Noni. She hates me. I saw her hit her daughter yesterday. In the parking lot. She's got the awareness of a two-year-old. She slapped her right across her face. Just because she wouldn't get in the car or something. I was watching through the window. She's a fucking bitch."

Julia's anger dried up her tears. Ray let the air clear and then spoke gingerly.

"Julia, you're making things hard for me." On the word "me" he felt his voice give a little, like a soft board in the floor. "I have to work in this place. This is my business.

"Think of me," he said, and again felt some emotion coming up. "You can't treat me this way. It's not fair. When you are at work, you have to be an employee. You know, do your job. It's not fair to use our relationship like that in the office."

As he spoke, Ray realized that Julia had never been that employee he was thinking of, even before they became involved with each other. Still, somehow, the whole thing seemed wrapped up with their relationship. Ray gave up trying to describe it and looked down. He played with a bit of gravel and some twigs.

He sensed Julia moving, and when he looked up she was walking through the sliding glass door back inside. He noticed a small rip between the elastic and fabric of her underwear.

Julia picked up the arm of the turntable and lay the needle down on the first song of the album. The room, back patio, back-yard, and whole south section of Santa Fe exploded once more into the incredible volume and intensity of Bette Midler's voice. Julia walked to the back bedroom and, in spite of the music, Ray thought he heard the door slam.

Ray supposed the conversation was over. He never quite knew in these situations. He was mad at Julia again. Angry at her for just walking off. Also, he was angry because it was always her temper, her feelings, that set the stage. In her presence there was no room for his own timid self.

Ray walked through the living room and out the front door. Just as he pulled the door shut, he had the urge to slam it, so he opened it again and with a jerk slammed it shut. The small side window vibrated. The music dimmed to a mild roar. He looked at his watch—1:05. He had time to go to Burger King before meeting Scott at the office.

At the Cemetery

Betsy dropped Jesse and Zach off at Ray's office Friday afternoon along with the usual suitcases, games, diaper bags, and other paraphernalia of separate households. Zach was clutching a new stuffed giraffe as he sidled up against Ray's leg.

"Thanks," Betsy said, referring to Ray's willingness to take the children at three in the afternoon. He saw her begin to explain something, watched her as a thought turned over in her mind and her mouth began to form to let it out. She was going to tell him why she needed to drop Jesse and Zach off early; he could see it. It was a reflex, an "I'll be back at five" sort of comment, but she caught it before it escaped.

"See you," she said instead, looking at him tight-lipped.

In the car, Jesse realized immediately that they were not headed to Ray's apartment.

"Where are we going?" he asked.

"To the cemetery, to visit your brother Sean."

Jesse said nothing.

"Go cemetery. With Mommy," Zach said.

Ray parked as close as he could to Sean's grave and, after unbuckling Zach from his car seat, walked over and stood in front of the bronze plaque. He sat down in the green grass. Zach and Jesse ran off, experienced in the amusements available at the cemetery. The markers were all laid flush with the ground and sitting, Ray thought he could have been on any well-kept lawn in Short Hills, New Jersey. He looked out toward the horizon, at the Jemez Mountains to the west. The peaks were white with snow. Seven years earlier Ray had stood looking at these mountains during Sean's funeral. It had been windy and colder then. Ray had read something, words he had written the night before. Dimitri had cried and hugged him and told him how brave he was. Ray had looked at the mountains fading off to the north in a haze as his mother-in-law's minister read from a red prayer book. What is this guy doing here? Ray remembered thinking. All of Ray's brothers had come, and his mother. In seven years, Ray had not returned to this place.

Sean had died suddenly. In his crib in Betsy and Ray's bedroom, nine days after he was born. Betsy had gone to bed early. Ray had been watching a PBS special on TV, *I, Claudius*. Claudius's wife, the queen, had challenged the most famous whore in Rome to a contest. In adjoining rooms, they were fucking one man after another until one of them could no longer continue. The queen won. Ray could not remember how many men she fucked, hundreds. Even the whore's sense of propriety, of decency, of what was human, was stretched to the point of horror. She emerged from her room disheveled and disoriented. The queen came out looking refreshed, rejuvenated. She was contemptuous of the whore and clearly disappointed that the contest had not been more challenging. Ray had been sleepy. He balanced a half-empty can of Budweiser on his stomach as he lay on the couch watching. He had worked outside in the cold all day and he was worn out. He and Scott had had a few beers at the Green Onion before Ray left for home. Scott stayed throwing darts. The language of the TV show was stiff and difficult for Ray to understand.

"Ray," Betsy yelled from the bedroom, "something's wrong."

When he arrived, Betsy had laid Sean across the foot of the bed and was fiddling with the snaps of his light blue sleeper. When she exposed his small, bony chest she pressed on it a few times and then leaned her head down to his, her ear next to his nose. She stuck her finger in his mouth and wiggled it about and then pressed a few more times on his chest.

"I can't tell if he's breathing," she said without shifting her attention from him.

Some milk dribbled out of Sean's mouth.

"Shit," Betsy said, and picked him up, turned him over, and pressed against his back with one hand while her other one held him on his chest. More milk came out of his mouth and dribbled down on the red quilt.

"Shit," she said again and laid him back down on the bed.

Ray took a few steps toward Betsy and Sean. There was not enough of Sean for Ray to help, not enough baby for both of them to touch, press, and poke, even if Ray had known what to do. Ray had thought Sean was too small for both of them to be handling him all the time, so Betsy held him and nursed him and dressed him. Ray had been waiting for him to get a little bigger, a little less fragile. Ray stood, leaning slightly forward, his hands opening and closing at his side.

Is he going to be all right? he wanted to ask, still in a stupor.

"I can't tell if he's breathing," Betsy repeated, more urgently than before. "We need to get him to the hospital."

Ray could finally do something. "I'll get the car. I'll phone the police."

Where they lived at the time, in the country, was too far for an ambulance. Ray dialed the number for the state police from the front of the book. He made an effort to speak slowly, saying everything clearly, so he would not have to repeat it. Only when he began to speak did he realize that his throat was choked.

"This is Ray Griffey. I live in Alcalde. My son is sick; I don't know what is wrong. My wife and I are bringing him to the emergency room. We will be in a white Chevrolet Nova, New Mexico plates. I don't know the number. We will be going very fast. It would help if one of your cars could meet us and turn on its lights and get us through town as quickly as possible."

"I'll notify the patrolmen," the dispatcher said after getting his phone number.

Betsy got in the back of the car with Sean. She knelt on the floor, in front of the seat. All the way to the hospital she continued to massage his chest and breathe into his mouth. She worked steadily, silently.

Ray drove the old Nova as fast as it would go, which did not feel fast enough. Familiar roadside landmarks went by as if he were just on his way to work: the Pojoaque elementary school, the truck weigh station, the Cuyumungue stone yard, Camel Rock. Time was too ordinary. Is he going to be all right? Ray still wanted to ask, not clear anymore what "all right" meant.

At the Tesuque turnoff a black state police car overtook him, pulled in front, and turned on the red, twirling lights on the top of his car. Like race-car drivers, bumper to bumper, they roared up the Tesuque hill, past the Opera, past the turn for Tano Road. As they crested the ridge, the lights of Santa Fe spread out in front of them. The night was clear, quiet, and cold. The street lights and house lights twinkled in the winter air. Far to the right Ray could see the long stream of headlights of the cars on the highway to Albuquerque. At the bottom of the hill, a city police car fell in line, turning on his lights.

A man and a woman with a gurney met the car as they pulled into the semicircular drive of the emergency room. Betsy ran alongside as they rushed Sean away. Ray noticed the two policemen leaning against the bumper of one of their patrol cars, talking with each other. One of them was smoking. He wanted to go up to them and thank them for helping out. He wanted to ask them if Sean was going to be all right.

Ray and Betsy sat in chairs outside the two large gray doors of the emergency room. The doctor came out in a green medical suit. Before he said anything, Betsy started crying, wailing. He sat next to her, waiting patiently. When she quieted, he told them what Betsy already knew, had known, probably, all along. That Sean was dead.

Ray had floated through the next hours as if in a dream. They had gone to Betsy's mother's house. The world had descended like a torrential rain. Betsy had kept up her wailing with the endurance of a child. After a while, it was dawn. More people, more phone calls. Yet mentally, emotionally, Ray remained stuck back on the couch, half awake, half asleep, a fourth beer balanced on his stomach, the TV going, men and women in Roman togas speaking a malevolent, lyrical English. Stuck even in the moment before that, in the plain English of a plain life. Until Robin had found him wandering the halls and, like a hypnotist snapping her fingers, had started the walls crashing down around him, and the pieces of that old life had begun their slow tumble.

"Are you going to cry?" Jesse asked quietly from behind Ray.

Ray turned to look at him. "Did your mother cry?" he asked.

Jesse nodded his head.

"Did you cry?"

Jesse shook his head no.

"I cried then, when he died," Ray said. "When we had the funeral, here, seven years ago, Dimitri cried. Sean was only nine days old when he died. Still, you cry. Maybe someday you'll want to cry, and you weren't even born."

"I don't know," Jesse said skeptically, "maybe."

Today Ray felt the sadness of Sean's death not as tears, but as a mystery which pressed hard against his understanding of the world. It unbalanced him, as if he were dizzy, only his head was clear. He felt tilted from a force in his solar plexus, where his breath started and ended. Sean had died before he had ever lived, and that was what caught at Ray and pulled him. Except it was more than just Sean; it was all children forming that vast pool of trust and innocence; and in a strange way it was Ray himself. It felt almost as though his life had gone on without him, and he was left looking back on his own innocence in wonder, as if it were an empty pair of boots left standing in the road, the owner somehow yanked out of them.

Certainly Sean's death was part of the reason that Ray had left Betsy. Ray could now admit that to himself. But it was a complicated piece in a largely unsolved puzzle. Betsy had never really recovered. Her grief had filled all the spaces of their relationship like a giant balloon filling a room. Finally Ray had run gasping for air. Yet he also knew that this death had been a simple moment of pressure that had snapped their relationship as if it were balsa wood. The weakness of the vessel, therefore, and not the storm had brought Ray to this place. He had come, finally, to visit Sean's grave. And suddenly it all made sense. Here he was, at the cemetery, standing at the crossroads of his life. At the point where his life had broken, and at the point where he might once more pick it up and put it back together.

Ray hung his head and took a deep breath, searching for a way back to solid ground. Zach ran up to them, the bulk of his diapers causing his legs to swing as he ran.

"Sean's house?" Zach asked, pointing at the brass marker.

Ray nodded.

"I want more balloons. One, two, three, four, six balloons. I want giraffe. Daddy?"

"Yes, Zach?"

"I want party." Zach raised his arms and gave a little hop to demonstrate how big and how much fun the party would be.

"Let's go," Ray said, getting up.

Jesse and Zach raced back to the Toyota. Ray looked back to the west at the mountains. The clouds were gathering. Near Los Alamos a large, curved column of snow stretched down to the ground from a field of clouds. In New Mexico you could do that: stand in one place and watch someone else's weather. The far horizon let you see so much of the world. Such a wide view impressed on Ray how much of an observer he had always been. Even in his own life he had stood aside and watched, as if he were just someone he knew.

Just a
Word

It snowed all weekend. After a mild January with no snow, February had arrived cold and full of snow. Saturday it had snowed over two feet at the Santa Fe Ski Basin and over three at Taos. That night it was predicted that the temperature would drop below zero for the third night in a row.

The onslaught of snow had Ray thinking about skiing again. He had not skied since he graduated from college twelve years earlier. Why had he stopped? He had skied all his life, since he was five. Every weekend his mother had hauled him and his brothers to a small hill sixty miles northwest of Philadelphia, near Allentown. Ray remembered lace-up leather boots with cabled "bear trap" bindings on wooden skis. He remembered spending years on what his mother called the baby slope, forever wrestling with the ice-slick rope tow, which ran through his hands like a buzz saw until he tightened his grip and was jerked forward, his arms pulled so sharply that he thought they would pop out of his shoulders, his body snapped forward so that he almost came out of his boots, and his skis suddenly crossed, tangled and dragging, as if they had been frozen to the ground.

"Get up and do it again," was one of his mother's essential statements of philosophy. She never actually stood out on the slope and told him that; she mostly stayed inside the lodge with a book and a cup of hot chocolate, ready to warm, comfort, and reequip any child of hers who might, at any moment, come stumbling in from the cold. She did not ski herself because her husband, Ray's father, thought it would be unwise. What if she broke a leg? How could she then take care of the children?

Ray must have gotten up and done it again many times, because he eventually became good enough to compete in slalom races when he was a freshman at college. He only raced briefly, never having enough ambition to become really good, but he kept his old yellow-bottomed Head 360s busy around the New England ski areas until he graduated. Then they were put away and never taken out again until his mother found them and donated them to a private elementary school for their auction. By then the skis and bindings were completely out of date, and the school was advised not to offer them for sale.

Betsy, too, had grown up skiing, but she and Ray had never done it together, as if as a couple they had retired from such activities. Ray and Julia had yet to go skiing, but they continued to talk about it. They had talked about going the following weekend, and earlier that afternoon Ray had gone to Alpine Sports to see about renting skis. Once there, he instead decided to buy himself a pair of gray Salomon rear-entry boots, blue Rossignol skis with Tyrolia bindings, and black Scott ski poles, all on sale and all much more high tech than the sport used to be.

It had given him a certain bounce, buying that equipment. He had felt pleased, even creative, as he had jockeyed his new skis through the open windows of the Toyota. He still felt expansive, lying on his bed, his new gear stowed in the front hall closet. Spending that money had been a good thing, he assured himself, suddenly anxious to go skiing, as if, after waiting all these years, he could not wait another three days.

Just then he heard Julia come in the front door. She fussed with her boots (new midcalf dark brown leather boots) and her jacket, then he heard her slap an envelope down on the kitchen counter.

Waiting for her to walk through the bedroom door, Ray heard nothing more. He got up and quietly walked down the hall to the kitchen. Only the faint evening light lit the rooms. Ray stood still. It was so quiet that it was spooky. He saw the bulky envelope on the empty counter. He walked through the kitchen and looked around, straining to see in the dim light. Finally he picked Julia's shape out in the far corner of the living room, sitting still amid the collection of pillows there.

He wanted to tell her about his new skis, and then he wanted to ask her what was wrong, but he said nothing. He retreated a few steps and picked up the envelope. As quietly as he could, he took out the papers. They unfolded to a full fourteen inches and he could tell right away that they were legal documents. He strained to read them. He could make out a lot of *whereins* and *herebys* but could not make much sense of it. He saw Roget's name, and Julia's, but still the meaning of it escaped him. Then, with a suddenness, he realized what it was. It was a divorce decree. Julia and Roget were divorced, officially, finally, legally.

Ray put the papers back in the envelope slowly, quietly. They seemed private. They *were* private. Ray had had no idea that Roget and Julia were getting divorced. There had been talk, but nothing about this, nothing about a date, an actual event. He stood in what had now become total darkness trying to sort it out in his mind.

He was, of course, pleased. It was an unexpected victory on behalf of their relationship in which Roget had always seemed to stand as a third party. But it was a victory full of foreboding. Julia was not, it was clear, doing a victory dance in the darkness in the corner of the living room. Ray listened for some indication of what she was doing, but heard nothing. For his part, this divorce was so unannounced, so unheralded, that he did not fully believe it. He had held tangible proof of it in his hand, yet he felt no truth about it. It was a piece of paper; even more irrelevant, it was a legal document.

Yet, to give Julia credit, she had done it. Or maybe Roget had done it. Whichever, it was more than he had done in regard to his relationship with Betsy. He had not even broached the subject of divorce, even though he had no doubt that they would get divorced. He had been pestering Julia since he knew her about her ambivalence toward Roget and had held himself forward as an example of firm and decisive action; yet here she was, suddenly divorced, and here he was, still married. Nothing had changed at all.

Ray walked over to Julia and knelt in front of her. He sat back on his heels and was immediately uncomfortable, but he did not move. He could make out that Julia was leaning her forehead on her forearm, her head down so that he could not make out her face.

"Was it bad?" he asked.

She lifted her head but did not look at him.

"Horrible," she said in her flattest Nebraska accent, the *r*'s deep in her throat.

"How many years has it been?"

"It's not that."

Julia paused, not feeling like long explanations. Ray kept silent. Finally Julia went on.

"He shows up with his lawyer who keeps asking me about you, are we living together and stuff. He uses words like adultery, the prick. I kept looking at Roget, who never looks at me, as if he's not even there hearing this shit from this guy, as if Roget never slept around, as if he were some angel or something. I didn't know it was going to be like that, with lawyers and sitting up there in front of the judge. I thought we were just going to sign some papers. That's what Roget told me, the motherfucker."

The darkness was insulating, as if the world were only outside. Ray and Julia, just a breath away from each other, were as far apart as if they were in different rooms. Julia's voice was hard as she continued.

"Then the lawyer starts asking me about when I used to work for Roget, when I used to do the ordering for him, and hire his salespeople, work on Sundays. He asked me a lot about when I did the ordering, and finally I get it, finally it sinks in to me, I'm so stupid. Roget's afraid I'm going to want some of his business. I got so angry right in the middle of one of this little bald-headed lawyer's questions, because I finally get it, and I go a little crazy.

" 'I don't want any of his goddamn business,' I yell at him, and that gets Roget's attention. Finally, for the first time, he looks at me. The lawyer was a little surprised and doesn't say anything. I talk right at Roget.

" 'You know I made that place what it is, and you're scared. That's why you hired this creep, isn't it? But I wouldn't want any part of that tourist dump. I don't want one penny of anything from you. You keep your precious little inheritance, your precious store. This was Jocelyn's idea, wasn't it?'

"I could tell from the way he looked that I was right. She would think of something like that, and Roget, as smart as he is, really doesn't know shit from perfume. They've been fucking for a long time, I know, and she was always scared of me. I hired her, the bitch."

All Ray knew about Jocelyn was that she worked for Roget at his store and that she was one of the handful of black people who lived in Santa Fe.

" 'You should have just asked,' I yelled at him. 'Why didn't you just ask?' "

Julia's voice softened, almost breaking. The muscles in Ray's calf were cramping but he did not move, as if moving might set off some delicately fused explosive, might destroy the moment that seemed to be going somewhere. But where?

"If he had asked," Julia said quietly, her voice composed again, "I could have saved him a lot of money; he wouldn't have had to hire that lawyer.

"That lawyer made me feel like shit. When I was done yelling he just sat down without saying anything else. The judge was a lady. I don't think she was used to such hysterics. 'Let's just sign the papers,' I told them, and we did."

Julia laughed. "I must have been pretty mad; they tiptoed around me as if I had the plague."

"How many years has it been?" Ray asked again.

"It depends if you count the years that we weren't talking to each other," Julia said, laughing again. "I met Roget when I was nineteen."

Ray felt Roget's presence in the room, between them, stronger than he ever had before. He rocked to the side, off his heels, and sat next to Julia with his back against the wall. His feet started to tingle as they came back to life.

"I found a place," Julia said. "I'm going to move in with Lucia for a while. It's small, but it's what I need now. I came to get my things."

Ray was thinking about Julia and Roget at nineteen. That's young, he thought, and a long time ago, over ten years. He felt insignificant in comparison, displaced by the sheer complexity of Roget and Julia's relationship.

Julia got up after a while and Ray heard her packing in the bedroom. She was back, with her hard tan suitcase, surprisingly quickly.

"I guess I'll go," she said to Ray from the hallway. They could not see each other in the dark.

"Julia," Ray said, looking for some point of entry, looking once more for a way to turn her away from Roget and toward himself. His sense of himself as an intruder confused him.

"Julia," he began again. "Why are you leaving?"

"I need to be alone. I need a place to think, to get away." She sounded a little angry.

"You could have had a place here," Ray said, suddenly tired and willing to let her go. He had loved her, and he believed that she had loved him. This was not the proper ending. "You're walking out on love," he added.

Julia was quiet for a moment. "It's simpler than that; I just need some time," she said, no longer angry.

Ray did not believe her.

Ray discovered later that Julia had left her divorce papers on the counter. She had also left a blue flannel bathrobe with white piping, a bathrobe he had often watched her take off. It was in one of the closets, hanging by itself.

• • •

One day a few weeks later Ray arrived at work just after Scott and a crew had left for the Blue Sky Ranch. The job had mushroomed quickly and motor starters, disconnects, meter cabinets, and other high-priced controls were being ordered and installed in a frenzy. It was beginning to take time away from the shopping-center job. Ray had sent his first request for payment in on Friday and was worried that the amount might shock them—over eight thousand dollars. Scott said that Pedro had a crush on Charlene, who worked in the front office there.

"She's nice, but she's all religious," Pedro had told Ray when he asked him about it, not so much discouraged as perplexed.

"Girls like that expect you to be nice, to be polite, and clean," Ray advised him.

"I know. I don't know if I know how to do that," Pedro answered, laughing.

"Can you ask her when we might get paid?"

"Sure."

The first call of the day was from Robin.

"How's it going?" she asked.

From Robin, this was not an idle question. When Ray asked her, she answered in detail. He caught the "OK" before it got out of his mouth and tried to think for a moment how it really was going.

The disappearance of Julia from his life had been abrupt. She was gone from work and the house at almost the same moment and what had been a whole, dimensioned life with her had quickly been reduced to a few painful phone calls and dinner twice at the new Indian restaurant downtown. In one stroke, his life had been pruned beyond recognition.

"Not so good, I guess," he told Robin, finding it difficult to admit. He decided not to elaborate, since Robin did not seem to consider his problems with Julia to be very significant.

"I called for two reasons," Robin said after a short silence. "First, I want to invite you, with Jesse and Zach if you have them, down for the weekend the second of April. If you want. I'm part of a small show at the university; there's going to be a party, and it might be nice to have some time to visit."

Ray liked the idea immediately. He liked any idea that involved help with the boys. Just the distraction of having other people around eased the persistent pressure, the baffling oppression of their presence. Also, he liked the idea because he felt this invitation was something new; Robin had never wanted to get together "just to visit" before.

"I'll be there," he said immediately, double-checking his calendar as he did.

"Good. Can you come Friday night? That's the opening."

"Yes."

"Great. Number two. I was talking to an old friend from Santa Fe, an artist. He's older than us; really, he's more a friend of Dimitri's than mine. But he was divorced a while back and went to this psychiatrist, and just the way he talked about him, the things he said, it made me think of you. I mean, he made this therapist sound so good that I almost wanted to go see him. But I thought you really might want to, so I got his name."

"Go ahead," Ray said, picking up a pen. Ray wrote his name, James Hough, as Robin spelled it.

"Anyway, there it is," Robin said.

After he hung up, Ray crumpled the piece of paper up and threw it in the trash. He had another phone call before he could give it another thought. This time it was Julia. Ray was surprised.

"I was talking to Mary Ann, waiting for you to get off the phone," Julia told him.

"She's working out great," Ray said.

"Good, I'm glad. I thought she would. She's a lot smarter than I am. And a lot more stable." Julia laughed.

Ray did not agree or disagree, but he knew already that having Mary Ann in the office instead of Julia was a lot easier on his nerves. And Noni was happier. Even Scott was happier. Ray was not sure that he was happier, but the tension had eased. Julia, too, seemed more relaxed and more cheerful.

"I'd like to drive up the Pecos Canyon this weekend," Julia said. "To visit a friend who lives in a cabin up there. He writes all week and then on the weekend his girlfriend comes to visit. She's actually a better friend than he is, but I know him too. I thought maybe you'd like to come along. It would be nice to spend the day with you. We could make a picnic."

"How about skiing?" Ray asked, thinking about his unused new skis.

"It's getting too nice to ski, don't you think?"

Ray had to agree. The weather had turned warm and seemed like it was going to stay that way.

"Yeah, you're right. That would be great," Ray said, wondering if Julia had forgotten that he spent most weekends with Jesse and Zach. The following weekend, though, they were staying with Betsy. Her father had arranged a trip of some kind.

Then Bud called. He was blasting in a road at a subdivision south of town and the developer had decided that as long as they were blasting they should put in conduit for small streetlights. Ray agreed to meet him on the site late that afternoon.

When his phone rang again, it was Betsy. He could tell from her voice that she was upset.

"Can you get free for lunch today?" she asked, trying to sound congenial, casual.

Ray wished he had made a lunch date with Bud.

"Sure," he told her.

They made arrangements to meet at La Choza at noon. Ray's good mood disappeared abruptly.

Ray thought La Choza was the best New Mexican restaurant in Santa Fe. Good, for New Mexican food, meant steady quality, consistently the right mixture of cheese, onions, beans, and, of course, good chile. Gourmet was not a relevant word for New Mexican cooking; if it was gourmet, it was something else. The mocha cake at La Choza, however, was something else, and whenever Ray ate there, he always had his heart set on the mocha cake.

They sat in the front room with the small pink tables. The sun streamed in the south window. Ray ordered enchilada with red chile; Betsy asked for a side order of a tostada. The waitress filled their water glasses and left some garlic bread on the table. Ray was so uncomfortable that he could not find any small talk to fill the spaces. Betsy had her hair pulled back and she looked severe.

"Ray," Betsy said, "I thought that if I went away on this trip with the boys, I thought that if you had some time to yourself, that things might change for you, that you might think about it, that you might feel differently."

Ray had sensed this, but had hoped that the trip might be more for her benefit than for his. "I don't, Betsy. I'm sorry."

"You know, I was trying to help. I was trying to give you some space. I thought maybe you might think about us."

Betsy paused and then continued.

"I understand you took a trip with Julia."

Ray hesitated before answering. Betsy was no longer looking at him and she was not waiting for an answer.

"You know, I'm really angry about this, Ray," she said. "I don't think you're giving me much of a chance."

Ray nodded his head; not because he agreed with what she was saying. He thought that the two of them had had years of chances, and she did not sound particularly angry. In all those years, she had never gotten angry.

"I mean, to walk out like that—*bam!*" she said, now somewhere between hurt and angry. "To just leave. No comment, no discussion, no reason. What is that? Is that something human?"

In this last sentence Betsy fully tapped her anger. She let it flow.

"You think that it's OK to just leave when you feel like it. You made commitments. You made promises. I've invested my life in this marriage. We have children, you know. Where have you been these past years? What have you been doing? How many little affairs before Julia? How many you never told me about?"

"None," Ray quickly put in.

"Right. None. I bet none. You're a little turdhead running after women. Having affairs."

Ray remembered that Betsy's mother had called Betsy a "turdhead" when she got drunk.

"How stupid can I be?" Betsy continued, chopping with her

hands as she talked. "I thought we had a family; I thought we had a marriage. I thought we were making something. But you were doing something else. I feel like an idiot. What the fuck was I doing?"

Betsy was yelling without raising her voice. Her anger came from her chest. Her face was red.

"You told me that you weren't leaving me for Julia. You think that you can just lie to me like that?"

Julia had moved in and then back out again between this and the last conversation he had had with Betsy about Julia, Ray thought. "We're not living together," Ray said, looking for a proper tone to use in answering Betsy's anger.

"You think that you can just lie to me like that?" Betsy repeated. "Jesse's at home saying, 'Julia' this, 'Julia' that. Why do you lie to me?"

Ray started to explain that Julia had lived with him briefly while she was looking for another place, but Betsy cut him off. He didn't mind; she was right.

"Of course, I'm sure this isn't the first lie. You know, I trusted you. I really trusted you." Betsy started to cave in on herself, but snapped back. "This is the most violent thing that has ever happened to me."

Ray knew, on the scale of things, where that put him. Betsy's parents had been alcoholics and had fought physically, frequently, until their divorce. Betsy's father had often hit her, too. Then, her boyfriend, who was a drug addict, had beaten her sometimes and once had carved a small half-moon on the side of her neck with his knife.

"You think that when you want to, you can just move on?" Betsy continued. "And what of all of us? You think that we can just pick up and march on as if nothing happened? Are you crazy? I mean, we are small children here."

Ray noticed her slip on the pronoun, but said nothing.

"What about Jesse and Zach?" Betsy continued. "What about us? You have a new girlfriend. You dance on. But what about us?"

Betsy paused, waiting for an answer.

"It's not 'us,' Betsy," Ray said, finding some of his own anger to match hers. "I'm not leaving Jesse and Zach. They're my children too. It's you and me, Betsy; we're over."

Whatever hope Betsy had held for mending this tear, whatever fantasy she had held that this might be a temporary problem, crashed at that moment. Ray could see the flames of the wreckage running across her face and hollowing out her eyes. Betsy dropped her head, her red bangs falling forward in a neat row.

At that moment, the waitress delivered their plates. "The top one is hot," she told Ray and left.

"Do you have any idea how that makes me feel?" Betsy asked, her tone softened. She was once more looking at him. The color had left her face.

Ray thought that he did. He was pretty good at understanding how Betsy felt.

Looking into his eyes, she continued. "When you say nothing, what am I meant to think? Things run through my head: that I'm ugly, that I'm stupid, that I'm no good in bed, that I don't know how to make you happy. That I'm no good."

She blinked slowly, her voice trailing off as if everything inside her might stay in place if she stayed very still. It was the moment that Ray had been dreading since he left Betsy. He had brought her back to her deepest pain. He had loved her once, or thought he had. He had never intended that they would one day be here. Yet as clear as the despair on Betsy's face, here they were. There was nothing for it.

"I think maybe I'll go," Betsy said after a long silence. "I'm not very hungry." She reached into her purse for some money.

"It's OK. I'll pay," Ray said.

Betsy put three dollars on the table anyway and left without saying anything. Ray started on his enchilada. Betsy's untouched tostada and her empty chair were his silent guests. Today, he thought, he might need two pieces of mocha cake. Or maybe none. He put his fork down and leaned back. He was suddenly not hungry. He sat quietly, trying not to think. After a few minutes, he decided that he was done and left, paying on the way out.

• • •

When he got back to the office, Ray fished the crumpled piece of paper out of his wastebasket. He looked up the number for James Hough in the phone book. After three rings, a machine answered the phone. Ray hung up. He sat thinking. He redialed the number. Pretend it's a general contractor, he told himself. When the machine answered, he paused for a moment, wondering how to explain himself, wondering exactly what it was he wanted. He settled for just leaving his name and number.

Fifteen minutes later, James Hough called back.

"I'm returning your call," he said.

Ray imagined an old man with the face of Freud.

"I don't really know how to do this," Ray told him. "I guess I'd like to come in for ten or fifteen minutes so we could check each other out." That didn't sound quite right to Ray, but he left it at that.

"Fine," Dr. Hough answered crisply, flipping some pages. "Would it work at noon April second, the first Friday of April?"

Ray had immediately lost interest in doing this, but he said, "OK." That was the Friday he was going to Albuquerque to see Jack and Robin, but noon would work.

"Good," Dr. Hough said. "Friday April second, at twelve. I'll see you then."

Ray thought he sounded positively upbeat.

"Fine," he answered and hung up.

Noni told him Joe Steppe was on the phone.

"Hello," Ray said.

"Old friend. Good news. Rankin has finally paid up. I've got a check for you."

"Good," Ray answered, suddenly indifferent to this money the company needed so desperately.

"Aren't you glad?"

"Yes. Yes, I'll come get it now."

After picking up the check from Joe, Ray drove out the Old Las Vegas Highway to meet Bud. He followed the directions through a network of newly carved dirt roads to the base of the foothills and parked next to Bud's truck at the beginning of the new road they were blasting. Bud was warming himself in the cab and drinking coffee from the tin cap of his thermos. Ray heard the dynamiter's air drill from around the bend as he crossed to sit in the cab with Bud.

"Coffee?" Bud offered, raising his cup.

Ray shook his head. Bud's nose was red from the cold and his shoulders were drawn up around his neck. The radio under the dash delivered a burst of static and broken words. Ray could make out the voice of Bud's secretary, but nothing that she said.

"I can't read you, Michelle. Come again," Bud said into the mike.

"I said your lawyer wants you to call him right away," Michelle said, the signal suddenly clear.

Bud reclipped the mike with a sigh.

"I'm finally getting divorced," he said, and then laughed. "I guess the lawyers realize we've run out of money.

"It's a joke. I don't even know where Fran is, where my children live. She says she feels threatened. The court says OK. The lawyers talk to each other. Over three hundred dollars an hour, combined. You know, we had some arguments over the years. Sure, I lost my temper a few times. But, you know, I never hit her, I never even threatened her. I'm not a threatening guy."

Ray agreed that Bud was as meek as they come, yet part of him did not believe Bud. The part of Ray that believed, naively, that people get what they deserve and that the courts always have a reason for what they do, resisted what Ray knew from his own experience to be true, that Bud was as meek as they come.

"Now we're getting divorced," Bud continued. He laughed again. "Whatever that means. After all that I've been through, what is divorce? I don't even know. Just a word."

"I know," Ray said. "I just had lunch with Betsy. We're getting divorced too."

Bud did not respond, may not have even heard him. Ray thought about the lunch, about Betsy. By circumstance, Bud and

Betsy were more closely aligned, but he understood what Bud meant. Divorce was just a way of defining something that cannot be understood. It sorted out things about property, ownership, stuff like that, and it allowed life to go on, to move, but the hollow sound beneath it tugged like a deep cave.

They got out of the cab and walked up the rocky path toward the sound of the air compressor. It was getting late and whatever warmth the sun had offered had dissipated. When they rounded the corner Ray saw the truck that held the giant air compressor and the yellow drilling rig mounted on metal tracks, attached to the truck by hoses. A bit, guided down through a small tower by an operator, hammered a hole into the rock as water was pumped through holes in the bit to settle the dust and firm the walls of the hole. A small cone of gray mud marked where each puncture had been made. The noise made it impossible to speak.

When the drill operator finished the hole he was working on, he conferred by hand signal with the truck driver and they slowly backed their rigs down to the spot where Ray and Bud had parked. They were done drilling for the day. When they shut their machines off, the absence of noise was overwhelming.

Another worker, wearing an insulated jumpsuit, was following behind the drilling machine setting the charges. He measured the hole with a rod, to make sure that it was still clear, and then dropped in the dynamite, which trailed one red wire from its detonator. Then he poured some powder from a large bucket into the hole. After the powder, he shoveled four scoops of pea gravel from a wheelbarrow with a large gardening trowel and dropped it down on top of the dynamite. The rest of the hole he filled with dirt and gravel that was lying around.

Bud showed Ray where the trench was going to be for the lighting conduit and they measured how many lights were going to be needed. When they returned, the worker in the jumpsuit was moving his wheelbarrow over to the last hole. Bud walked up behind him as he dropped the dynamite down the hole and tapped him on the shoulder. Bud squatted down next to the worker, took his wedding band off his finger, and asked him if he could drop it down the hole. The worker nodded. Bud knelt next to the hole and dropped in the ring, looking in after it like a young boy who had dropped a stone down a well, as if he might hear or see when it hit. After the pea gravel was in, Bud helped the worker scrape in the dirt and stones.

"Meet me over there," the worker said, pointing to a large group of boulders at the beginning of the bend.

He moved his tools and wheelbarrow out of the way, and then connected one firing wire to all the red leads poking up out of the holes.

"These aren't actually wires," the worker explained as he joined Bud and Ray at the detonator and began making the final hook-ups for firing. "It's some sort of silver foil in there that lights, like a lightbulb. I guess this one's yours," the worker told Bud as he stood up. "Just push that button there on the side of the box."

Bud smiled. His face became happy. Ray thought it was the first time he'd seen Bud actually look happy. Bud took one hand out of his pocket, leaned over, and pushed the button. Ray could pick out each charge as it fired milliseconds after the one before it and the earth shook with a dull thud. A moment later they heard debris coming down through the trees like a light rain.

I Don't
Know What
Went Wrong

After Julia and Ray spent the day in Pecos, they had a pizza at Tony's Pizzeria and Julia spent the night.

"I should have left a toothbrush here," she said, laughing. "Can I borrow yours?" Julia was meticulous about brushing her teeth, and her teeth were as large and healthy as her Nebraska homeland.

Julia did not come when they made love, she rarely had, but she pulled Ray into her with the longing and love of haunted dreams, and when he came they both felt the closeness of their skin pressed hard against each other. They slept spooned together, Ray with his arm looped around Julia's small waist. Early in the morning, Ray woke up and entered her again as they lay, from the rear, and Julia squeezed his forearm as she moaned.

Their relationship might be scattering in the wind, but the intensity of it didn't seem to be diminishing at all.

The closeness of such moments confused Ray and ultimately made him feel worse, made him regret that their relationship could not hold any of the same heat. He decided that it would just be better to end it altogether. Julia was coming over for dinner Thursday; he would announce it then. He had invited Dimitri as well, but then called him back and told him he needed to be alone with Julia.

"I'm going to break up with her."

"*Verdad?*" Dimitri asked, as stunned as he had been when Ray broke up with Betsy.

"Yes, it's over."

"You fool. You got the best-looking woman in this city and you let her go?" Dimitri laughed.

"This is the moment you've been waiting for. You can park outside my door Thursday night and pick her up when she leaves."

Ray was not at all sure it would go that way. He felt a little sophomoric, talking about breaking up as if it were a high school prom. Maybe they wouldn't break up after all. Maybe they would make love, like on Sunday. What did it mean, to break up? What, for that matter, did it mean to be together?

These doubts plagued him on Thursday when Julia arrived forty-five minutes late. He had a plan for the night. They would eat. He was going to cook scallops, deep-frying them the way they did in the little stands on the back roads of Cape Cod. They would talk and laugh over dinner. Julia would be impressed by the meal; Ray had never cooked anything so elaborate before. They would experience a depth of friendship that would buffer the news to come. After dinner, Ray would announce, clarify really, that their relationship was over. They would both nod their heads, recognizing the truth, sad nonetheless. Before long, Julia would make one of her wise-ass remarks, one of those wry, full-of-worldly-knowledge-but-still-it-hurts comments, and they would both laugh, and their friendship would be recemented and they would go their separate ways, connected to each other for life. Or maybe she would spend the night and they would make love three times before they went their separate ways. Ray was ambivalent about this last possibility. Sex with Julia was not something that he was prepared to give up, yet if she stayed he thought it might cloud the message, the whole point of the evening.

Things did not go as planned. The oil was too hot and immediately burned the breading on the scallops. Julia had driven to Albuquerque for the day, looking for a place to rent and finding only dumps that all cost too much, including one in which the landlord had tried to kiss her. Because there was no dinner and no dinner conversation, Ray accelerated his schedule.

"I feel like it's over for us," he said.

"What?" she asked loudly, distracted and confused.

"Over. Us. Done with." Ray could see that this part of the plan was falling apart too. Julia was not prepared for it; she was not going to make it easy. Ray was taken by surprise. He thought he was stating the obvious. Suddenly he wanted to take back what he had said. He wanted to wait on this conversation, but it had already begun.

Julia stood staring at Ray. They were both in the kitchen, leaning against opposite counters. She was absorbing his words. She was sorting out that this was different from upset, that this was different from "I'm hurt," that this was over. Yet she still wasn't sure. She stared and waited.

Ray was now going to have to say it one more time. He began to equivocate.

"Julia, you've been leaving for weeks, months even, since we began." He noticed that his tone was pleading. He wanted her to help. He paused, took a deep breath, and dived in on his own. "It's over, Julia. You and me. I don't want to go on anymore."

The emotions were plain on Julia's face; she was angry. "What kind of bullshit is this?" he expected her to yell, but she turned away from him and walked quickly into the middle of the living room.

She stood with her back to him, her head bent. Ray was focused on her, trying to divine her thoughts, her mood, but he didn't learn much from her back. Then Julia walked toward the couch, stopped, and walked back across the room. She began pacing, in small steps, back and forth, her long legs awkward, her knees locking from time to time, so she looked like a crane. When she finally spoke, she spoke clearly, almost wisely, as if her feelings elevated her understanding.

"You, of all people," she said without stopping her pacing and without looking at him, "I never expected this of you."

Ray felt the truth of it. It was as if he had been caught lying. As if he were some snake-oil product that had advertised itself as good for growth, good for health, good for life, and had hung around town too long and now someone who had bought the product, someone who had believed, was staring him down with the naked truth of it.

He looked at Julia and he could not remember where they had started, what they had come through. He only saw her there, accusing him for his betrayal. Betsy too, with her "what about's": What about when you told me you loved me? What about when we drove to Albuquerque to buy a pizza? What about Sean?

Ray felt haunted by the empty blue bottles left around which betrayed that he had once been there, as if they all had "Ray Griffey" stamped on the bottom. Haunted by the snake oil they once contained, by the promises and the hopes he had once presented so boldly.

"You never wanted this relationship, Julia," he said. "From the beginning, you've been pulling away. Now you're even moving away." Ray heard his voice rise as he ended the last sentence and didn't say any more for fear that it might get away from him altogether.

Julia stopped and looked at him. He met her eyes. "I'm sorry" is what he wanted to say but didn't. He had said too many "I'm sorry's" lately. Julia walked over and sat down on the edge of the couch, her knees together, as if she were in an office waiting for a job interview. She worked at keeping back her tears.

"You, you would just leave like that?" she asked.

Ray had not moved from his place in the kitchen. Smoke from the burned scallops clung to the ceiling. The scallops floated in the oil like black lilies.

She's got it all wrong about who's leaving, he thought, but said nothing; over is over, let it just be done. Julia had been content just being in a relationship; he had wanted more. He pushed himself off the counter and sat down next to her on the couch.

He would miss Julia. She had taught him how to fold blue jeans, how to steam broccoli, and how to be depressed. She had sparked him. It was as if, when she left, all this would go with her. He wanted to take it all back, to grab hold of her and convince her to stay, to say nice things to her and make love to her on the rug. But they had done all that before. She had stayed. Love had seemed more real, briefly. This turn was to be different. He took her hand, and like teenagers they wove their fingers together and continued to just sit.

He was emptied, like a tire without air, crushed flat. For Ray Griffey, whose name at that moment sounded foreign even to himself, there was nothing left but his imperfect memories of the places he had stopped along the way.

"I've felt so good with you," Julia said, sounding resigned. "So safe. I guess I've really blown it, huh?"

Ray softened and wanted to dive back in with her, but he had drawn the line. He had bungled it, but there it was, laid down nonetheless, and he wasn't going to stop and pick it back up again now. He had come to understand the pain of doing the same thing over and over.

After Julia left, Ray glanced up and down the street to see if Dimitri was there. She had driven off without looking back at him. Ray stood under the black, wide night, constellations of stars indifferently shining through. He sensed himself soaring, rising above all this. He felt his trajectory, his orbit. Betsy was a fading spot on the earth and Julia was a meteoric occurrence. Ahead of him was the infinity of space. Walking back into the house he felt light and a little lost.

Ray was working late on an estimate at the office when Noni, who had left less than an hour earlier, called.

"I think you better go up to Scott's house," she said.

"Why?"

"Glenda left him."

Ray did not immediately see why this problem needed his attention. He knew that Noni had arranged for Jonathan, Scott and Glenda's son, to go part-time for day care to the same lady as her daughters.

"Is there a problem with Jonathan?"

"Jonathan's still at Estrella's, at day care. Glenda left them both. Just packed and left."

"Where did she go?"

"I don't know. She didn't say. She left a letter with Estrella to give to Scott when he came for Jonathan after work. Evidently Scott read it and got a little crazed and ran off. Without Jonathan."

Ray was resisting fully understanding and sympathizing with this information because the bid he was working on was due at ten the following morning. Also, he had had enough of marital drama lately.

"Glenda was a sourpuss," Ray said.

"She was more than that," Noni answered with a laugh.

"What do you mean?"

"What I mean is that she slept around all the time. With bikers mostly, but she wasn't picky. Right there at the house. When Jonathan napped."

"How do you know all this?"

"Everyone in town knows. Everyone but Scott."

"And me."

Noni laughed. "My husband bowls with some guys that have slept with her. They tell stories."

"You think he's at the house?" The thought of Noni and everyone else knowing every day about Glenda, and Scott not knowing, had suddenly made Ray full of concern.

"Probably. I think you should try to find him."

"Thanks, Noni."

Scott lived behind the El Gancho Tennis Club, in the foothills. His driveway was steep, with sharp switchbacks. As Ray negotiated the final curve, he could see Scott's pickup parked among the old Chevy Novas and motorcycles. He stood outside his Toyota a moment listening. The lights were on in the living room. Everything was quiet.

Suddenly, Ray saw the flicker of a shadow through the windows seconds before he heard a loud crash. Then he heard Scott roar, sounding like a lion. There was another crash, more like a thud, like someone hitting a punching bag. Scott roared again.

Ray was momentarily frightened to go in. He had never seen Scott angry. Finally, though, he walked up the five steps to the door and knocked. Just as he did, he heard another thump. Whatever Scott was beating would not be holding up well, Ray thought; Scott was a strong, big man. He tried the door. It was open. He cracked it to peek in but could see nothing, so he opened it all the way and stepped inside.

Scott did not see or hear Ray. He was standing in the same brown shirt and blue jeans he had worn that day to work. With both his hands, he was holding a dirty drive shaft from a Chevy Nova, and the wall in front of him, the wall between the living room and the kitchen, looked as if it had exploded. Sheetrock hung in broken chunks, and the framing itself had started to pull loose from the ceiling.

As Ray was watching, Scott wound up for another blow, swinging the drive shaft like a mythic Norse hero beating back his enemies with a jawbone. As his steel club swung over his head and then around like a baseball bat, Scott bellowed, closing his eyes and throwing back his head. When he made contact, Ray felt the whole house shake.

Ray waited for the moment of impact to pass. "Scott," he said to him.

Scott looked at him quickly, his eyes wild and distant. For an instant, Ray was truly frightened, and then Scott's blue eyes focused and registered recognition. Scott lifted the drive shaft, showing it to Ray, and then tossed it at the bottom of the wall.

"Glenda left," Scott said, and he staggered over to the couch and sat down. Ray went to the broken wall, fingering the gashes. He picked up the drive shaft. It was heavy, and hard to grasp because of its thickness. Ray stepped around in front of the wall as if he were a batter coming to the plate. With difficulty, he raised the end of the drive shaft and started a backswing, but he could not support the weight. He moved his right hand down and, as a child might first try to swing a bat, muscled the drive shaft around for a meek tap low against the wall.

"You're pathetic," Scott said.

Ray tried again, this time delivering a more satisfying blow. He did it twice more, each time with more authority. He was beginning to sweat. He took off his jacket and picked up the drive shaft again. He had momentarily forgotten about Scott. He swung once more, this time breaking the sheetrock.

Then he remembered pictures of Olympians in the hammer throw. They twirled, their arms stretched straight out, centrifugal force creating the momentum needed to lift and throw the implement. Ray picked up the end of the drive shaft with both hands extended in front of him. With a grunt he began his spin, trying to raise the end of the drive shaft up as he did. It dragged along on the floor, caught momentarily on the carpet, and then became airborne. He threw back his head for counterbalance, spun once, twice, and then with a loud shout he let go. The drive shaft crashed through the wall and, like an arrow, came out the other side. It stuck for a second, and then slid all the way through until just the U-joint stuck out and up toward the ceiling.

Ray shouted again, smiling. The blood pounded in his temples. He could smell his own sweat. He turned to Scott.

"You're too fucking much," Scott said.

"Yeah," Ray shouted, raising both fists as Zach might.

After walking around a few times to cool off, Ray sat in the chair next to the couch. "What happened?"

Scott shook his head. "I don't know, man. I just don't know. She left. She left me a letter at day care. It just said she was glad to be rid of us and she wasn't ever coming back."

"You've got Jonathan," Ray said.

"I don't know what went wrong."

Ray sat silent. He was having trouble feeling Scott's problem. Ray had never liked Glenda. Now, with what Noni had told him, he thought they should all be glad to be rid of her. Yet he knew Scott. He knew him to be a loyal man. Scott would never have seen Glenda as anything but his wife. He never would have caught any hints about what was really going on, and there must have been plenty.

Scott was loyal to Ray in the same way he'd been loyal to Glenda, and to Prime Time Electric. Suddenly, Ray saw a connection: Prime Time Electric was not doing well, yet Ray was always making it seem that everything was OK. He was deceiving Scott as Glenda had. He had been thinking about just closing the doors. If he did, it would be like Glenda's leaving. He decided to confess.

"The company's not doing well," he said, finding it very hard to say.

Scott looked puzzled.

"I don't know," Ray went on. The thoughts kept jamming in his brain; the words kept catching as he tried to speak them. Ray was discovering how much he had invested in keeping up the good appearances of Prime Time Electric.

"I don't know. I can't quite get a handle on it. The bills seem to get further behind. I feel squeezed all the time. We get more work; jobs go well; the money is bigger and bigger. But it never gets easier. In fact, I think it's getting harder. I've been thinking about getting out."

"No," Scott said quickly, on the edge of the couch. "We can make it work, Ray. I know we can."

Ray wanted to believe him. Scott could make almost anything work. It was what made him beautiful. But there were a few things that were out of his reach. Glenda had obviously been one. Ray thought that business might be another. What Ray had learned about business was that there were only winners and losers. He suspected that people like Scott and himself did not want to win badly enough to stay out of the losers category.

At that moment, though, it appealed to Ray to stay with Scott. He nodded his head.

"OK," Ray said. "We'll try."

Scott put out one of his huge hands and Ray shook it.

"Let's go get Jonathan," Ray said.

• • •

Ray called the first ad for a color TV that he read in the *Thrifty Nickel.* The man who answered said his name was Chad and told Ray that he could come over right away. He gave Ray the address. It was an apartment behind the Episcopal church downtown.

"Why are you selling it?" Ray asked when he arrived, thinking that this question might flush out any burned-out tubes that Chad was trying to hide.

"Because I got a new Sony," Chad answered, pulling an old sheet off his new TV. Chad smiled with pride. He had a day's growth of beard and wore an old green army T-shirt. His apartment was only one small room and was cluttered with boxes, books, papers, and large plastic garbage bags stuffed full.

"Are you moving?" Ray asked.

"No," Chad answered simply.

Ray thought he must work a night job and that he was getting up. The only thing of any value he seemed to own was his new TV, camouflaged under its sheet to blend in with the rest of the mess. The old TV sat, uncovered, in a corner on top of a green dresser. Chad worked his way over to it and turned it on.

"Two years ago," he explained, "this TV was state of the art. Remote control; programmable buttons."

He played his hand across the buttons, making the picture snap from one show to another. He left it on an undersea Jacques Cousteau movie. Cousteau's heavy accent narrated as dimly lit sea plants waved in the currents.

"We did not know what to expect," Cousteau said. "No one had ever been in these waters before." He spoke his sentences in distinct phrases.

Chad's apartment looked like the Undersea World of Jacques Cousteau. The heavily shaded lamp in the corner was the only light, and it was as if the clutter everywhere was placed at the whim of some eternal currents washing through. Everything was the same green of Chad's T-shirt, even the walls, the same inky green of the ocean depths.

Chad wanted a hundred and fifty dollars for his TV. Ray decided that Chad knew TVs and that a hundred and fifty dollars was probably a good deal. He didn't really care so much about making a good deal. He was ambivalent, still, about owning a TV at all. He stood silent, letting his ambivalence swim along with the camera man in the documentary.

Chad's apartment was Ray's worst nightmare about TVs. It seemed to him implicit that a TV came with all the dim messiness of that apartment. Your living room might not suddenly clutter it-self up, but your mind did. TV turned everything in your brain a thick green color. Your interior rooms suddenly became inhabited by derelicts and bums. You ate Twinkies for dinner. You became impotent. And yet, thought Ray, it was just a box, just program-ming.

"I'll take it," he said. "Can I write you a check?"

Chad did not want a check, so Ray extracted a promise from him not to sell it to anyone else and returned the next night with cash. Chad had not shaved, and nothing in his apartment had moved. He was wearing the same army T-shirt. They wrestled the TV off the dresser and loaded it into the back of Ray's Toyota. A light wet snow was falling. In the orange glow of the streetlights, it looked as if it were not falling at all, but hanging in the air.

This TV will keep me company, Ray thought as he fiddled with the heater in his car. Tomorrow I will get Cable TV to run me a hookup in the bedroom.

Moving the TV by himself was next to impossible. Ray realized that he had not considered portability in his purchase. With great effort, he finally settled it on the end of his desk, turned so that he could watch it from bed.

The phone rang. It was Dimitri.

"It's over," he said. "With Eleanor."

"I thought it was over two months ago."

"No, it's over now. I'm moving out."

"Do you want to move in here?" Ray asked. "I have a new TV."

"Maybe, for a little while. You don't have much room, with the boys."

"They're only here on weekends. We'll make it work. Come on over."

•　•　•

Dimitri arrived with a bag of groceries. He wore his wool cap, scarf, and so many layers of clothing that he looked blown up, like an air mattress. He began taking off some of the layers and piling them in a corner of the living room: his coat, his sweater, his flannel long-sleeved shirt, his cotton long-sleeved shirt. Finally he was down to his blue polypropylene long underwear. He began unpacking the groceries.

"No clothes? Just food?" Ray asked.

"Are you hungry?"

"I ate, but I'll have something." Ray never turned down Dimitri's cooking. "It's almost ten o'clock," Ray added.

Dimitri laughed, never stopping his urgent unpacking and arranging. His hands moved with the dexterity of a shell-game operator's at a carnival.

"Where's the frying pan?" he asked.

Ray pulled out the cast-iron frying pan and moved to a stool across the counter. Dimitri turned on the light in the exhaust fan over the stove and began twisting the control knobs for the burners. The light played through Dimitri's thinning hair and cast deep shadows across his face. Ray remembered times that he had sat across the counter on a stool watching Julia, seduced by her dances with food. Dimitri was a more complex and confident cook. He never slowed down, like a one-man band, going from instrument to instrument. In comparison, Julia's cooking had been like folk music, a simple guitar. Dimitri beat two eggs in a bowl. Clearly his spirits were improving.

"What happened?" Ray asked when they finally sat down to their breakfast burritos with pan-fried potatoes and slices of avocado and tomato.

But Dimitri was not yet ready to talk. First he had to sample the food. He retrieved the pepper grinder from the kitchen. Finally, after he had taken six or seven bites, the frantic momentum of his orchestration began to slow into the sensual gratification of the meal. Dimitri eased himself into an entirely different state, as if he were slipping into the womblike warmth of his hot tub.

"She's sleeping with someone else," Dimitri said, when talking seemed all right.

"Eleanor?"

"Of course Eleanor, you idiot. Who did you think I meant?"

Ray shrugged his shoulders. Dimitri continued.

"I think she's been sleeping with him for a long time."

"Let me back up here. What about the letter you showed me? What about the divorce? What about it's all over?"

"I know, I know. But I didn't know she was sleeping with this guy."

"That would have made a difference?"

"Well, I like to know these things. All that time I'm trying to have sex with her and she refuses me, she's really sleeping with another guy."

"So all the more reason that it's over."

Dimitri mopped his plate with a quarter of a tortilla. His mood changed from angry to reflective.

"It's funny, isn't it? I want it to be over; I write her a letter giving her a divorce. But when I find out she is sleeping with someone else, I cannot let go. I still think of her as mine. Why is that?"

"You're Greek. It's in your genes to possess women."

Dimitri was done eating and he lay on the rug against the wall with a pillow under his head. Ray lay on his side at Dimitri's feet, his head propped on his hand.

"What is it, Ray?" Dimitri asked, exploring the tragedy. "Why do we do these things? What is it that we want?"

Ray had no answer. Dimitri went on, not waiting for one.

"You leave your wife and your beautiful children. You live in this—this hideaway."

With a sweep of his hand Dimitri demonstrated his feelings about Ray's apartment, although he liked it far better than the first one.

"And because you do these things, something in me is triggered. And now I leave my wife, and it turns out that she is sleeping with another man."

Dimitri began to cry. He pinched the bridge of his nose to stop himself.

"Do you think that because of what I did, you left Eleanor?" Ray asked.

"Not because. I am not blaming you. Only when you came and brought me to that place and told me you had left, something in me was woken up. Not at first. At first I was horrified at such a life. But slowly, with time, I saw that you did not die, I saw that you keep your relationship with Jesse and Zach; something in me began to wake up.

"But what is it? What is this thing in us, Ray, that makes us do these things? What unhappiness?"

His tone had turned philosophical and was laced with the excitement of discovery.

"Did you know that I had been married to Eleanor for almost twenty years? And all those years, there was so much unhappiness. So much that was not said. And she too is unhappy, not just me, obviously, because she is sleeping with another man. But all those years, we stick it out. We are miserable. Until now. Why? Why now?"

"Because it is time?" Ray said.

"Time? What time? It has happened, I know, but I don't understand why."

Dimitri began to cry again. This time, he did not try to stop himself.

"I am an old Greek," he said. "We have no control over our feelings."

Ray grabbed another pillow from the corner and lay against the wall next to Dimitri.

"I can't stay here," Dimitri said after he stopped crying. "This is your place."

"Pay me a little: a hundred dollars. You can be my roommate. I would like that."

"You have no room, with the kids."

"When they're here, I'll sleep with them. In fact, I'll sleep in that room all the time. You can have the room with the TV. I didn't really want a TV anyway."

Dimitri was finally persuaded. Ray claimed the single bed that Jesse slept in. He would get a double mattress. It would fit without a problem and Jesse could have his single back and Zach had his crib.

Ray lay in bed with his hands behind his head. He heard the TV in his old room come on and he fell asleep to the drone of the late-night news.

Man
Reaching

Ray had trouble finding the office of Dr. James Hough. It was in a house on a small backstreet he had never seen, even though it was only a few blocks from his Silver Street apartment. There was a waiting room with two chairs and a side table covered with old copies of *The New Yorker.* Under one of the chairs a noise machine was plugged in and making a steady sound like a deep-throated snake. There was a sign taped to the door of the inner office asking patients not to park on the small street out front where Ray had parked. He thought for a moment about running back out and moving his car and then decided that his ten-minute visit exempted him from the rules.

Just as he sat down, the inner door opened. James Hough, looking nothing like Sigmund Freud, introduced himself and shook Ray's hand. As he entered, Ray's fingertips were tingling.

"I have to turn on my answering machine," Dr. Hough said. "I'll be right back."

Ray sat in a large leather chair. He imagined the torments of other patients trapped in the smooth surfaces. James? Doctor?

Jim? Where do you start with this? Ray wondered, feeling suddenly as if he should have thought this through a little more, should have had a game plan.

Dr. Hough sat directly across from Ray and put on a mute, cat-like grin. Ray considered an array of things to say, ridiculous comments about Dr. Hough's office: the pictures on the wall, the color of the carpet, the difficulty of the location. He noticed the switches and plugs: the switches were the old pushbutton kind and the plugs were two-pronged, ungrounded. He considered commenting, but said nothing. Finally, he simply shrugged his shoulders.

"Why don't you tell me something about yourself," Dr. Hough suggested.

Ray was suddenly struck by the similarity of their ages. Yet Dr. Hough sat in the doctor's chair and Ray sat in the patient's. What had he been doing all his life, Ray thought, that the two of them would end up in opposite corners of the office this way?

He ran through his mind the story of his life, looking for places to begin.

"Last fall," he said, "I separated from my wife, left my wife, really. And children. I had this girlfriend. I also just broke up with her."

It washed across Ray how much this story was like a tawdry romance novel. He was about to say how Julia worked for him: boss sleeps with bookkeeper, leaves wife. How many times had that plot drifted out into the air of the converted living room in which he now sat? It was embarrassing to Ray and he flushed red. Even the disasters of his life lacked imagination. He stammered a little, looking for some identifying quality, some unique part of his life, something to make him different.

Dr. Hough sat patiently. Another one of these guys, Ray imagined him thinking. Ray did not want, had never wanted, to be another one of those guys. He felt the desperate pull of it, the oppressive sameness of it, as if he would drown. He was one small, bobbing head, far out at sea, weak with the effort of trying to reach land, weak with the hope of ever getting there. He felt the pull of it. He gave up just a little. He sighed and shrugged his shoulders again.

"We could meet on Wednesdays," Dr. Hough said, opening a three-ring binder he used as an appointment book. "I have an opening at ten o'clock on Wednesdays."

Ray nodded his head solemnly, but kept sitting. Dr. Hough wrote in his book. Ray felt too heavy to move. There was more, he thought, more to say, more to do.

"Wednesday, then," Dr. Hough said, closing his book and looking at Ray with the same catlike grin.

Ray descended the five outside steps on Dr. Hough's stoop with leaden feet. He felt horrible. He had wanted Dr. Hough to clap him on the back and tell him that he was fine, to shoo him out of the office with a gentle scolding for wasting the valuable time of a psychiatrist when there was nothing the matter with him, to tell him that Betsy and Julia were sick and they should be in there, not he, not Ray.

Only he had been booked in for a lifetime of Wednesdays without saying more than three sentences. That guy's a quack, Ray thought angrily. What the hell can he know from just a few comments? His anger had no spine, though, and caved back into his glum mood. Ray felt like a criminal who had just been sentenced. Suddenly, he was a child, wondering what he had done wrong.

"What did I do wrong?"

He had never asked his mother that. He was always meant to know what he had done wrong, so he had never asked. He remembered the red Formica table in the kitchen with the wood chairs painted red. He saw himself on one of the chairs, his chair, his legs dangling, too short to reach the floor. He had done something wrong. No one was yelling at him; the yelling was over. He was alone. He had eaten a lot of peanut-butter-and-jelly sandwiches sitting on that chair. There would be many more. But for now there was just little Ray, lost. He looked as nondescript as Jesse and Zach had when they returned from St. John. They were, all three of them, just little boys, blended into life's landscape and forgotten.

• • •

On the way to Albuquerque, Ray explained to Jesse and Zach about art shows. He was hoping that telling them about the commerce of art might impart enough sense of seriousness that they would behave at the opening.

"You mean Robin makes pictures and people buy them?" Jesse asked, amazed.

"That's right."

"How much does she sell them for?"

"I'm not sure. Four or five hundred dollars, I think."

"For one picture?"

"That's right. For one picture."

"What does she make pictures of?"

"Robin likes to draw horses. They don't always look exactly like horses. Some of them are abstract. Abstract means they don't really look like the thing, more like the idea of the thing. Sometimes, they aren't even of a thing."

"And she gets five hundred dollars?"

Ray nodded his head. Jesse leaned over and snatched the bag of games and toys from the floor of the backseat. He took out the pad of paper and the crayons and one of the large picture books to use as a table. He was soon hard at work.

"I want coloring," Zach said.

Jesse quickly set Zach up and returned to his work.

"Maybe we could get some of Robin's friends together and sell them our pictures?" Jesse said as he worked.

"How much are you going to sell them for?" Ray asked.

Jesse stopped to think about it. Five hundred was a lot of money, but Robin was a lot older. "Do you think they'd pay one dollar?" Jesse asked.

"I don't know. You could try."

"Look," Jesse said, holding up his first work. "I'm going to sell it. For a dollar." It was a horse. In the corner, in blue, he had written $1, with the dollar sign backward.

"Great," Ray said. "Do another."

"Look," Zach said, holding up his first work, more abstract than Jesse's. "I going selling too. For a dollar."

They drove straight to the gallery on one of the side streets off
Central near the university. Jesse brought in one of his drawings to
show Robin, who was standing in front of a large painting talking
to three matronly ladies. Jesse and Zach clung to Ray's legs. Robin
noticed them and came over. She had a way of walking that put
herself forward, on her toes, as if she were always a little off-bal-
ance.

"Hello, Jesse, hello, Zach," she said after giving Ray a hug.

"Look, Robin," Jesse said, holding his drawing out for Robin.

"Jesse, that's great. Can I see it?" She took it from him. She
started to laugh. "Kids do such great art. I wish some of my horses
looked like this."

Jesse beamed. "I was thinking. Zach and I wondered. Maybe
tomorrow or something we could get some of your artist friends to
come by and look at them and maybe some of them might want to
buy one."

"Better yet," Robin said, "maybe we could have an auction."

"What's that?" Zach asked her.

"That's where you hold your pictures up one at a time and people yell out what they'll pay for it and each person has to bid
higher than the first one. It's really fun. People go crazy and you
get a lot of money."

Jesse's eyes lit up. "Yeah."

"In fact," Robin said, "some friends are coming over after the
opening. Maybe we could do it then."

Jesse's eyes brightened even more.

"Come see this painting," Robin said.

Ray noticed Jack against the far wall, his black hair combed
back in a wave like Elvis's.

The painting Robin wanted to show them was of an abstract figure. His arms were raised and curving off to the left. The whole
painting was shooting off to the top left corner, as if a hurricane
were grabbing hold of everything.

"This is new for you," Ray said, "doing people."

"I know."

"What is it?" Zach asked.

"You tell me," Robin answered. "Who's that a picture of?"

"My dad," Zach yelled immediately, jumping up as he said it.

"Right." Robin laughed. "And what's he doing?"

"Reaching," Zach answered quickly, again.

"Right." Robin laughed more. "And what's he reaching for?"

The burden of being right twice weighed on Zach and he retreated to one of Ray's legs as he thought. Finally he answered.

"Me!" As he said it, he jumped again, jubilant.

"That's right." Robin stomped her foot and slapped her thigh as she laughed. "That's absolutely right."

Robin took on Jesse and Zach's auction as a project.

"Come to our art auction," she told her friends at the opening.

Jesse went to the car with Ray and brought back some paper and his crayons to fill out his portfolio. Jesse told Robin that if she wanted she could make some pictures for the auction too. When the crowd thinned, she sat on the floor next to him and made two drawings of horses.

"You're good at horses," Jesse told her.

After they returned to her house, Robin set up the auction in their living room while Jack and Ray made grilled cheese sandwiches.

"That's the most fun I've ever had at an opening," Robin said as she collected the sandwiches for the boys. "I'm really glad you guys came," she told Ray.

When enough people had arrived, she sat them all on the living room floor and put Jesse and Zach together on an overstuffed chair facing them. Robin stood next to the chair and explained the rules.

The bidding was slow at first. Zach sold a minimalist red line for fifteen cents; Jesse sold a patch of blue for twenty. Then things began to pick up. Zach held up a looping yellow abstract with a brown intrusion coming in from the right that bid up to seventy-five cents. Jesse's first horse brought fifty. The guests were showing some discrimination, giving little for the lazy drawings and more for the ones they liked better.

When the pile of coins on Jesse's lap was larger than he had ever hoped for, he pulled out one of Robin's horses from behind him and gave it to her.

"You can do yours now," he told her.

Robin held it up. There were some scattered boos.

"What do you bid?" Robin asked, laughing.

"Five cents."

"Ten cents."

"Come on," Robin pleaded. "This is my work. People pay hundreds. Soon it will be worth thousands."

"Fifteen cents."

"It's not worth more than fifteen cents," one of the original bidders said.

"Come on," Robin said.

"Twenty cents," Jesse bid. Everyone laughed.

"No one will bid more than twenty cents?" Robin asked.

"Going once. Going twice . . ."

Jesse handed Robin twenty cents. She pouted over such a low price.

"Don't worry," Jesse told her. "Money's not the most important thing in the world."

Robin laughed. "What is?"

"I know," Zach said.

"What?"

"Gravity."

For a moment, the room was utterly silent. Zach glanced desperately at Ray, wondering what he had said wrong. Then, led by Robin, everyone laughed and the auction was over.

Most of the guests had left when Ray went outside and sat on the steps from the kitchen looking over the tattered, leaning garage. It was April and almost warm. He thought for a moment about Dr. James Hough. He realized that he was frightened; afraid of being exposed. Not that he thought he had done anything wrong. It was abstract. He was afraid of what might happen if Dr. James Hough peeled back his protective layers. Afraid that, being so naked, he might shrivel up and die: overexposure, sunstroke. If people didn't need clothes, they would be walking around naked.

Ray alternated between feeling combative and angry with Dr. James Hough for wanting to strip him, and submissive and open to whatever he might suggest. Everyone's frightened when they go to the doctor, he thought; we want to get well, but we don't want to have to change anything to do it.

Robin spotted Ray through the window in the door and came out and sat next to him.

"You OK?" she asked.

Ray shrugged. Robin looped her arm through his and leaned her head on his shoulder. Her touch was new and different, the touch of a friend, and it gave him comfort. Ray was transported back to that moment after Sean died and Robin sat next to him on the couch and they both cried. His insides softened and he thought he might suddenly cry again but it passed. He took a deep breath.

"Are you going to fix up your garage?" Ray asked after a pause. "Prop it up? Straighten it?"

"I don't think so. We have a lot to do on the house. There are some electrical things I want to ask you about. I like the garage the way it is. I think we'll leave it. I've been thinking of doing a painting of it. I've never done any buildings, but there's something special about the garage: the old, faded blue color; the way some boards are missing; how it leans without falling. It doesn't look like it's going to fall, does it? As if, even though it's leaning, it's still totally solid."

Ray nodded his head.

"It's special, somehow. I don't think I'll ever really do a painting of it, but the fact that I want to means it's special. I think we'll just leave it."

They listened to the traffic from Isleta Boulevard: the car horns, the trucks as they shifted gears, the whine of a motorcycle, an occasional shout. The darkness settled around them.

"I'm glad that opening is over," Robin said. "They make me so nervous."

Ray felt that much was over.

"What's next for you?" Robin asked.

"Is that like 'What are you going to do when you grow up?' "

They both laughed. Ray thought about it. He had been so involved with disentangling himself from Betsy and entangling himself with Julia that there never had been a tomorrow. Now both women had dropped away at the same time, as if they were a pair. He had scheduled a meeting with a divorce mediator for next week, and he had heard that Julia and Roget had gotten back together. For the first time in as long as he could remember, he had a tomorrow.

"I suppose I'll keep on with Prime Time Electric," he said, thinking of Scott. "For a while, anyway."

Zach opened the door behind them, looked at Ray and Robin for a long moment, and then ran back inside.

"Neat kids," Robin said as she laughed.

Ray nodded his head.

"I went to see that shrink you told me about," he told Robin.

"And?"

"He's young. Our age."

"And?"

"I feel like I missed some turn. Everyone else has moved on, and I look up, and everyone's gone. I'm left playing some child's game by myself."

"I don't think of you that way. You're an electrician: hands full of lightning bolts, a business, in charge of the world."

"I know," Ray said. "But I think that's the game. I keep playing at it. It seems important; it feels important. But it's not."

Ray had a sudden image of sunlit fields, playing fields: soccer, football, basketball courts. Lakes with eight-man crews stroking across glass surfaces. His memories all had athletes with uniforms running through them, and the uniforms all had numbers.

The games are over now, he thought. Although the smell of the cut grass and the sun, like Robin's leaning garage, lingered in his mind and haunted him.

"Time to back up and start over again," Ray said, realizing as he did that it was not really true. He was not going back and forth over the same strip of hard concrete. Re-starts were not part of the mathematics of human life. Geometry did not contain enough dimensions to describe his course. He was reaching backward, forward, and standing still all at the same time.